I Hear You

Jonny Mendez #2

Andre Gonzalez

M4L Publishing

GET EXCLUSIVE BONUS STORIES!

Connecting with readers is the best part of this job. Releasing a book into the world is a truly frightening moment every time it happens! Hearing your feedback, whether good or bad, goes a long way in shaping future projects and helping me grow as a writer. I also like to take readers behind the scenes on occasion and share what is happening in my wild world of writing. If you're interested, please consider joining my mailing list. If you do, I'll send you a free time travel thriller as a thank you!

You can get your content **for free,** by signing up at BookHip.co m/KAWWBK

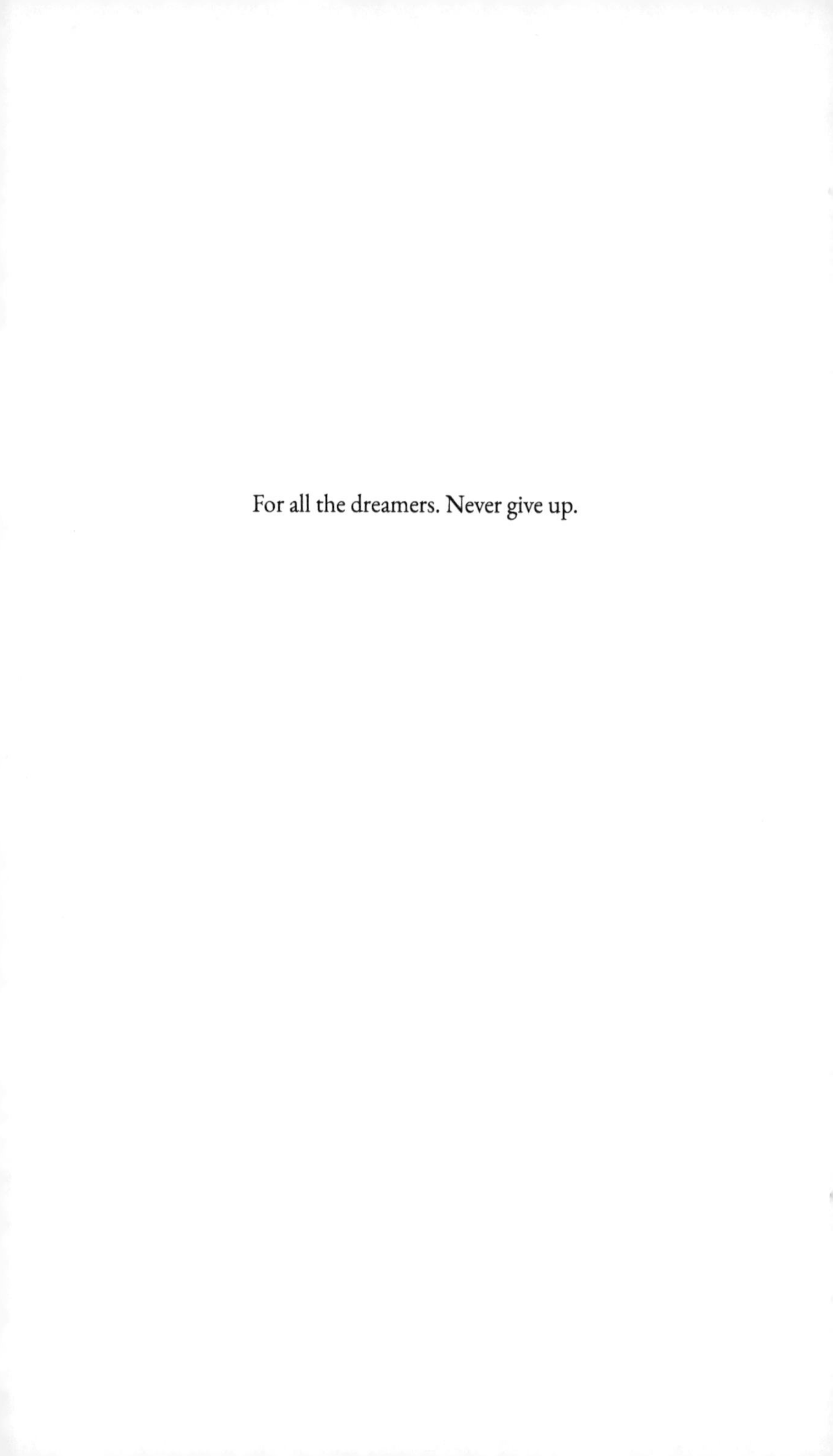
For all the dreamers. Never give up.

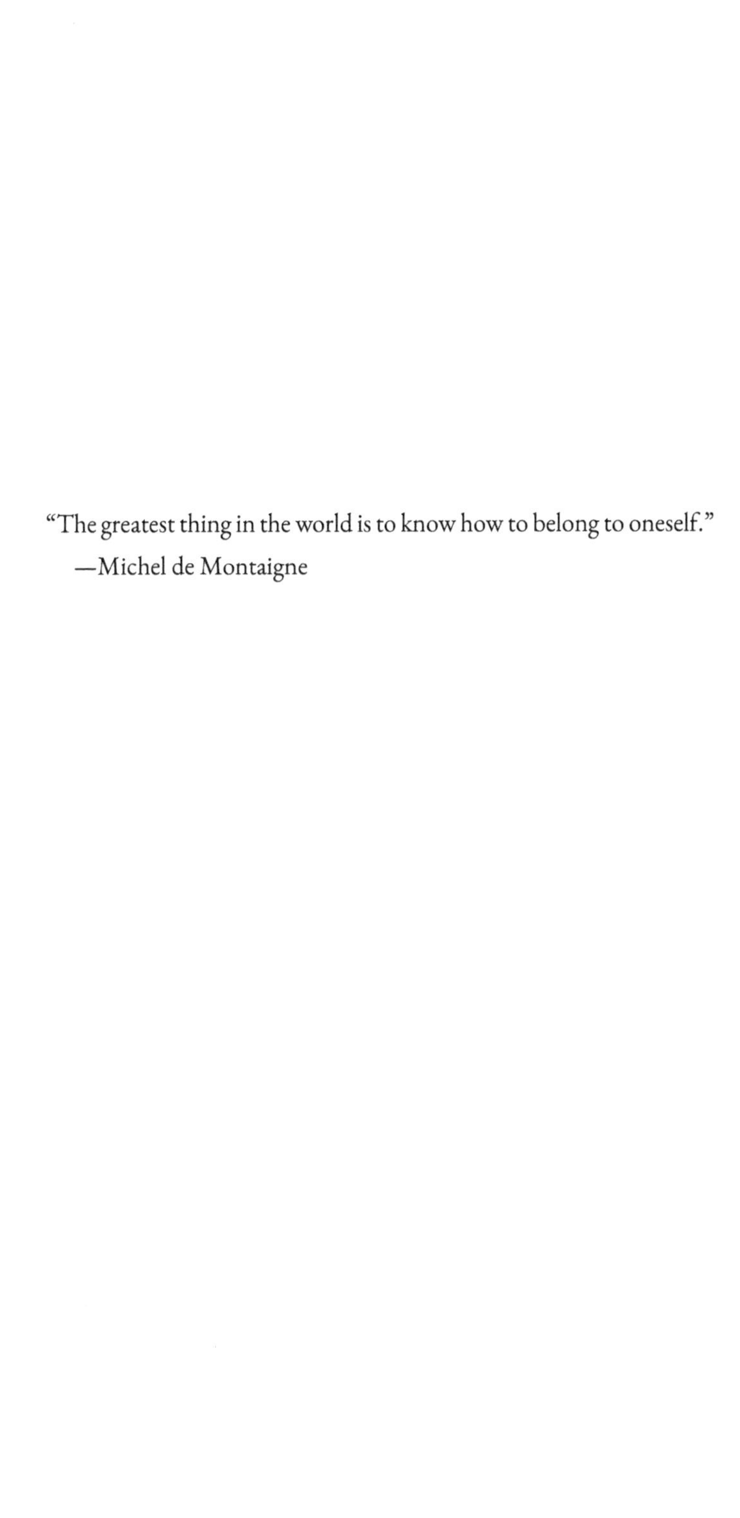

"The greatest thing in the world is to know how to belong to oneself."
—Michel de Montaigne

Chapter 1

I had never seen a human body splatter on concrete before today.

Sure, I'd seen things I'd rather not speak of during my years with the SEALs. But that was in war, and expected.

I was enjoying lunch at the Royal Hotel in Redwood, Oregon. The hotel stood seven stories tall, the biggest in this city of 100,000 in central Oregon. They had a cafe on the main level with an option to sit inside or outside.

I had always enjoyed sitting outside to eat. We had plenty of Mexican restaurants with outdoor seating in Laredo. Those large spaces with a dozen oversized umbrellas to provide shade. Something about sipping on a margarita just hit differently while outside on a warm day.

Unfortunately, this cafe didn't serve booze, and the hotel bar wouldn't allow me to take a drink beyond their boundaries. So I settled for a Coke to go with my ham and turkey sandwich. The next best drink choice.

I had just finished my sandwich when the server came over.

"Anything else, sir?" he asked.

"I'm okay for now," I said. "Thanks, Sammy."

I came here about three times a week and had Sammy nearly every time. He was working his way through Redwood Community College for his first two years of school, with plans to complete his degree at the University of Oregon.

Sammy nodded politely, flashing a quick smile before turning away to another table.

I sat right at the edge of the metal fencing separating the cafe from the sidewalk. It was Friday afternoon, and I had the day off from the landscaping company I'd been helping with since I arrived in Redwood four months ago. I usually put in twelve-hour days Mondays through Thursdays. The work kept me in shape. I rarely felt the need to go to the gym after hauling rolls of sod and wheelbarrows full of rocks around all day. If we ever got rained out, I'd head to the gym, but that was rare during the summer.

Redwood came to life once summer break started. The city enjoyed a steady flow of tourism, mainly for the outdoorsy types. Campgrounds, rafting, fishing, and hiking were all available at the nearby Deschutes National Forest. Even better, the city had a growing scene of local breweries. There were at least fifteen that I knew of, and I'd been able to visit all but five so far.

Where I visited once a week, however, was the Borders bookstore. Yes, *that* Borders. Apparently, when Borders shut down their business, only the corporate-owned stores were closed. This left a dozen of franchised Borders in operation, until they eventually dwindled down to this last remaining store in Redwood, Oregon. They were officially dubbed The Last Borders, and became a major tourist attraction because of their unique status. Book nerds from all around the country came to Redwood just to browse the shelves and experience the nostalgia of Borders one more time. My kind of people. Hell, I remember going to the Borders in Laredo when I was a teenager for the midnight release parties of the new *Harry Potter* books.

Life had been good to me in Redwood. Four months and no drama might have been a record. I wouldn't say I've made any friends, but I enjoyed close acquaintances through the landscaping job. People to grab a beer with after work. With an added bonus of keeping my Spanish sharp.

"Use it or lose it," my late mom used to tell me.

I'd been using it all summer and was delighted to find I hadn't missed a beat.

I roamed the country, refusing to settle down in any place. While Laredo was my hometown, I hadn't been back there in almost a year. Usually just to check on my mom's house and other matters.

I had no family aside from a nephew who was looking to begin college. And my father, who I'm pretty sure wanted me dead. Another reason I stayed on the move.

My life had been nothing but a cluster of complications ever since my mother died. Going home always made me nauseous. Like there was some life that should have been there for me. But it had all been wiped out. It was like visiting a ghost of my former self, and who the hell wanted to play that game?

I'd much rather explore this beautiful country I had dedicated ten years of my life to serving. Few people understand the sheer magnitude of the United States. While each city, no matter how big or small, had their shared similarities, each had its own unique charm. Like a fingerprint that belonged only to it.

Redwood was a busy and booming city, yet the people still had that small town neighborliness. Kids played in the street. There were block parties. People knew each other within their smaller communities around town. The politicians actually worked together to improve the livelihoods of their fellow citizens. I never sensed polarization.

Sometimes I wondered if I was even in the same country depicted on the news channels.

People didn't leave Redwood. Generations stretched back to the 1820s when the earliest pioneers discovered the city and lived in harmony with the Native Americans already in the area.

I liked to move every six months, but Redwood was a hard place to imagine leaving. I needed peace in my life, and I had found it here. But I knew peace couldn't last forever.

Especially today.

I finished my Coke when Sammy dropped off the check. I paid with cash and left a generous tip, remembering the struggle of paying my way through college.

"Any plans this weekend?" Sammy asked as he collected the cash and stacked my two dishes on the corner of the table. He wore black jeans and a black button-up, a white apron wrapped snugly around his waist.

"It was a tough week," I said. "Temps in the upper 90s every single day. Might grab a new book and just lounge around the house this weekend. Not feeling up for doing much. How about yourself?"

Sammy rolled his eyes. "Got a term paper to work on."

"You're only taking two classes over the summer, right?" I asked.

Sammy nodded. "It's the most I can manage. But these papers are a real pain in the ass. And this one is about how the US stock market affects international policy. Couldn't be a drier topic, even for an economics major."

"Goodness," I said, shaking my head. "Well, you have fun with that, and I'll see you next week."

Sammy clapped me on the back. "Have a good weekend, Mr. Mendez."

I grinned. "I've told you to call me Jonny. Or even just Mendez, like they did in the military. None of this *mister* stuff, okay?"

Sammy shrugged. "Just how I was raised, Mr. Mendez."

"Fair enough."

Sammy left me alone to stare out at Palmetto Drive.

Across the street, I noticed a couple walking hand-in-hand. They halted and were pointing up. Maybe they had spotted a bald eagle. The tourists always got excited when one showed up. I had seen them at least twice a week as long as I'd been here.

A family of five were walking along and stopped next to the couple, also looking up.

I looked further down Palmetto Drive and spotted several more people looking in the same direction, some running for a closer look. I'd seen when a group of tourists spotted the bald eagles before. It usually caused a commotion that lasted a few seconds before the eagle flew away. But something was different this time.

When I heard a woman shriek from the opposite direction, my stomach sunk. I looked to my left and saw her sprinting toward the hotel, hand outstretched as she pointed upward.

"Noooo!" she screamed. "Don't do it!"

I looked up out of instinct, but the patio was covered. I hopped over the fence and landed on the sidewalk. When I looked up, I saw what was causing such a frenzy.

A man stood on the edge of the hotel's roof, hands at his sides, looking down.

Traffic came to a halt on Palmetto Drive, as people poured out of the businesses and onto the street and sidewalks. This was a busy block with several shops, tourist centers, restaurants, and, of course, the Royal Hotel.

Within thirty seconds, I estimated eighty people had made their way outside. Every single one of them looking up at the hotel's roof.

A man darted by me, bumping into my shoulder, talking into his cell phone. "Yes, officer," he said. "Get down here right now. He's going to jump!"

Hearing the words spoken aloud in such a panic startled my instincts awake. But there was nothing I could actually do. As many times as I'd been to this hotel, I never strayed from the cafe and bar area. I assumed the elevators were near the check-in desk, but how long would they take to get to the top floor? Could I even access them without a room key?

I jogged out toward the center of Palmetto Drive, where the still growing crowd had formed, and subconsciously left a space open where this man would land if he jumped. The man looked down, undisturbed by the scene unfolding on street level. I supposed anyone in his predicament gave second thought to actually jumping, but my gut told me his mind was already made up.

A police car flashed its lights as it moved down the street, the crowd clearing a path. Two officers jumped out, one with a megaphone. He shouted into it.

"Sir! Jumping is not the answer. Step away from the edge and let us help you down."

His voice was both authoritative and nervous. He probably had the proper training to handle this scenario, but this was likely his first time using it. Practice was one thing, but when reality greeted you with a slap across the face, you had to trust your instincts and let them take over. I experienced that both in the SEALs and CIA.

The man on the roof said nothing. Didn't even acknowledge the officer.

"Think about everything you have to lose!" the officer shouted. "There is no coming back from jumping. Give yourself a second chance!"

This officer was trying his best, but he arrived at this situation cold. No idea who the man was, or what had pushed him to this point. His words made no impression. Landed flat. I swung my gaze back at the man. I couldn't make out his facial expression from this distance, but I could tell his eyes were narrowed on a certain spot. The space everyone had cleared for him.

"Sir!" the officer shouted, desperation now thick in his voice. Others in the crowd were shouting similar things, begging this man to back off the edge.

No one had a chance.

The man stepped forward, his foot hovering over the edge for a quick second before the rest of his body's weight followed behind it.

His fall was graceful. No tumbling. No screaming. The entire crowd, which had now grown to at least two hundred people, fell deathly silent as we all watched the man soar through the air. He spread his arms and legs out, and just before he hit the ground, I clearly saw his face.

He looked focused. Like he was completing a job. Not ending his life.

Then he hit the pavement.

The sound was like someone slapping the surface of a swimming pool with their bare hand, only amplified so it could reverberate through the darkest halls of my memories forever.

People shrieked and sprinted away. Blood splattered in every direction, some getting on the hotel's brick facade. The man lay in a lifeless heap on the ground. Even the officers had to look away from the scene, the one with the megaphone dropping it to clutch his stomach.

I stepped back. I'd seen too much death in my life and didn't need a front row to yet another gruesome scene. Although it was much too late for that, anyway.

I turned and left, just wanting to get back to my house. I didn't need to stay as a witness. We all saw what happened, including the police officers. Sirens sounded in the distance, drowned out by the commotion taking place on Palmetto Drive.

Little did I know, this was just the beginning.

Chapter 2

I returned home and immediately turned on my television. It was a forty-eight inch screen mounted to the wall in the living room, easily the biggest TV I've enjoyed during my life of bouncing from rented houses to hotels and motels.

I lucked my way into this house. A cottage-style home just outside of downtown Redwood. A guy I worked with let me know his uncle lived in the house, but returned home to Honduras for six months out of the year. After a couple of phone calls, I was in, paying an unbeatable rent of two hundred dollars a month, and that included access to the Toyota Camry that was sitting in the driveway when I arrived. Only condition for the using the car was to keep it clean and follow the oil change schedule.

I had no driver's license, but no one needed to know. I knew how to drive and would avoid any traffic violations. No one drove too crazy in Redwood, so I wasn't worried about accidents, either. If this was Los Angeles, I'd reconsider.

This little cottage had become my personal paradise. One bedroom, one bathroom, a kitchen with everything I needed, and the living room where I spent most of my time. A young couple with three kids lived on one side, and an elderly couple lived on the other—the

Walkers. They brought me freshly baked cookies every two weeks and only wanted to chat for five minutes.

As much as I despised unexpected visitors knocking on my door, the Walkers were fine, and let me be.

The TV was on a commercial when I'd turned it on, and it finally returned to the breaking news story. I pretty much only watched the local news, unless I wanted to fall asleep on the couch watching reruns of *The Office* or *Parks and Rec*.

The daytime news anchor, Alana McGregor, spoke in a grave tone while the camera feed showed the scene unfolding outside the Royal Hotel. Firetrucks and ambulances had created a perimeter, all for the better. No one needed to see that shit on TV.

"We return to our breaking news coverage of a man who jumped off the roof of the Royal Hotel this afternoon," Alana said. The screen cut away from the hotel and was replaced by an image of a man with dirty blond hair and a scruffy goatee. "The deceased has been identified. Authorities found the wallet of Jackson Green among the remains and confirmed with hotel staff that a man by that name had checked in late last night. Mr. Green was a resident of Redwood, who attended Redwood High School, and recently worked for the parks department. He leaves behind a wife and two children. Hotel staff is cooperating with the police department to understand how he had gained access to the roof."

The feed cut to the news station and showed Alana. Jonny enjoyed watching her in the afternoons. She had the prefect smile and a soothing voice. And dreamy blue eyes to get lost in.

"Redwood has not had a reported suicide in nearly two years," Alana explained. "Take this moment to reach out to those closest to you. Check on them. Sit down and really ask how they're doing. I lost a friend to suicide in high school, and it's such a gut punch. You'll always wonder if there was something you could have done. I urge you, right now, to stop wondering and reach out."

Tears welled in Alana's eyes. News casters usually had the best poker faces, but this had clearly struck a nerve.

She gathered herself enough to say, "We're now going out to the field, where Rick Sanchez is live on the scene."

The screen returned to the hotel and Rick Sanchez standing in front of a firetruck, microphone held to his chin.

"Thank you, Alana," Rick said. "So many in Redwood are seeking answers today. Jackson Green was well known within the parks community. I've had the chance to speak with a few of his colleagues, and they all described a man with an intense work ethic and passion for the local parks. Mr. Green led the project to expand the availability of youth soccer and baseball fields, which resulted in a fifty percent increase in Redwood children registered for sports in just the one year following the project's completion. I'm joined by Jackson's colleague from the parks department, Jennifer Murphy."

The camera panned out, and a woman with bloodshot eyes shuffled in next to Rick.

"Thank you for talking with us, Jennifer," Rick said. "What can you share about Jackson?"

Jennifer sniffled her nose and wiped her eyes free of the tears before speaking. "I worked closely with Jackson for the last three years. He was a man of faith who loved his family, his coworkers, and even people he never met. He was driven by a passion to make the world a better place, and he did that through parks. In a time where we're all so distracted with technology, Jackson held his belief that parks were still the best way to bring a community together. He didn't just fight to have the parks built, he made sure they were maintained, and always planned events. People don't know it, but those Friday night movies at the park, the bubble events for kids, Easter egg hunts, all of it was planned and organized by Jackson. Losing him is such a big hit for this city."

Jennifer couldn't contain her emotions any more and continued sobbing.

Rick nodded, thanked her, and had the camera shift its focus back on him.

"Thank you, Jennifer, for a touching account of Mr. Green's impact on Redwood. We want to take this moment to share with you the phone number for the National Suicide and Crisis Lifeline. Just dial 988 and you'll be connected with a trained expert. They also have text messaging and online chats available, and are available twenty-four hours. Share the number, and if you need it, don't be afraid to use it."

A graphic flashed the number across the bottom of the screen. Rick held a finger against his earpiece, nodded, and started walking.

The cameraman kept up while Rick spoke. "I've just been informed the chief of police is moments away from a press conference to address today's incident."

Rick rounded the firetruck and stopped in front of the outdoor patio I had just been sitting at moments earlier. A podium with microphones was set up in front of the black fence, a heavyset police officer with a stern expression standing behind it.

The officer was staring into the crowd of reporters and bystanders gathered around and nodded before clearing his throat to speak into the plethora of mics.

"Good afternoon," he said in a clear, confident tone. A graphic appeared on the bottom of the screen, introducing this man as Redwood Police Chief, Mason Barker. "This is a dark day for Redwood. One we'll never forget. I personally knew Jackson Green. We went to high school together. Played football. Even won a state championship during our senior year. He was always a quiet guy who kept to himself, but no one ever doubted his integrity. We didn't stay in touch after high school, but reconnected once he started his job with the parks department. I ran into him plenty of times at City Hall and always enjoyed hearing about his work and family. He was no longer the quiet one. Instead, Jackson became a fierce advocate for Redwood and those who call our fine city home. We spoke with Jackson's wife a few minutes ago at their residence, and she has requested the family be left alone while they process today's events.

"I want to thank the Royal Hotel for their cooperation. From what we've gathered based on preliminary information, Jackson had checked into the hotel last night at nine-fifteen. Following his key card activity, he went up to the top floor, where the hotel has a swimming pool. Camera feeds show him walking around the pool, fully dressed, and what appeared to be him talking to himself. We will run a toxicology report to determine if drugs or alcohol played a role. The parks department confirmed Mr. Green was expected at work today, and never called in. They called him twice throughout the morning, but he did not answer.

"As for today's event, Mr. Green returned to the top floor shortly after noon, but never appeared near the swimming pool. We believe he accessed the emergency stairwell and climbed up a flight for roof access. The hotel confirmed having recent issues with the door's locking mechanism requiring keycard access. Mr. Jackson could open the door without issue and gain access to the roof. From there, it's fairly straightforward what happened. Everyone who came in contact with Mr. Green yesterday confirmed he was acting his usual self and had no reason to suspect suicidal thoughts. We will speak with his family in more detail when they are up to the task, so that we may have a better understanding of the *why*.

"Mr. Green appeared to be alone during his stay at the hotel, and no foul play is suspected. For now, we only ask you to contact the police department if you have any information regarding the last couple days of Mr. Green's life. Thank you."

Chief Barker turned away from the podium and did not take questions.

The feed returned to a still graphic of Jackson Green. It was an official government photo, probably the same one on his work badge for the parks department. He had light blue eyes to complement his wavy dirty blond hair.

I paused the TV and stared at the image. "What were you hiding?" I asked the screen. If Jackson lived in Redwood, worked in Redwood, and had his family in Redwood, where was he going at nine o'clock at night?

"What were you doing at that hotel?"

Chapter 3

The landscaping crew worked on Saturdays. In fact, they worked every day of the week.

I had made it clear I was only interested in part-time work, and that I wouldn't be available most weekends. With my insanely low rent, I didn't exactly *need* extra money. What I made each week was enough to pay my rent, gas, and food. With a few extra dollars left over to splurge on things likes books and coffee shops.

After having a hard time falling asleep Friday night, I decided I'd work on Saturday. I had too much nervous energy, and it would be better put to use hauling heavy shit around on a summer day. Something about the Jackson Green story wasn't sitting right with me. And I knew myself well enough to know I needed to stay away from the matter before getting sucked in. I never intended to play hero, especially in these smaller towns I visited. But my years of training and experience had molded my brain into seeing situations differently from everyone else.

I understand no one wants to speak ill of the dead, or jump to conclusions, but why the hell was no one questioning *why* Jackson Green was at a hotel only ten minutes from his house?

I had watched the evening news, late night news, and the morning news segments to see if any more details had emerged. But they only played the same clips and sound bites I had already seen.

My first assumption was an affair. A man leaves his wife and kids at nine o'clock and drives to the most expensive hotel Redwood has to offer. He is alone and checks in. For what reason? There had to have been a woman who met him there. Or maybe a man. Those kinds of sex scandals weren't uncommon. However, the hotel reported no calls from Jackson's hotel room. Plus, there was the footage of him wandering around the swimming pool, also alone. My theory had weak legs to stand on, if any.

He could have gotten into a heated argument with his wife. Instead of sleeping on the couch for the night, maybe he wanted luxury. Only his wife could shed light on that possibility.

That left one last option. Jackson had planned to take his life and knew exactly what he wanted to do. If he was the family man people claimed, then he wouldn't have wanted to take his life at home for his wife and kids to find. Perhaps the scene at the swimming pool was him talking himself out of taking his life. Or talking himself into it.

There were too many unknowns, and if I had stayed at home, the puzzle would have driven me toward insanity.

But I should have known better.

When I arrived at the house across town for a xeriscaping project, everyone was talking about the man who jumped off the roof. Our crew fluctuated day by day, depending on the project, but there were already twelve guys when I parked down the street and walked from four houses over.

"Well, well, well," our crew leader, Eduardo, said with a wink. "Look who it is. Señor Mamado."

Everyone cackled as I walked up and replied, "Buenos días, cabrónes. I knew you missed me doing all the heavy lifting."

Eduardo had been leaning against the side of his truck and stood up to give me an embrace and slap on the back.

"You have a nice day off?" he asked in a thick accent. "Sipping your little coffees at the bookstore?"

Everyone laughed.

I loved these guys. The shit talk flowed like a river every day, and no one was off limits.

I grinned. "You should try taking a day off sometime, Eddie. Maybe your wife will love you again if you take her on a date."

Eddie's jaw dropped before he broke into hysterics. He always talked about his wife who had left him ten years ago, but many of us in the crew suspected she never actually existed. Naturally, it became a running joke.

"No mames!" Eddie cried, shaking his head while everyone else joined the laughter.

"We did Spanish on Thursday," I said. "So, English today?"

We had a diverse mix in this crew. A handful of guys from Mexico. A couple of white boys working a summer job and learning the ropes of landscaping. Plus a few others from Latin descent that didn't speak Spanish. When I joined the crew, Eddie was eager to improve his English, while the others were hoping to learn Spanish. We made an agreement to alter which language we spoke every other day.

"Ahh," Eddie said, having grown proud of his vast improvement of the language. "English today. Did you hear about the man who jumped off the hotel yesterday?"

A few of the crew dispersed to the back of the truck to load materials into wheelbarrows, while others carried shovels and rakes onto the front yard that weeds had overtaken.

"Hear about it?" I said. "I was there."

Eddie's eyes bulged. "You were there? For what?"

This caught the attention of the guys, who promptly stopped what they were doing to circle around me and Eddie.

"I was having lunch at the hotel," I explained. "Was actually sitting outside when everything happened."

Eddie's face soured as he shook his head. "So...you saw?"

I nodded. "Sure did. Wished I hadn't."

The group fell silent, most of the guys looking down at their feet as they imagined what it might have been like to stand there when the body hit the pavement.

"Are you okay?" Eddie asked, placing a hand on my shoulder. Despite all the ribbing from this group, we all cared for each other.

"I'm alright. Can't get the image out of my head, but I'll be okay."

And it was more than the image I couldn't clear from my thoughts. The sound. The screams. Even the scent of blood that filled the air right after the impact. I'd seen people shot in the head, blown up from bombs, and even mauled by a tiger. But none of that compared to what I witnessed yesterday.

"And it was really Jackson Green?" Eddie asked.

"The face I saw matches what's been on TV. So, yes."

Eddie nodded. "Well, it's unfortunate, and I'm sorry you had to see it. But at least we can know the world is a better place now."

I frowned. "A better place? Did you know Jackson? Everyone says he did so much for Redwood."

Eddie pursed his lips and jerked his head from side to side. "Sure, he built some parks. Made the city better. But he was an evil man."

"Evil?"

Everyone in our group nodded.

"So you all knew him?" I asked.

"We all *worked* for him," Eddie said. "Who do you think he hired to do all that work on those parks? We're the most reliable landscaping company in town. He wanted quality work done for his precious projects, so he hired us."

"So you had a poor working relationship with him?" I asked. "That doesn't seem fair to call a man evil."

Eddie let out a laugh as he crossed his arms and leaned back against his truck. "Jackson Green was one of the bad ones. The worst."

"El diablo!" a guy named Jesus shouted, gritting his teeth.

"Jackson Green hired us to build three soccer fields," Eddie said. "I met with him at his office, and we got all the details sorted out. He even gave me a check that day to pay for the first field—labor and materials. And so we started. City jobs are the best. If you do a good job, they'll always hire you again. So this was our chance, and we wanted it all to go perfect. And it did.

"We finished the first field in six weeks. Jackson came out and inspected the field. He loved it, but said we were ahead of schedule. The city gave us eight weeks to finish the field. Because of that, he couldn't pay us for anything besides the materials to start on the second field. He said he'd have the money for the labor in two more weeks. Something about the project being split into three parts since it was three fields. I told him that was fine, and we'd get started.

"We knew what we were doing the second time around, so we were quicker. Built the second field in four weeks. We never received the payment he said we would, but when he came out to inspect, he paid for the materials for the third field, and paid for half of the labor costs for the second field. Told me there were issues with accounting, but it would all be sorted out. I took the half payment as a sign of faith, and so we knocked out the third field in another four weeks, knowing a big payday was coming..."

Eddie stared into the distance, his fists clenched.

"He didn't pay you," I said, knowing long ago where this story was headed.

"It wasn't just that," Eddie said. "When he showed up at the inspection after the last field was built, he came with some lawyer in a suit."

"A lawyer?"

Eddie forced a sarcastic grin. "An *immigration* lawyer. I'm not here legally, even though I've lived in Redwood for fifteen years and applied for citizenship twelve years ago. Lots of us are in the same boat. We want to become citizens, but there is always some excuse why our applications keep getting delayed.

"The lawyer thanked me for my work on the soccer fields and said that we were all settled. I told him that was incorrect. I was still owed one hundred thousand dollars. We had forty guys on that crew that needed to be paid. The lawyer said everything was square, and that if I caused any problems over it, he would call ICE to round all of us up and send us back where we came from."

My stomach twisted in knots. Eddie was right. Jackson Green was evil.

"Did Jackson say anything?" I asked. "Or did he hide behind his lawyer the whole time?"

"I was angry and shouted things at Jackson. In English and Spanish. He told me if I ever approached him, he had no problem shooting a spic, and that everyone would believe him it was self-defense."

"Pinche diablo," Jesus said, and spit on the ground.

"And that was it?" I asked. "You didn't fight at all?"

"I couldn't," Eddie said, frustration boiling over. "We split the money we had, sold some of the leftover materials, and had to move on. When they threaten ICE, there's nothing we can do. It wouldn't have mattered to me, but these other guys have families here. Or families back home relying on their paychecks."

"Did you speak to any lawyers of your own?" I asked.

"Claro. But we never had anything signed with the city. Back then, we never signed agreements for any work. Just agreed on a price, a time, and got the job done. We did it that way for three years before this city project, so didn't think any different."

"He had that planned from the start," I said. "Probably heard about you not signing contracts and made a plan."

"Exactly. We know that now. Always get something in writing, just in case. Haven't had an issue since. But that was the biggest job of our lives, and we only got paid for half of it. It ruined my reputation. No one wanted to work for me. Took a long time to get back where we are today."

"So it's safe to say there are at least forty workers in town that are happy to see him gone," I said.

Eddie grinned. "My friend, there are forty people who are mad they didn't get to kill him themselves."

Chapter 4

When I woke up Sunday morning, I had a logical mind for the first time in two days.

Something about the information Eddie had shared yesterday wasn't sitting right with me. How could a well-known local figure like Jackson Green have such a stellar reputation despite being a horrendous human being? Did his family know his true colors, or did he go through life faking his personality for the masses?

It also made me second guess the suicide. Now, I knew what I saw with my own eyes. Jackson was on that roof on his own, so it's not like someone had pushed him. But could someone have threatened him? Dug up his dirt and blackmailed him into taking his own life? It seemed drastic, and I still couldn't make sense how it all tied in to him going to the hotel late Thursday evening.

There was more to this story, and I had nothing but dead ends. The only way I could gain more information was to get involved with the police department. Cops always hated me when I showed up. Probably because I knew more than them. Big Mexican dude with arm tattoos shows up to your town and is naturally better at your job than you. I couldn't blame them for the hatred, but wished they could put their egos aside and welcome the help.

Nope.

I wasn't about to go down that path again. I'd stay in my house and mind my business. We had a busy week ahead with work, finishing the xeriscaping project we had started yesterday. Then I was going to spend Thursday and Friday with the irrigation guys to learn how sprinkler systems worked. Seemed like a good life skill to have.

I fried an egg for breakfast, made some toast, and washed it all down with a glass of orange juice. This was my typical breakfast when I got to cook for myself, something I'd rather been enjoying during my time in Redwood. I learned plenty about cooking from both my mother and aunt when I was growing up, and was surprised how much stuck with me after going several years without touching a pot or pan.

During my recent trip to the famous Last Borders, I grabbed a copy of David Baldacci's newest release and had been enjoying it as company during meals. After breakfast, I cleaned the dishes, took a shower, and returned to the living room couch where I planned to spend most of my day reading, and maybe watching some baseball games.

When I turned on the TV, my stomach immediately dropped.

The news channel was still on, and it showed a new breaking story.

A male reporter stood in the middle of the woods, crews of emergency responders pacing around frantically in the background. I cranked up the volume.

"I'm here in the parking lot of Ben's Trailhead," the reporter said. "Just west of town, where authorities have reported finding the body of a man who appears to have taken his life by gunshot."

A graphic signaled the reporter's name as Andrew Leonard.

"There is a residence about a tenth of a mile from this parking lot," Andrew continued. "Those living in the home reported hearing a gunshot from the direction of the hiking trail, and called police to report it. Coincidentally, police received a call this morning from a woman concerned about her brother, as she believed he might be a danger to himself or the public. Police have confirmed the two calls were related, identifying the deceased as Timothy Summers, a long-time resident of Redwood."

"Another suicide?" I said to the TV, looking around the living room as if the walls had answers. On Friday they said there hadn't been a suicide in Redwood for almost two years. Now there had been two in three days.

They flashed a portrait of Timothy Summers, a man in his mid-forties, jet black hair slicked to the side, a wide grin on his face.

As if hearing my thoughts, Andrew continued. "This is the second suicide to shake Redwood this weekend, both of which occurred in a public setting. While authorities are still trying to understand the reasoning behind the first one that happened on Friday afternoon at the Royal Hotel, there is now another case in need of answers. We reached out to the local center that handles calls on behalf of the National Suicide and Crisis Hotline, and they have not reported a particular influx in calls, nor had any reasons to suspect any of their callers escalated to the point of taking their own lives."

"What the hell is happening?" I asked the TV, standing up from the couch.

"The trail will remain closed for the day while crews assess the scene. Police are asking anyone with information on either of these suicides to please call. For channel four news, this is Andrew Leonard."

The feed cut back to the news studio, where two anchors looked shaken to the core. A man and woman, both in their late fifties and with plenty of makeup caked on, stared into the camera with a nauseous look on their faces.

"Ladies and gentlemen," the man said. "In my thirty years of covering news for Redwood, I have never witnessed anything like this. We must come together as a community and show support for each other. Pray to whatever higher being you believe in. Our town needs healing, and it needs it quickly."

The woman anchor nodded along, licking her lips before speaking. "Thank you for that, Ed. Timothy Summers was born and raised in Redwood, and lived with his sister on the west side of town, not even fifteen minutes from the hiking trail where his body was found. Friends and family called him Timmy. He worked at Big Ed's Tires for the past nine years. His manager said Timmy was at work yesterday and seemed his normal self. The tire shop is closed on Sundays, so Timmy was not expected at work today. Coincidentally, Timmy was also a member of the 1999 Redwood High football team that won the state championship, along with Jackson Green, who took his life on Friday afternoon."

I turned off the TV.

People took their lives every day, but two people on the same weekend? And now I'm learning they played football together over two decades ago? This wasn't exactly a small enough town for that to be a coincidence. Yet, here we were.

I sat in the silence of my living room, trying to fend off every urge to burst out the front door and start asking questions. There had to be more of a connection than playing on a football team together. Maybe they had stayed friends because of their time together in the sport. But to take their lives two days apart...what was their angle?

Nothing was adding up. My instincts insisted I get involved. The town was too rattled for critical thinking. If this police chief had played with these two men in their high school days, he likely wasn't having logical thoughts, either.

Maybe this was why I got sucked into these scenarios whenever I bounced around different towns. I saw things differently because of my life experiences, but I also had no attachments to anyone involved.

The football connection made me think something was at play. They said this team won the 1999 state championship, which was obviously a big deal for Redwood, considering they had mentioned it both times.

The town's library would have records of those golden days, but today was Sunday and they were closed. I hadn't grabbed a cell phone during my time here, but really wished I had one right now. The guys liked to tease me, call me Amish. But they, better than most, understood my desire to stay off the grid.

The convenience of being able to look up some information right now would make my Sunday better. This Timmy Summers guy had a sister in town. Maybe she could provide some insight.

An idea popped into my head, and I rushed out the front door. This was one of those safe neighborhoods where I didn't feel the need to lock my door. It also helped I had nothing worth stealing, and could pulverize anyone who dared break and enter.

I cut across my small yard and went to the Walkers' home next door. Their main door was open, leaving a raggedy screen door as the only separation between me and entering their house.

I knocked hard, knowing they had difficulties hearing.

The husband, Herb, came strutting down the hallway, dressed in his usual attire of jeans and a flannel button up. His wife, Rochelle, trailed behind him, wearing a flowy summer dress.

"Is that you, Jonny?" she called out, squinting her eyes. They could probably only see my silhouette standing in the doorway, but there was no mistaking my mammoth figure.

"Good morning, Herb," I said, waving. "Rochelle. Hope I'm not intruding."

Herb reached the door, a wide grin on his face. They knew I was introverted and probably never thought they'd see the day I came knocking on their door. He pushed open the screen door, speaking in a raspy baritone. "Come on in, Jonny. You are never intruding."

Rochelle caught up with her husband, and the three of us stood in their foyer. My mother always taught me to not enter someone's home and ask for something right off the bat.

"How are you two on this fine Sunday?" I asked.

"Oh, just wonderful," Rochelle said. She kept her silver hair tied up in a short ponytail, revealing plenty of lines and wrinkles along her temples. Yet her smile still had a youthful charm about it. "Tended to the garden this morning. Watched the replay of the Mariners game."

"Oh, and how did they do last night?" I asked. This was how most of our conversations usually went.

"Lost three to two," Herb said, shaking his head. "Another one run loss. If these dummies could just score some runs, they'd be unbeatable."

"Tough night," I said. "Bats can't stay cold forever, right?"

Rochelle nodded along. "Eventually, I suppose. So what brings you over on a Sunday morning, Jonny?"

"I was wondering if you have internet I can use. And maybe a computer."

"You don't have internet?" Herb asked, frowning. "I thought everyone had the internet these days."

Rochelle rolled her eyes and slapped her husband on the arm, which he promptly rubbed without giving a second thought.

"Don't be so rude," Rochelle said to him, then looked at me. "We have internet, Jonny, and you're welcome to use it. In fact, you can even see if the signal will reach your house. I'm not sure how all that works, though."

"That's incredibly generous," I said, flashing Rochelle a smile. "I don't actually have a device at my house to even use the internet on. But if I get one, I'll keep that offer in mind."

Herb frowned even harder at me. "No internet or tech gadgets? Who are you?"

Rochelle slapped him on the arm again, but he didn't rub it this time, just stared at me in amazement.

I let out a friendly laugh. I usually got these questions from people my age or younger.

"I've never had an interest in those things, although I understand the practicality they provide. Like right now."

"You gonna watch some naked ladies?" Herb asked, shooting me a wink.

"Herb!" Rochelle cried.

I chuckled. "Relax, Rochelle. I won't watch naked ladies on your computer. Just hoping to research some stuff about these two suicides that happened in town."

Herb's brows moved from the frown into an elevated curiosity. "Those are tragic. Lives taken too early, no matter how you look at it."

Rochelle nodded. "Research? What kind of stuff do you want to know?"

I shrugged, not even sure of the answer myself. "Just some background into the two men. I find it odd that they played football together in high school and then both take their lives within two days of each other all these years later."

"Just a shame," Rochelle said. "I'm sure Carissa is a mess right now."

"Who's Carissa?" I asked.

"Timmy's sister."

My heart beat a little faster at this information. "You knew Timmy? And his sister?"

"Of course, dear. They used to live in the house next to yours. Timmy would cut our grass in the summers, and they'd both shovel our driveway when it snowed. Good kids."

Maybe I wouldn't need the internet after all. I also didn't want to seem too aggressive. But sometimes you had to seize the opportunity in front of you.

"Do you by chance know where Carissa lives?"

Chapter 5

I took the Camry to the west side of town, driving past the trailhead that had been all over the news this morning. Sure enough, the scene had yellow tape and still a half-dozen police vehicles, along with the county coroner's meat wagon.

I drove past it, wishing the site was cleared so I could look around. Not that there would have been anything of relevance for me to find after the authorities swept the scene.

But still.

I always found value in trying to get into the mind of murderers, terrorists, or whoever I'd been tasked with targeting. In this case, a man who took his own life from the confines of wilderness.

I pulled up to the house of Carissa Summers ten minutes later, wondering what the hell I was doing. This woman had just gone through a nightmare this morning. Who was I to come knocking and start asking for information about her brother? She'd probably refuse, but I needed to show my genuine interest and tell her I had some suspicions. Maybe her brother and Jackson had forged some kind of blood bond during their high school years. Others could be involved. As much as I wanted to ignore my inner voice, my gut told me there could be more suicides to come.

Carissa lived in a small, light blue ranch on Fern Road. Half the homes on the block were lined with white picket fences. A cluster of kids played a game of street hockey further down the road, their little siblings sitting on the sidewalks cheering them on.

The neighborhood was peaceful, making it even harder to imagine Carissa Summers sitting inside in misery.

I stepped out of my car and drew in a deep breath. One thing I loved about Redwood was the fresh air. While a decent sized city in its own right, it was practically dead center in the state of Oregon. Nowhere near another metropolis like Portland. And with the surrounding forests, a simple drive to the outskirts of town welcomed visitors with crisp, natural air.

Carissa's home did not have a picket fence. Instead, I followed the concrete path decorated with rocks along the edges. She had a hummingbird feeder to the right of the entrance, and a welcome mat that said "THE PASSWORD IS: I BROUGHT WINE"

The blinds and curtains were closed all along the front of the house. It was entirely possible Carissa wasn't even home. She could have been off with family mourning the death of her brother. But I saw two cars parked in the driveway, and rang the doorbell.

I stood there for a minute, staring at the door. Didn't want to give off creeper vibes by stealing glances toward the windows. I rang the doorbell a second time and gave a gentle knock to go along, just in case the chime wasn't working inside.

I was just about to turn away when I heard the clacking of the deadbolt being unlocked. The door swung open, revealing a woman with dark circles under her eyes. Her black hair was a frazzled mess. There was no mistaking this was Carissa Summers.

The tip of her nose was red, raw from blowing and wiping it repeatedly.

"Can I help you?" she asked, staring me up and down like she had never seen someone so large standing before her.

I bowed my head. "Good afternoon, miss," I said. "My name is Jonny Mendez, and I was hoping to schedule a time to come back and speak with you about your brother. Whenever you're ready, of course."

I could've used an alias. But my name was common enough where I never worried about being caught during my brief stints in small town America. I vanished as soon as anyone believed they understood me on a personal level.

She blinked rapidly, still looking me up and down as if she was trying to piece together a puzzle. "I'm sorry. Are you with the police?"

"I'm not. I'm not with any law enforcement agency. However, spent several years with the Navy SEALs and the CIA. Your brother's death, combined with Jackson Green's on Friday has raised some suspicions for me."

Carissa rubbed her temples. Exhaustion clearly had a stronghold over her, and I wasn't making matters any better. Maybe she thought I was an illusion of sorts.

"And you're from Redwood?" she asked. "Sorry, this all seems a bit odd."

"I'm not from Redwood originally, but have been living here for the past few months." I always found it best to be direct and honest with people, especially when they were under duress. "My neighbors are Herb and Rochelle Walker. They told me I could find you here."

"Herb and Rochelle?" she repeated. Hearing those names brought a flicker of life to her countenance. A smile touched the corners of her mouth. "Wow. I haven't heard from them in years. How are they doing?"

I shifted my weight to the other leg. "Well, I obviously can't speak for how they were in the past. But they are lovely people to have as neighbors."

"Does Rochelle still bake cookies?"

I grinned. "She brings me a fresh batch every two weeks."

Carissa's smiled faded, and her lips started trembling. Tears rolled down her cheeks as she shook her head. "Sorry."

I raised a hand. "Carissa, you have nothing to apologize for. You've gone through a lot today, and that's why I want to come back another time to talk."

She shook her head again. "No. Come in."

Carissa stepped aside to allow me to pass. She wore a pair of athletic shorts and a t-shirt, but I glimpsed her upscale coats hanging on the rack in the foyer.

The house was dark, and the temperature felt glorious as the air conditioning blasted. To my left was the kitchen, where a tea pot waited on the stove.

"I really don't want to intrude today," I said.

"It's fine," she replied, yanking a hair tie off her wrist and pulling her hair into a messy bun. "I don't mind the company."

"Not to sound rude," I said. "But do you not have any family coming to spend time with you today?"

Carissa drew in a long breath, placing her hands on her hips, and let it out as a sigh. "Afraid not. It was just me and Timmy. Our parents were killed when we were in high school. They were bicyclists. Hit by a drunk driver trying to pass the car in front of him. Drove on the shoulder and wiped both of them out."

I pressed my hand against my heart. "I'm incredibly sorry. I lost my mother at a young age, too. And have never met my father."

She looked into my eyes, and I saw the pain in hers. Not just the pain of losing her brother this morning. But the pain of losing her parents. A pain that never left the body, no matter what you tried to do. It clung to your soul like a leach.

"So you're like us," she said. "Tough. Independent. You never had a choice for another way."

I nodded. Sharing this type of bond with someone was always both comforting and awkward. There always arose a desire to swap stories. Compare who might have had it harder. But we always knew it wasn't a competition. We just liked to think somewhere out in the cold world, maybe someone had it worse than us.

"Let's sit down in the kitchen," Carissa said. "Would you like a cup of tea?"

"That sounds great," I replied, following her to the round kitchen table covered with piles of mail and magazines.

She scooped up the mess into a single pile and placed it on the empty seat backed against the wall. Carissa shuffled to the stove, turned the knob off, and opened the overhead cupboard to grab two tea cups.

As she stretched, I couldn't help but notice her curvy figure. I promptly looked away, gazing down at my intertwined fingers on the table. Never approach a woman in a vulnerable state. That had long been a rule of mine. It wasn't fair to either person involved.

Carissa returned to the table and placed the tea cups down, pulling out the open seat on my immediate left.

"Do you need milk or sugar?" she asked.

I wasn't much of a tea drinker and didn't know all the rules and etiquette. "No thanks. I take it straight."

No idea if that was a thing tea drinkers said.

Carissa pulled her cup to her lips and took a sip.

"So, your name is Jonny Mendez. You're not from Redwood. And you're not with the police. But you have suspicions? I'm not sure what you want from me exactly."

"Let me take a step back," I said, shifting in my seat and taking my first sip of tea. That shit was scalding hot. "I have no involvement with anything happening this weekend. But because of my background, I can't help but notice when things seem...off. Now, I understand suicides aren't typically investigated, especially ones that seem straightforward on the surface. But I don't think these were as straightforward as they seem."

Carissa scrunched her face in confusion. "How do you figure? Jackson jumped off the building. And my brother shot himself in the head."

"Again," I said. "That's what we see on the surface. Do you not find it strange that these happened two days apart? And that they both knew each other from high school."

Carissa shrugged. "A lot of those guys from that team still talk to each other. They all get invited back every five years to celebrate the anniversary of their championship."

"How close were you to your brother?" I asked.

Carissa sipped her tea, and when she put it down, tears welled in her eyes. "We were all we had for each other. His house is three blocks down. We lived together for the longest time. Until seven years ago, then agreed it was best to live our own lives. He started a serious relationship and didn't want to bother me. Still promised to always be close by, and that's why he moved within the same neighborhood."

"So you both lived in this house together?"

Carissa nodded. "We moved in here after my brother turned eighteen and could legally buy property on his own. I'm—sorry, I *was*—two years younger than him. I was fifteen when my parents passed, Timmy seventeen. Technically, we should have both been sent off to foster care. But my family has been in Redwood for generations, so the city held a special hearing to decide our living circumstances. With my brother only a couple of months from turning eighteen, the Walkers offered to check on us every day, so we could keep living in our house. They were granted some sort of temporary guardianship that expired when Timmy turned eighteen."

"Wow," I said, sitting back in my seat. "That seems like quite the workaround for you two."

Carissa smiled. "We like to handle matters on our own in Redwood. Always have, always will. No one on city council wanted to get the state involved after our parents' death, so the arrangement was kept a secret between those involved. We're forever grateful, and that's why we vowed to never leave this city."

I drank my tea, glad it had cooled down enough to be bearable.

"I understand a phone call was made to the police before your brother took his life," I said. "That was from you, right?"

Carissa scratched her head, blinking away a fresh batch of tears. "Yes. I had a feeling something bad was going to happen. I just didn't know what."

"How?"

Carissa drew invisible circles on the table surface with her finger. "He called me at four o'clock this morning. It was weird because he sounded completely fine. Like he was calling to just check in and catch up. Only that's not what he called for."

"What did he say?" I asked, shifting forward in my seat. My tea was going completely cold, but I didn't care right now.

"He told me he loved me. That he was proud of me. Of us. We'd gone through so much together, and he believed I'd be okay living on my own without him."

Carissa stopped, her shoulders jolting as she cried more. She wiped her face clear and drew in a deep breath. "I begged him to tell me what was going on. He'd been having some...episodes over the past few months. This wasn't the first time he'd called me in the middle of the night. But the other times he sounded—I hate saying this—crazy. Like he was in a trance. But this time was different because he sounded so normal. Confident. I could tell he came to peace with whatever he was battling in his mind. I jumped out of bed and drove to his house. But Timmy wasn't there. And he wouldn't tell me where he was. That's when I called the cops."

Carissa paused again and stared blankly across the room. Her hazel eyes seemed to glow with the constant layer of moisture covering them.

"Had he said anything about Jackson after what happened on Friday?" I asked. I wanted to reach out and comfort Carissa, but knew it would have been way too forward of a move.

"We talked about it Friday night," Carissa said. "Timmy was plenty upset, as you can imagine. Was beating himself up for not having reached out to his old friend recently. I think he was just going through the typical guilt of losing someone and not having had proper closure. He stayed in Friday night. I offered to come over, maybe watch a movie together, but he insisted he was fine and would go to bed early to sleep off the grief. I should have just gone. Maybe he'd still be here today."

Carissa appeared to have run dry of tears, but her voice carried the same amount of sorrow.

"Was there anything else going on in Timmy's life that could have pushed him to do this?" I asked. "Sorry to make you relive all this so soon. I'm just trying to get a clear picture."

Carissa nodded. "It's fine. I understand. My brother hated his job. Hated his boss. You wouldn't think working at a tire shop came with so much drama. But it did. The shop owner, Ed, created a lot of chaos. Stretched workers thin. Shortened their breaks, refused to give fair raises. I'm not even sure the last time my brother had a Saturday off. All of them get asked to work every Saturday. But Timmy always gave a facade that he was fine. Didn't mind the overtime pay. And ever since him and his girlfriend broke up two years ago, he claimed he had nothing better to do on weekends. So he just took the punches."

"A toxic work environment can take a toll on people's mental health," I said. "I saw it in the military and in the CIA. If you don't get it addressed, it can make you crumble under the pressure. I might ask around his tire shop and see what his coworkers have to say. They may have more insight than your brother was sharing."

"Good luck down there," Carissa said. "Big Ed runs a tight ship. If he sees you snooping around and not trying to get new tires, he'll call the police on you for trespassing."

"Sounds like a real winner."

Carissa chuckled at this. "That's one way to describe him."

"How did your call with your brother end?"

Carissa glanced at the wall and bit her bottom lip. "His last words were what really set me off. He said, 'I'm sorry for what I did. I never wanted to get involved. Please ask them to forgive me.'"

Chapter 6

That night, I parked in front of Timmy's house just after nine o'clock. Carissa didn't give me the address. She said he lived two blocks over, so I parked at different sections of the block to monitor the activities of each home, eliminating them until finding Timmy's.

Plus, a couple had stopped at Timmy's house and placed a wreath of flowers on the doorstep. Most of the homes in this neighborhood looked similar, and Timmy's was no different from Carissa's. The driveway sat abandoned, and I presumed his car was still parked at the trail where he had taken his life, or already towed to the impound.

I had taken a lunch break to grab a bite from a place called Snazzi's Sandwiches. It was the closest dining option to Big Ed's Tires, and I wanted to scope the area with plans of returning when they were open this week. Folks in Redwood took their Sundays seriously, as I found few people out and about.

I had to wait for nightfall before making my move into Timmy's house, and didn't move my car to his property until the sun made its encore.

The neighborhood had been quiet most of the day. The afternoon grew brutally hot, keeping most of everyone inside. Except for a man five houses down who spent his day washing two cars in the driveway while tending to a six-pack of beers.

Some kids came out around seven o'clock, tossed a football around for an hour, then returned to their air-conditioned homes. It still blew my mind how rarely kids played outside. Growing up in Laredo, we had plenty of days with one hundred-degree heat. And that never stopped us. I'd leave the house at eight in the morning, find a group of friends at the baseball or soccer fields, and play until lunch time. After lunch, it was right back outside until ten o'clock on most nights. Life was fun. Simple. I credit my upbringing to the man I am today and wouldn't trade a single one of those memories for something as trivial as a cell phone or tablet.

I brushed the memories aside as I stepped out of the car and scanned the neighborhood. Most houses had their front porch lights on and their curtains drawn. Crickets chirped, and somewhere in the distance, a car backfired. A fox moved through the shadows on the opposite side of the street, paying me no attention.

I found it hard to imagine someone living in a deep depression in such a peaceful neighborhood. But I suppose we all hide our demons away in the back closets of our minds.

I strolled up the pathway to the front door, taking careful steps over the flowers laid out on the welcome mat. I gave a half-hearted turn of the knob to find it locked and promptly skirted around the house to head for the backyard. No point in breaking in from the front where anyone could see me, including the camera doorbell that now alerted no one at the other end.

A raccoon scared the shit out of me when I reached the back. It took its sweet time in the tin dumpster, knee deep in an old tub of vanilla ice cream. The creature scurried away when I shouted—more to myself—and vanished into the night.

A crescent moon hovered in the sky, providing me with a mere glow as I examined the back door. It was also locked, so I examined the surrounding area for anything that didn't quite look natural. Timmy kept a garden hose rolled up next to the door, along with two potted plants which I couldn't make out. And that's when I saw it. A large rock sitting on top of the soil in one pot.

I grabbed the rock, surprised by how realistic it felt, and turned it over to see the hidden compartment that held a key. This was practically the modern-day version of leaving your doors unlocked. Let me be the first to tell you, no one in Laredo was leaving a key hidden in their backyard. But being Redwood, I had a sense this was common practice.

I unlocked the backdoor and let myself in, feeling along the wall for a light switch. I flicked it on to reveal the kitchen. The room had a similar setup as Carissa's kitchen, and even the same table. They either shared similar tastes, or she had helped her brother decorate when he moved out.

The kitchen had little to offer, minus the package of Oreos on the counter tempting me. I proceeded through the house, only turning on lights that were away from the street-side. The layout worked to my advantage. Only the living room, a spare bedroom, and the bathroom ran along the front side of the house. This left me with total access to Timmy's bedroom.

I entered to find a room in shambles. The sheets lay tangled on the bed. An ashtray sat on the nightstand, filled with six spent cigarette butts. The carton they came from was tossed on the floor. A beer can appeared to have been thrown at the wall, the streaks dried but visible running down the surface. A short dresser stood opposite of the bed, a flat screen TV standing on top. The screen had a webbed crack in the center, as if it had been punched. The top drawer was open, shirts and boxers spilling out.

"What the hell happened in here?" I asked the empty room. Carissa had mentioned Timmy was having episodes over the past several months. But did she understand to what extent?

It was still possible Timmy hadn't done all this himself. Maybe someone was over and they got into a fight. I'm not sure why anyone else might be compelled to throw a beer can against the wall in their own room.

I opened the closet door and jumped back as a mountain of dirty laundry poured out. Behind it were old shoe boxes stuffed with family pictures and important documents like Timmy's birth certificate and social security card.

Nothing that suggested why he was pushed to take his life, aside from the obvious narrative the poor man had lost his grip on reality.

I turned off the bedroom light, disturbed by what I had just seen, and ventured down the hallway to the spare room. From what I could tell through the darkness, the room had been used more as an office. I shuffled in and closed the blinds, wanting to flash the light quickly to see if anywhere else in the house looked like Timmy's bedroom.

It wasn't an office, but a game room. There was a bed stuffed into the corner, covered with piles of clothes that at least looked clean. Clearly, the bed hadn't been used by a guest in ages, seeing as it didn't have sheets or a comforter.

Timmy liked video games. He had a TV stand below the window, with an even bigger television. Beneath it were two different X-Boxes, and both the fourth and fifth generations of Playstation. Cords lay in a clusterfuck along the carpet, but otherwise, the room was in much better shape than the last one.

I did, however, notice a manila folder on the middle rack of the TV stand, a couple of papers sticking out from the sides. I opened it to find a bill from Redwood Medical Center for twenty-three hundred dollars for a brain scan.

The papers behind the bill were printed images of what I presumed was Timmy's brain. Nothing was highlighted or circled, so I had no idea what I was looking at. The doctor on record was listed as Stephen Sowerby, head of neurology.

"Neurology?"

Brain disorders.

Carissa would have mentioned if Timmy had been diagnosed with anything in particular. Considering she told me he'd been having some mental issues lately, I don't believe she would have left this detail out. Could Timmy have been receiving treatment and never told his sister?

It seemed unlikely, considering their tight-knit relationship. But something like a mental illness could bring shame and embarrassment. Maybe Timmy didn't want to put this burden on his beloved sister.

The rest of the file was another ten sheets of brain images that made no sense to me. And finally, a prescription signed by Dr. Sowerby for Zoloft. I wasn't familiar with the drug, but made a mental note to look it up.

A phone rang from somewhere in the house, likely the kitchen. It startled me, so I stuffed the papers back into the file and fled the game room, sure to kill the light on my way out.

The phone rang six times before stopping, then rang again.

I hurried through the house, turning off all the lights. Maybe someone had noticed, after all, and was calling to see what was going on.

When I returned to the kitchen last, I spotted the phone. An old landline mounted to the wall next to the refrigerator. Reminded me of my childhood. We had a similar setup, and I remembered talking to girls on the phone, stretching that poor cord as long as it would go so I could speak from the privacy of the hallway, instead of the kitchen, where my aunt would eavesdrop while cooking.

The phone stopped ringing, so I turned off the kitchen light and exited through the backdoor. The raccoon stayed away, and I took cautious steps along the side of the house, watching the block from the shadows.

I saw no one, and sprinted for my car, zooming off into the night without another look back. My heart hammered in my chest as I kept checking the rearview. Home free.

At least, I thought so.

Chapter 7

A heavy knock banged on my door the next morning.

I knew it well. It was a universal sound that made everyone's stomach do cartwheels upon hearing it. The good ol' police knock.

Why the fuck were the cops at my house?

I was enjoying a deep sleep, my head spinning as I hopped out of bed. I glanced at the clock in the living room as I passed through. It was 8:07.

A second knock came. Heavier. Louder.

I looked through the peephole and saw two police officers standing outside, thumbs hooked in their belt loops.

Always good when they didn't have their weapons drawn—something I'd encountered on plenty of occasions, thanks to my vigilant behavior.

I opened the door, and both cops looked at me through their sunglasses. One was bald, with more arm tattoos than me. The other had a short buzz cut with a thick mustache covering his upper lip.

"Good morning, officers," I said, clearing my groggy throat. "How can I help you?"

"What's your name, sir?" the bald cop asked.

"Jonathan Mendez," I replied. "May I ask what this is about?"

"Where were you last night?" mustache asked me.

God dammit. Someone saw me in the neighborhood.

"I was here at home," I said. "Sleeping. That's why my hair looks like this."

I pointed to my messy hair, feeling one side matted flat against my head, the other side a frazzled shit show.

"Let's call it last night around 9:15," baldy said, crossing his arms.

I could take on the mustache guy, but baldy would put up a fight.

I wasn't sure how to play this. I could lie, but I got the sense these guys *knew* where I was last night. Why else would they be standing on my doorstep right now?

I took too long thinking, so baldy spoke again. "Sir, you're gonna have to come with us. We have video footage of you at the residence of Timothy Summers last night. With no one having let you in, we have to consider this breaking and entering."

"B and E?" I asked. "But there was a key. I was supposed to be there. And what video footage are you talking about?"

"Save it for the station," mustache said, reaching into his belt to pull out a pair of handcuffs.

I raised my hands peacefully.

"Officers," I said. "I think there is a misunderstanding here. I'll go with you down to the station. No need for handcuffs. Am I under arrest?"

The cops exchanged a glance.

"No, sir," mustache said. "But we need to detain you for questioning. I'll keep the handcuffs as long as you cooperate. Got it, *Jonathan*?"

I nodded. "So, should I follow you guys there?"

Baldy laughed. "No, you'll be riding with us."

I cocked an eyebrow. "Can I call shotgun?"

Baldy laughed again. "Are you always so chummy with law enforcement?"

"I try."

"Get in the car, smart ass," he said, and the two officers parted to clear a path for me to pass them.

Guess that was a no on the shotgun matter.

I dragged my feet to the police cruiser, wearing nothing but flip-flops, a pair of shorts, and a rather thin wife beater. Or whatever they called those shirts now to not offend the new generation of softies.

I waited for one of them to open the rear door and let me in. Baldy did so and drove us to the station.

"Busy time of year for you guys?" I asked. I couldn't help but keep the mood light when dealing with the police. It was only a matter of time before they learned my identity and background, and understood I wasn't actually up to no good.

Neither man responded.

"How long of a drive are we looking at?" I asked.

Mustache looked over his shoulder at me. "Do you ever shut up?"

"Well," I said. "I haven't been told I have the right to remain silent."

"That's because you're not under arrest, jackass," baldy said, glaring at me in the rear-view mirror.

"Jackass?" I said. "That's rude. Look guys, I was at Timmy's house last night. Yes. But it wasn't breaking and entering."

"Save it for the station," mustache said. "We're almost there."

It ended up being a ten-minute drive to the police station, in which we drove in silence. Except for the occasional crackle from the radio up front. Dispatch reported a shoplifting incident at a liquor store, plus a report of domestic abuse during the drive over.

We pulled up to the station and drove around the back, where all the police cruisers were parked. The building looked more like an event center from the outside—welcoming, with perfectly manicured shrubs and trees running along the perimeter. Several windows peppered across the light gray stone facade.

We parked, and baldy opened the door for me to step out.

"Ladies first," he said, extending an arm to direct me toward the door below a portico engraved with REDWOOD POLICE DEPARTMENT.

I entered the building like I belonged. An older officer sat behind the reception desk, staring at a computer screen through his bifocal glasses.

Mustache took the lead and guided us down a hallway to the right, where we passed a handful of offices before stepping into Interrogation Room #3, as noted on the sign hanging outside.

"After you," mustache said, holding open the door for me.

I entered and took my seat at the steel table, and waited for the two officers to sit down on the opposite side.

Only mustache sat down. Baldy leaned against the wall, arms crossed.

"You're just here for questioning," mustache said. "You *do* have the right to speak with an attorney, but we'll keep this light. Okay?"

I nodded.

"Let's start with your full name and date of birth," mustache said, taking out a notepad and pen. This was my first glance at the nametag on his uniform. Chambers.

"Jonathan Christian Mendez. Born November second—"

"Cut the crap," baldy interrupted. "Do you have any identification?"

"Passport at the house. It's expired, but it's all I have right now."

"So, no driver's license?" baldy asked, stepping forward. "You drove that Camry without a license."

I shrugged. "There's no proof of that."

I knew my way around the justice system. Evidence was a bitch.

"Roman," Officer Chambers said. "Run a check in the system for Mr. Mendez here. Anything we should know about on your record?"

"Ten years of service with the SEALs. Five with the CIA—not sure if that actually shows on my record."

I knew it didn't, but fuck these guys. They needed to know who I was.

Officer Roman glowered at me before leaving the room.

Chambers smiled—he was the good cop. "Excuse me for a second, too. Would you like a glass of water?"

"Sure," I said.

If these asshats only knew how many times I'd sat in interrogation rooms, maybe we could cut all the posturing. I knew the drill. They wanted me relaxed so I'd cooperate. See Chambers as my friend. But not too relaxed. That's why Roman was there. To scare me. Though, I feared no man.

The room was chilly to keep me alert and a tad antsy. Maybe I'd spill a juicy detail and incriminate myself.

Dumb asses.

Fifteen minutes passed, and I sat completely still while waiting.

They returned, and Chambers handed me a paper cup filled with water. Roman trailed behind him with a tablet in hand, surely where he had all my information pulled up.

Now they both sat. Chambers spoke first.

"So, Mr. Mendez. Your background is exactly what you told us."

"Why would I make that up?" I asked.

Chambers chuckled. "You're in an interrogation room. People are inclined to say just about anything once they pass through that doorway."

"I'm not a regular person," I said.

"Yes, I see that now. So tell us, Mr. Mendez, what were you doing at Timmy Summers' house last night?"

The mood had shifted to one of relaxation. Like we were old friends catching up for coffee. I wasn't sure if the shift was genuine, or part of Chambers' gimmick.

"I'm friends with Timmy's sister, Carissa," I said, taking a gamble I could only pray would work out.

Chambers raised an eyebrow as he scribbled on his notepad. "I see."

"She wanted me to check on the place," I continued, never afraid to double down. "Said it was too soon for her to step into her brother's house. She just wanted to be sure the stove hadn't been left on. Things like that."

"How do you know her?" Officer Roman asked, monotone and pissed off. I could see it in his eyes. He was hoping to lock me up here today, but saw that opportunity fizzling out with each passing second.

"I've only been here a few months," I said. "My neighbors are the Walkers, and they connected me with Carissa shortly after I moved in. Said I needed to spend time with people my age. Now, I haven't spent a ton of time with Carissa—I much prefer to not leave my house if it's not necessary. But I checked on her after I saw the news about Timmy. That's when she asked me to do this favor."

Chambers kept writing. Roman kept glaring.

Officer Chambers folded his hands on the table. "Clearly, this was just a misunderstanding, Mr. Mendez. And I apologize for that. We're just doing our job—I'm sure you understand."

I nodded. "Of course."

"It was all by dumb luck we even saw you at Timmy's house," Chambers continued. "Our team was processing Timmy's belongings last night, which included his cell phone. Just so happened it was that exact moment when you set off the doorbell camera he had, and the notification popped up on the phone. We tried calling to see if anyone would answer…"

"Yes. I heard the phone. But I was raised to not answer the phone in someone else's house. So I let it go."

"Very well then," Chambers said, sitting back and tossing his hands up. He looked at Roman. "Anything else you want to ask? Doesn't seem we have any issue here."

Roman finally broke his glare from me as he met his partner's eyes. "Nope. All good."

"Well, Mr. Mendez," Chambers said. "We have no reason to take up any more of your time. Thank you for coming down to chat with us."

"I do have a question," I said.

"Shoot."

"This may sound odd, but have the police looked deeper into these two suicides?"

Chambers furrowed his brow. "In what sense?"

I leaned forward. "It can't be a coincidence, can it? These two men take their lives two days apart. And they've been connected ever since high school. And not just friendly waving in the hallways. They were bonded by something special. That state championship I keep hearing about."

The officers exchanged glances, then shrugged. "We understand the connection between the two men," Chambers said. "But we also investigate suicides to look for any signs of foul play or involvement from third parties. There was no such evidence at either scene. At this point, we have to believe it *is* a coincidence."

"Understood," I said, standing up from the table.

"We'll get you a ride back to your house," Chambers said, standing and extending his hand for me to shake. He was no longer playing the good cop routine.

Officer Roman did not offer his hand, and only stared at the table as I shuffled out of the room.

Chambers walked me to the lobby, found the first young officer we crossed paths with, and had him give me a ride home.

The young officer's name was Santos. He was a scrawny kid who needed some time in the weight room. He shared his life story with me. Freshly graduated from the academy. Family from Guatemala. Wanted to propose to his girlfriend this year. We griped about the lack of authentic Latin cuisine in Redwood.

He dropped me off at home and we went our separate ways. It wasn't even noon yet, but already the day was scorching. No one was outside on my block, but I knew the Walkers were watching. They had surely seen the police arrive and take me away earlier. Even if I couldn't see them, I knew Rochelle had a radar for anything happening on this block.

I strolled up to my door and let myself in, freezing when I saw a small piece of paper lying on the floor inside.

I frowned as I squatted to pick it up, flipping it over to read two typed words:

BACK OFF

Chapter 8

I returned to Carissa's house on Tuesday morning.

As much as I wanted to go straight there after finding the note left at my home, I couldn't possibly justify bothering her two consecutive days after her brother had taken his life.

I spent my Monday afternoon inside, Glock by my side as I tried to piece together who the hell left me the note.

Back off from what?

Did someone in town know I was actually snooping around Timmy's house? The only person who came to mind was Officer Roman, but we had been in the same room yesterday and he wouldn't have had time to beat me to my house before I showed up.

This meant it had to be someone from Timmy's neighborhood. They must have seen me and jumped to their own conclusions. They would've had to follow me home Sunday night to know where to leave the note. Considering my eyes had been glued to the rearview during my drive home that night, I knew that wasn't a possibility, either.

So who was it?

I had no way of knowing.

But the note proved one thing in my favor: I was on to something.

And whoever was behind the note didn't want me to continue following my suspicions. The suicides must have been planned. Orchestrated. And the call to back off had to mean there were more coming. Why go through the trouble of leaving such a note if you were done with whatever sick game was being played?

The note also opened the door to a new reality. Someone was watching me. But for how long? And why?

These questions swirled in my mind as I strode up to Carissa's door and knocked, the note folded in my hand.

She pulled open the door, and I felt the air get sucked out of my lungs.

Carissa was in shambles the last time I was here, and for good reason. Right now, though, I had to look away from her tight jeans and crop top that showed a most tempting sliver of her silky skin.

"Hi," I said, sure she had noticed my initial shock.

"I've been expecting you," she said. "Thought you'd come yesterday."

"Why is that?"

"Come in," she said, pulling the door open all the way and stepping aside.

She closed the door before leading us into the kitchen, where we took our same seats as Sunday.

"I got a visit from Officer Chambers yesterday," Carissa said, raising her eyebrows at me. "And he told me all about you."

My throat tensed. I couldn't read her mood.

"I'm sorry," I said. "I didn't mean to drag you into this. But I had to make up a story on the spot. Didn't think they would actually follow up with you. I gave them plenty of details to make it seem legit."

Carissa grinned. "You did well. I'm impressed. Mentioning the Walkers as our mutual connection. Brilliant."

"So you're not mad?" I asked.

She shook her head. "Not about your cover-up story. I am mad you went into my brother's house without asking. If you had just asked, I would've said yes. Even would've gone with you."

I felt both relief and stupid at the same time. "I didn't want to hassle you after everything that had just happened."

"That's fair," she said. "But still. Just ask. I let you into my home on Sunday. Clearly, I'm intrigued by what you have to say about all this."

"So you agree there is something bigger at play than just two random suicides?"

Carissa paused and seemed to consider this. "I think it's *possible*. But I need some proof. Sure hope you found something at Timmy's house."

"We can come back to that in a minute," I said. "I found something at *my* house yesterday."

I unfolded the note and slid it across the table.

Carissa read it with a quick glance before looking at me. "Back off? What does this have to do with anything?"

I scratched my head. "I was hoping you could tell me. It was slipped under my door while I was at the police station yesterday morning."

She read the note one more time. "It's rather vague. Could be in relation to anything, I suppose. Are you dating anyone with a crazy ex? Or are you implying this is because of you snooping around my brother's death?"

I shrugged. "Definitely not seeing anyone. Plus, I keep to myself. I go to work and come home. Might stop for a bite somewhere in town. Try not to speak to people when I'm out and about. At home, I chat with the Walkers a couple times each week. And that's about it. That's why I think it is me being in your brother's house. Someone must have seen me."

Carissa sighed. "Well, the police obviously caught you if they took you in for questioning. So there's no saying who knows about your visit the other night."

That was true. Police could gossip as badly as teenage girls, especially if they were having a slow night. And there were always members of the press who lurked around police stations.

I rubbed my temples, growing frustrated. "But this is proof, right? I'm not just making this up in my head."

"Proof of what?"

"That someone is behind these suicides. I mean, if they were actually random like we're led to believe, why would this note turn up? I'm the only one in town who believes something is suspicious. Now, I haven't acted on that suspicion aside from going into your brother's house. That's why I'm narrowing it down to someone in that neighborhood. No other explanation."

"Do you feel threatened?" Carissa asked, shifting in her seat and studying me.

"I wouldn't say that. I'm concerned someone outside of my tight circle knows where I live. But if anyone wants to start trouble with me, they'll find they won't get very far."

"A macho man," Carissa said. "I see."

"What's that supposed to mean?"

She smiled. "Big tough guy with scars and tattoos. Of course, you're not going to admit you're scared. You have a reputation to uphold."

"I'm sorry," I said. "Are you a therapist or something? You've been analyzing me since I walked in."

"I'm a middle school counselor with a background in psychology," she replied. "Most of my time is spent studying adolescent behavior, but that doesn't mean I can't pick apart a grown man."

"Pick apart? That seems intense."

Carissa laughed. "I'll back off. Promise."

"Hold on," I said. "Are psychology and neurology related at all?"

Her eyes fluttered as she considered the question. "They're two branches of the same tree. Psychology is more abstract—understanding people's thinking, emotions, and behaviors. Whereas neurology is more concrete—studying the brain and nervous system. A neurological disorder can cause psychological problems."

"Do you have any neurology education?" I asked, leaning forward and planting my elbows on the table.

Carissa shook her head. "Took a high level introduction to the subject in college, but that's it. My expertise lies more in the abstract. Why are you asking all this?"

"In your professional opinion, would you say your brother was suffering from any psychological issues?"

This question caused a sheet of seriousness to take over Carissa's face. I was sure she had already given this some thought in the past, but had never been directly confronted about it.

"I believe he was suffering from a mental breakdown," she said. "A mild one, perhaps. Like I told you on Sunday, he'd had these episodes before where he'd call me in the middle night in a panic. But those instances were sporadic. To define them as something more serious, there would need to be some consistency."

"Did you know Timmy was seeing a neurologist?"

Carissa turned pale as she gazed into my eyes. "Excuse me?"

"I saw a file while I was in his game room. It was full of brain scans, but there were no notes. Also, a prescription for Zoloft signed by a Doctor Stephen Sowerby."

She clapped her hands to her face. "Why wouldn't he have come to me?" Carissa's lips trembled, on the verge of crying. But no tears came. "Doctor Sowerby treats a wide range of mental disorders. Zoloft is an antidepressant. Timmy knew something was wrong if he went to see Doctor Sowerby. But why didn't he tell me?"

Carissa balled a fist and slammed it on the table. I recoiled, not expecting her abrupt movement. Her arms shook, lips pursed so tightly they were turning white.

"Carissa," I said, standing up. "May I give you a hug? I think you need it."

She nodded, eyes laser focused on the table, jawline popping out with rage.

I crouched down since she stayed seated and wrapped my arms around her. In my embrace, her shoulders tremored against my chest. Her body gave full resistance, stiff like she didn't actually want the hug. After thirty seconds, she softened, stood up, and leaned into my body, planting her face in my shoulder to let out the tears she'd been holding back.

"You've been dealing with this all on your own," I said, running a hand up and down her back. "That's not fair to you."

My t-shirt turned wet against my chest, soaking in her tears. She pulled back and looked at me through bleary eyes. "Thank you."

She sniffled and turned away to find a box of tissues on the kitchen counter, blowing her nose and wiping her eyes clear.

"Are you alright?" I asked, treading carefully.

She nodded. "I'll be fine. Emotions are all over the place. But you're right. I needed that hug. Human connection is so important during a time of mourning. And I haven't had any."

Carissa drew in a deep breath and waved her hands to cool off her face.

"I understand," I said. "I've dealt with plenty of deaths on my own."

"No one should have to."

"That's not what I came here for, but glad I could help."

Carissa nodded. "I actually feel a lot better. So, again, thank you. But I'm sorry to say, this information you just gave me might hurt your case that something malicious is going on."

"How do you figure?"

"Well, if Timmy was prescribed Zoloft, then he was diagnosed with a mental disorder. There are countless disorders that can result in suicide, so now I'm finding it unlikely he was part of some scheme. That there were two suicides on the same weekend isn't relevant. It's possible my brother was already dealing with suicidal thoughts, and seeing the coverage of Jackson's jump off that hotel may have been the final straw that pushed him to take his life. In fact, it adds up. Anyone in the throes of a mental breakdown is not capable of handling trauma. Jackson's suicide was random, but it came at the worst time for my brother."

Carissa paced frantically around her kitchen, grabbing her cell phone, purse, and keys.

"Where are you going?" I asked.

She stopped and stared at me, like she had forgotten I was even there. Her eyes blazed with anger and determination. "I'm going to see Doctor Sowerby to find out what the hell was going on with my brother."

Chapter 9

I went to dinner that evening alone.

Found a spot just outside my neighborhood that I'd been meaning to try and never had. A diner called The Oregon Trail.

I had skipped lunch, so went for an early dinner at four o'clock. The diner was filled with dozens of senior citizens at that hour, all enjoying coffees and breakfast foods for supper. Maybe I was an old soul, because all of that sounded perfect.

I placed my order of scrambled eggs, toast, bacon, hash browns, and extra bacon. I wasn't a coffee drinker and instead opted for a tall glass of orange juice.

My server was a plump lady named Kathy. With a K, she insisted. Kathy with a K chatted up a storm with me, asking where I was from, how long I was staying in Redwood, and yes, she knew the Walkers—they came in after church on Sundays.

The diner instantly gave me the small town vibes I always sought. There weren't many places like this in Redwood, but I finally found where the locals hung out. If I had to guess, a younger crowd and families would likely start trickling in around six o'clock, long after these current patrons would be back home, slipping into their pajamas and turning on the nightly news.

I sat in a booth alongside the window overlooking the parking lot. The diner was nestled on a quiet corner, no other businesses in sight.

Two gentlemen sat in the booth behind me, and their conversation was all about the two suicides that happened over the weekend.

They had no clue I was eavesdropping on their conversation, but they had my full attention.

"It's a damned shame," the man behind me said. I glanced over my shoulder to see he was wearing a gray fedora. His friend across the table wore glasses and browsed through a newspaper spread across the table.

"Makes me sick," the man in glasses said. "Jackson Green and Timmy Summers. Who would've thought we'd outlive them? Remember how invincible they seemed during that run?"

Fedora chuckled. "Our star receiver and corner back. Remember when Green got sandwiched on the sidelines in the first playoff game that year? The whole stadium went silent. Then he popped right up and scored a touchdown on the next play. That's when I knew we were gonna win in it all. That team had all the fight in the world. Plus the talent."

Glasses nodded. "I remember that playoff run like it was yesterday. Timmy with the pick-six to clinch the ticket to state."

I turned around in my booth. "Excuse me, gentlemen. I couldn't help but overhear your conversation. Were you guys part of that team somehow?"

Glasses met my eyes and chuckled. Fedora had to angle himself, albeit painfully, to look over his shoulder at me.

"Part of the team?" glasses repeated. "No. But we were teachers during that time. And being sports fans, we naturally took an interest in all the school spirit."

"So you knew these students personally?" I asked.

"Sure did," fedora said, turning back around.

"Why don't you come join us?" glasses said, sliding over in his booth.

"I don't want to impose," I replied. Deep down, I was ready to jump over the booth and join these gentlemen. But I understood the hassle of going through the pleasantries and politeness.

"You're not a bother at all, sir," glasses said, patting the empty seat next to him. "I insist. We've been swapping the same old stories for decades now. I don't know about Chuck here, but I always enjoy some fresh blood to add to our discussions."

Chuck adjusted his fedora and nodded slowly.

"Alright then," I said, grabbing my glass of orange juice and joining the older men at their table.

"Pleased to meet you," glasses said, extending a hand. "I'm Walter—you can call me Walt. And my friend here is Chuck."

I shook both of their hands as I shifted to get comfortable in my new seat. These men looked to be in their mid-seventies, perhaps a little older. They both tended to cups of coffee. Chuck had a plate with chicken fried steak, and Walt had mostly cleared a dish of meatloaf and mashed potatoes.

"Thanks for having me," I said. "My name is Jonny. I'm still fairly new to town and have been learning a lot about its past after those two suicides this weekend."

"Welcome, Jonny," Chuck said, taking a swig of coffee. "What brings you to Redwood?"

I told them of my life on the move, feeling an instant trust. If these two men ever gossiped, I had an inclination they kept it between themselves.

"Life with nowhere to call home," Walt said. "Sounds both exciting and frightening at the same time."

I grinned. "It has its ups and down. But I got used to it being with the SEALs."

"The *Navy* SEALs?" Chuck asked, arching an eyebrow.

"Yes, sir."

"Wow," he said. "Don't think I've ever met a SEAL. Thank you for your service."

I nodded appreciatively. "The honor is all mine."

"So, why such an interest in our conversation?" Walt asked. "I suppose everyone in town is talking about the same thing. We don't exactly get a ton of breaking news stories around here."

I trusted these guys. But how much? They could have connections to the police department, or even the victims' families—not that it mattered in Timmy's case. I'd need more feelers to see what I could tell them, so refrained from sharing my involvement.

"Oh, I don't know," I said. "Just seems weird to me. These two guys take their lives so close to each other. What are the odds?"

Walt nodded. Chuck ran a finger along the rim of his coffee mug.

"We've been trying to make sense of it, too," Chuck said. "Now, we didn't keep in constant contact with either of them, but we'd still see them around. Even here a couple of times. I will say, and Walt can confirm, something seemed...off about Jackson the last time we saw him."

"Not the Jackson we remembered," Walt said. "We can tell you from firsthand experience, Jackson Green was always a bundle of energy. Not exactly a class clown, but never afraid to make a remark to lighten the mood. His presentations in class were colorful and always had everyone laughing. And they were good on top of it. Jackson was one of those kids who could get along with anyone. He just seemed to understand people and wanted to bring the best out of them."

I thought of the countless number of comedians who suffered from depression. It was always an interesting dynamic to me. People who were unhappy with their own lives channeled their sorrow and frustrations into comedy and joy, so that others in the world wouldn't have to feel like them.

"But you say that was a recent development?" I asked. "How long ago was that?"

"We saw him in here about six months ago," Walt said. "Now, he'd always greet us and give us big hugs. Happy to catch up. And that time, he saw us, waved and smiled, and went about his business. We didn't think much of it. Maybe he was busy and had to get going—he was picking up takeout, after all."

"But it was the next time we saw him," Chuck said. "In here also, three months ago. He walked in, looked at us. No wave. No smile. He was picking up takeout again, but this time he had an outburst."

"An outburst?"

Chuck nodded. "He went through his bag of food, checking everything was in order. They didn't put in those packets with the napkins and plasticware, and Jackson blew a gasket. Started cussing out sweet Kathy. Insulted her, asked her how hard it was to do a minimum wage job. All that kind of stuff."

"We found out later that's how he had become," Walt added. "Anyone who had an encounter with Jackson found him to be repulsive and offensive."

"It killed us to see him like that," Chuck said. "We don't know what made him that way. Looking back now, he must have been going through some sort of depression. That's simply not the Jackson Green any of us remember."

The table fell silent. Kathy must have sensed the tension, because she delivered my food and topped off their coffees without saying a word—or acknowledging I had moved tables.

"I've been talking with Timmy's sister, Carissa," I said.

"Ah!" Walt cried. "Carissa Summers is one of the best students I had during my career. Honor roll, extra curriculars, the whole package. Sorry, proceed."

"Yeah, she's pretty great," I said. "But she told me her brother had been dealing with some depression as well. She believes it played a role."

"Timmy Summers was the complete opposite of Jackson Green," Walt said. "Kept to himself. Very small group of friends. Probably saw him spend time with the same five friends all throughout high school. He was smart, but lacked discipline. Struggled with focusing and completing assignments on time. We cut him some slack, though, considering the living situation he was dealing with in his senior year. Losing his parents and essentially learning how to start his life on his own. All the while making sure his little sister never suffered."

Chuck nodded. "I always said Timmy had no need for high school. He'd lived through so much more than most adults, all before graduating. Looking back, we probably shouldn't have coddled him, but it just felt wrong to add any more burden to his life. All you can do is make the best decision when you're in the moment. And that was a trying moment. Not just for Timmy, but all of us."

"So both men suffered from depression," I said, scarfing down bites while they spoke. "And they both reached their tipping point around the same time."

Chuck shrugged. "That's how it appears. But I always wonder what winning that championship did to those kids. For most of the team, it was fun—a big celebration. But for the higher profile kids, they faced an incredible amount of pressure."

"In what ways?" I asked. It felt like my body was eating on autopilot. All I wanted was to keep learning about the two victims from Chuck and Walt while the eggs and bacon slipped down my throat.

"Well," Chuck continued. "The kids who played bigger roles, like Jackson, Timmy, plus the quarterback and running back, they got calls from colleges. They'd get asked whenever they were out in town which college they were going to. Only our quarterback, Tyrell Marshall, went on to play college ball. The others stayed in town. I don't remember their reasons except for Timmy not wanting to leave his sister behind. But they stayed in Redwood, and people were baffled. A newspaper article even went out on the one-year anniversary of the championship, calling out all four players for being a disgrace for not jumping on the opportunity."

"They called out the quarterback, too?" I asked.

"Tyrell? Oh yeah. He went to play for Oregon, but stayed in a backup role during all four years. Got one start and it was miserable. Threw four interceptions before halftime and never touched the field again."

Chuck finished his dinner with a couple more bites of the chicken fried steak.

"Aside from the negative news article, did anyone hate these guys?" I asked.

Walt stared into space, thinking back to the good ol' days. "No. Not really. There were some rumblings from smaller towns out east. See, Tyrell was the first Black quarterback our school ever had. Not an issue here in Redwood, but racism is still alive in well in the smaller towns. They didn't like losing to a Black quarterback. Shouted the N-word at him. Called the coach a monkey lover. The usual ignorant stuff."

"But nothing ever came from that," Chuck added. "Sure, it was tough for those kids to see and handle, but they stayed professional. And once they left those towns, no one ever thought of it again."

"I see," I said. "But no one from Redwood had problems? Maybe an ex-coach who got jealous of the team's success?"

"The basketball coach was a little grumpy at how much attention the football team was getting," Chuck said with a gruff laugh. "But it was all in good spirits. I'll never forget that week before the championship game. You couldn't go anywhere in Redwood without feeling that constant buzz in the air. Like everyone knew something special was going to happen, and we just had to wait for it."

I nodded. "I had friends on SEAL Team Six. Remember the exact feeling you're describing from the day they killed bin Laden."

A wide grin spread across Chuck's face. "That's incredible. I'd love to hear more about that another time."

"We can arrange that," I said, scraping the last remnants of hash browns from my plate. "But I really should get going."

"Already?" Walt asked, disappointment slipping into his voice.

"I have to get to an appointment," I lied. I liked these guys, but if I didn't leave, we'd end up sitting in this booth and chatting until midnight. "Thank you both for filling me in on this rich history of Redwood. I don't live far from here, so I'm sure we'll cross paths soon enough."

"We're here at least twice a week," Chuck said, standing up to shake my hand.

I slid out of the booth and stood to match him. "We have lots to talk about. Until then."

I shook Walt's hand, reached into my pocket, and tossed a twenty on the table. As I left the diner, my mind was on fire. My gut still insisted something bigger was at play. And now, I needed to find more players from the championship team.

Chapter 10

I went to work with the guys on Wednesday morning, not knowing my day with them would be cut short.

The day's work was at a golf course for repairs. Not on the course itself, but on the decorative walkway that led into the clubhouse. Apparently, some teenagers had taken their golf clubs to the flower beds and destroyed every plant in sight, plus the surrounding grass. It would be a full day's work to return everything to normal, and Eddie had a six-man crew to tackle it.

We started at eight o'clock, my mind elsewhere while I took a shovel to the earth. Could an event that happened over twenty years ago cause depression today? It seemed improbable, yet I still had plenty of instances where I fell into depression thinking of my mother getting blown up by the cartel.

That was different, though. That was a death. And I was there to witness it all. Still had the crescent-shaped scar across my cheek from a flying piece of shrapnel. I couldn't look in the mirror without remembering that day from hell.

These men from the championship team hadn't dealt with death, or even physical pain from their time as winners. Sure, I don't doubt reading such a vile news article had a negative psychological effect.

Especially for kids a few months removed from high school. But for that to linger this long? They all had grown up, started families and careers. Got on with their lives. It's not like people were still giving them shit every time they strolled into The Oregon Trail for lunch.

I was halfway through my assigned digging area when my colleague, Julio, started shouting, "Otro! Otro! Dios mío, otro!"

He was waving his cell phone in the air, shaking his head.

"Qué es?" I asked him, dropping my shovel and stepping over the mounds of dirt to join him. He had been leaning under a tree for a quick break, eating a breakfast sandwich from McDonald's and drinking a cup of coffee.

"Qué esta pasando?" he replied, shoving his cell phone in my face.

All the blood froze in my veins upon reading the news article on Julio's phone. The headline may as well have jumped out and slapped me across the face.

A THIRD SUICIDE REPORTED IN REDWOOD

"What the fuck?" I whispered, snatching the phone out of Julio's hand to read it for myself. A nauseous feeling swarmed my body as I read about the third victim. Tyrell Marshall. Redwood's first Black quarterback, and the one who led them in their historic run to eternal glory.

His wife found him early this morning, hanging from the rafters in their garage. Tyrell had fastened a noose from a forty-foot long extension cord kept in the same garage. No note. And no warning signs, according to his wife. He left behind two kids who both attended Redwood Middle School.

There was no further information, as the story was still under development.

I handed the phone back to Julio and ran to Eddie across the way, who had also been digging up the damaged grass to prepare for new sod.

"Eddie," I said, my breathing growing rapid. "I have to go. I'm sorry."

"Everything okay?" he asked, stopping and jamming his shovel into the ground to stand on its own.

"No," I said. "There's been another suicide. And I need to speak to the police about it."

"Go," he said, waving me off. No group of undocumented immigrants wanted to hear anything about the police.

"I'll call you," I said, and dashed across the parking lot to my car, fleeing the golf course.

It only took me seven minutes to race across town to the police station. I jumped out of the Camry and ran into the building, the officer behind the reception desk standing up out of caution. It was a younger woman today and her hand moved to her holster as I dashed toward her desk.

"Can I help you?" she asked, studying me up and down. She had brown hair tied into a ponytail, and reminded me of a younger Sandra Bullock, one of my top celebrity crushes.

"Yes. I need to speak to Officer Chambers. Is he in?"

She held her gaze on me for a few more moments before sitting back down. "Chambers," she repeated. "I saw him this morning, but I'm not sure if he's in the building. Let me call him."

My fingers drummed on the counter while she picked up the phone and dialed. She still watched me like she expected me to do something crazy. I suppose I looked absurd from her perspective. Big ass Mexican dude, sweating, panting for breath, and demanding a specific officer.

"Chambers," she said into the phone. "I have a man here to see you. Seems urgent." She looked me in the eye. "What's your name, sir?"

"Jonny Mendez," I replied.

"Jonny Mendez," she echoed into the phone. She nodded and hung up. "He's here. He'll be right out if you'd like to wait over there."

She pointed to a row of chairs to the right of the reception desk, all empty.

"Thank you," I said. "Sorry if I flustered you."

"Not a problem," she replied, watching as I dragged myself toward the chairs. I had no interest in sitting—I needed to do something. But a police station was no place to act a fool, so I sat down and fidgeted with my fingers for three minutes until Officer Chambers entered the lobby from behind me and clapped a hand on my back.

"Good morning, Mr. Mendez," he said. "I'm surprised to see you back here. Did you forget something?"

I stood up and shook his hand. "Officer Chambers, thank you for seeing me. Is there somewhere we can talk in private?"

His eyes narrowed as he studied me. But I saw the curiosity swimming behind his stare. "Alright. Follow me."

Last time I was here, we went down the hallway to the right. Today, we took the hallway on the left, lined with several doors, each with different names stickered onto the frosted glass windows.

We passed three doors and turned into an open one on the right. This room was simply labeled as *MEETING ROOM*.

I followed him to find a long table stretching the length of the room. The kind where big meetings happened. It could seat about ten people on each side, with two on each end. "Can I get you a water bottle or anything?" Chambers asked.

"No thanks," I said.

Chambers took a seat at the table, but I had too much energy to sit. Instead, I strolled to the opposite wall and leaned against it, arms crossed.

"So what's this about?" he asked, leaning back in the creaky chair.

"The suicide this morning," I replied. "Another one from the same football team. The quarterback this time. What have you all found out?"

The cop's eyes fluttered as he jabbed a finger in my direction. "Excuse me? Mr. Mendez, you have no right to barge into our police station and demand information. Now, I respect your background and understand it's probably hard for you to sit on the sidelines, but you're not a member of this police force. Unless you have information that can help us in any active investigations, our conversation here is done."

I balled my fists and uncrossed my arms. "I understand that. And I'm not trying to cross any boundaries. My concerns are as a citizen, and I genuinely believe something unusual is going on."

"No shit. We have three suicides on our hands in a matter of six days."

"And that's the problem. You're simply treating them like valid suicides."

"What do you want us to do?" Chambers asked, tossing his hands in the air. "One guy jumped off a roof. The other shot himself. And the newest one hung himself at home. None of those require setting up a crime scene. It's not like there's any evidence suggesting other people were involved. Mr. Green was alone on that roof. Mr. Summers was alone at the trail. And Mr. Marshall was at his house. Are you wanting me to ask his wife if she somehow hung her six-four, two-twenty husband from their garage on her own? Think about what you're suggesting."

"That's not what I'm suggesting. All I'm saying is the frequency and the common denominator behind these three suicides can no longer be considered a coincidence. What if these guys from the championship team made some sort of pact to take their lives all these years later?"

"Why the hell would they do that?"

I gritted my teeth. "I don't know. But it's lunacy to just sit here and pretend it's a coincidence. Three men gone within a week, all with the same link to the past. What you should be doing is trying to get ahead of the next one."

Chambers laughed. "You want me to go around and ask all the people from that championship team if they're having suicidal thoughts? I don't have the right to do that because of some hunch. And I hate to break it to you, but suicide isn't exactly a crime. It's a shitty and unfortunate thing, but it's not against the law."

I rubbed my forehead. I don't know why I was expecting them to welcome me with open arms to join their investigation. They'd already made it plenty clear there *was* no investigation.

A knock came on the door and it swung open. Officer Roman stepped in, the bright lights gleaming off his bald head. "Everything okay in here, Chambers?" he asked, scowling at me.

Chambers raised his eyebrows. And voice. "Oh, Mr. Mendez here thinks we need to go knocking on everyone's door and asking if they're having suicidal thoughts. Says there will be more suicides coming if we don't."

Roman's stiff expression softened into a grin as he laughed. "Wow. Did they teach you that in the SEALs, or the CIA?"

Both men laughed at this remark, and if I wasn't in the middle of a police station, I just might have thrown Roman through the goddamned wall.

"Wait 'til everyone hears about this," Roman said, still laughing.

I shook my head, regained my composure, and stomped across the meeting room. Roman stepped aside to let me pass through the door. Before I left, I looked over my shoulder and said, "The next suicide is blood on your hands."

Chapter 11

I returned home fuming.

This wasn't my first time dealing with a closed-minded police department. All I could do was take matters into my own hands. I couldn't fault them, either. It made no logical sense to have a police force checking on random citizens because a few people had taken their own lives. There was no correlation, even if the deceased all shared a bond.

It was a waste of time and tax dollars to do such a thing, especially when they needed to be out in the world dealing with actual crimes.

But I wasn't a cop. I didn't cost the taxpayer anything—a perk of having retired from the SEALs before reaching twenty years of service.

As much as I wanted to get started today, I'd wait until tomorrow. For now, I was glued to the TV, waiting for anyone in the media to make the connection and suggest what I was thinking. But they never did.

Sure, they mentioned how all three deaths in the past week were all Redwood natives, attended the same schools, and played on the championship team together. But much like the police department, they simply accepted this as a coincidence.

The only person who offered anything of substance was Tyrell's wife, Kalynn. But all she said was that her thoughts were with the members of the team. And she made a public plea for them to seek mental help if they needed it.

I only grew more frustrated with each passing hour. I skipped lunch and had cereal for dinner, in no mood to cook.

Shortly after seven o'clock that evening, a knock came from the front door. I presumed it was the Walkers from next door, but was surprised to find Officer Santos standing on my doorstep, dressed in street clothes.

"Good evening, Mr. Mendez," he said, bowing his head.

"Santos, right?" I said, looking around. He wasn't in a patrol car. A Chevy pickup truck was parked along my sidewalk. "What are you doing here?"

"Yes, sir." He looked around behind him. "Can I come in? I'd rather not speak out here."

I was always hesitant to let anyone enter my home. But Santos was as threatening as a newborn kitten. Plus, I was twice his size. I could probably throw him into the bed of his truck from my front step.

"Okay," I said, stepping aside. "Come on in."

Santos offered a polite smile before passing through the doorway. He stood in the living room and looked around.

I closed the door and hurried back to turn off the TV, which was now covering the story of a local hero tackling gang violence in Portland.

"Please," I said, gesturing to the couch. "Have a seat."

Santos looked at the couch, debating, then finally sat down.

"I take it you're not supposed to be here," I said.

"How do you know that?" he asked, eyes growing as they looked up at me.

"The way you kept looking behind you. Means you're worried about being seen. You're a police officer and not in uniform, insisting to come in. So you *really* don't want to be seen here. That also tells me it's urgent."

Santos gulped. "Yes, sir. Everyone at the station is talking about your visit today. I guess you scared Christina—she was at the front desk. But then Roman and Chambers have been telling all the other officers how you went in trying to tell them how to do their jobs. And that you were asking to join the force to help with the suicides. They mocked you."

I shrugged. "Well, I am an easy target for mockery, I suppose. What's this really about?"

"I'm still the rookie here, so no one really takes me serious," Santos said, looking at the floor. "I couldn't tell them I believe you."

"You believe me?"

Santos looked up, fear swimming in his eyes like he was taking a major gamble. "I do."

"And why is that?"

He shifted on the couch, and I sat down on the opposite end from him.

"I may be new, but it's allowed me to see things with a fresh perspective," Santos said. "Suicides don't happen in Redwood. They just don't. There have been three now and no one at the station seems concerned. I get the whole thing of it not being a crime, but I don't see why we don't make wellness checks on the other players from that team. It's a start. Maybe they know something about why the others took their lives. I just don't get why they wouldn't come forward on their own accord."

"Not sure if you ever played organized sports," I said. "But it's a brotherhood. No one on that team is going to say anything if there was some sort of pact. No one wants to be 'that guy' who ruins the fun. Even if this is their sick idea of fun."

"I get that, and I don't think that's the issue," Santos said. "It's messed up, but we don't have enough info. So far, it's three players from the team. And all three were the more popular positions. Notice it hasn't been linemen or kickers."

"You think that's relevant?" I asked.

Santos shrugged. "Just an observation. Football teams are big. There can be clicks within the team. Linemen hang out together. Defense. Special teams."

"So you did play?"

Santos grinned. "I may be small, but I'm fast. Played some receiver in high school."

I sunk back into the couch and placed my hands behind my head. "I'm glad you're seeing things as I am, but why are you here? What are you hoping to accomplish?"

Santos pursed his lips as he searched for the right response. "I'm here to help, Mr. Mendez. But I suppose the best question is, what are *you* hoping to accomplish? It sounded like you might have a plan. I obviously can't join you outright, but I can work on things from my side."

I stroked my chin, intrigued. This young cop was willing to cross a boundary for me. "If I could get you a list of names, would you be able to get me their addresses?"

Santos nodded immediately. "That's not a problem."

"What about call logs?"

He shook his head. "Need a warrant to get those. And I assume we don't want a paper trail of what you're up to."

"Good call. What about the cell phones of the victims? They found me snooping around Timmy Summers' house because they had his cell phone at the station. Could you get me the others?"

"I can look into that," Santos said, biting his bottom lip. "Since it's not a crime, I'm not sure how long our evidence team plans to hold on to those before returning them to the families. I imagine it's not long."

"Even if you can tell me where those phones end up going, that would be a big help. I can get access to Timmy's, so just the other two. I want to see if these guys were communicating with each other, or even had a shared contact. That could open up some possibilities for us."

I had learned to get reliable cooperation from others, it was best to use inclusive language like *we* and *us*. When people felt like they were part of something bigger than themselves, they never hesitated to help the greater cause.

"I'll see what I can find out," Santos said, pulling out a cell phone and typing a note to himself. "I'll need your number so we can stay in contact."

"I don't have one at the moment," I said.

Santos gazed at me with a childlike curiosity. "You don't have...a phone?"

"No, sir. I try to avoid having one for as long as possible. But it seems that time has come. I'll get one tomorrow morning. Why don't you write your personal cell number for me, and I'll reach out as soon as I get my phone."

I got off the couch and went into the kitchen, pulling open my junk drawer containing pens and small sticky notes. Santos joined me at the kitchen counter and scribbled his number on the paper.

"You're sure you want to get involved in this?" I asked him.

Santos drew a deep breath and sighed. "Yes. I see it as a low-risk, high-reward situation for me."

"How so?"

"Since I'm so new, I don't really get any serious assignments. Traffic duty, parking tickets, all that silly shit. And I understand. I have to pay my dues. My involvement will be low key, at least to start. I'll assist you in whatever way I can without risking my job. Worst-case scenario, you find nothing of significance and I keep doing what I've been doing. Or, you catch hold of something and bring me into the loop. I can take it from there and will earn the respect from my peers."

Santos spoke with a cool confidence, like he had rehearsed these exact lines on the drive to my house. I wasn't going to tell him if matters spiraled quickly, I had no issue taking it on myself. But hopefully it wouldn't come to that.

"Okay," I said. "I like the way you think. Make me do all the dirty work and you take all the credit."

The color flushed out of his face, panic settling into his eyes.

I laughed and clapped him on the back. "Relax, officer. I'm just fucking with you. I'm totally down with these plans—anything to keep me out of the spotlight."

Santos let out a nervous laugh. "Good one."

"And you'll let me know if you hear any internal rumblings about these suicides," I said. "It's only a matter of time. Now that word of my theory is spreading across the department, I'm sure it will be more than yourself who find it plausible. You also need to tell me if the cops have eyes on me. Not sure why they would right now, but I don't trust Roman. He wants to handcuff me so bad, it's almost kinky."

"Roman's a dick," Santos said, placing his hands on his hips.

"I've noticed." I glanced at the clock on the microwave. "Gotta call it a night. Long day ahead tomorrow. I'll shoot you a text as soon as I get my phone. I prefer texts over calls, but I understand if you don't want a trace of our conversations and need to call."

"Understood."

"Perfect. After I get the phone, I'll work on getting a list of everyone who played on that championship team. I'm sure I can find those in the archives somewhere in town."

"The high school will have it," Santos said. "But I'm not sure they'll give it to you. If I have time during the day, I'll swing by and see if they'll give it to me. I can help you with one name from that team right now. Mason Barker."

"Mason Barker? Why do I feel like I know that name from some-where?"

Santos looked me dead in the eye. "Because he's Redwood's chief of police."

Chapter 12

I got an early start on Thursday morning.

I arrived at the town's Walmart at 8:15 and bought a burner phone. As much as I loved the smaller towns, I couldn't complain when a city was just big enough to have a Walmart and other chains. It was an added convenience. I'd been in small towns where only one person sold phones, and if they happened to be away on vacation, I was simply shit out of luck. Or had to drive an hour to the nearest town that had a semblance of civilization.

The library opened at nine, so I grabbed breakfast at the small cafe in the front of the Walmart, enjoying a bacon and egg sandwich while my new phone charged from the nearest outlet on the wall.

Once finished, I made the ten-minute drive across to Redwood's downtown library branch. Even for a bigger town, I could still get anywhere in ten minutes, fifteen during rush hour. That was nothing compared to Los Angeles, where I had recently stayed. The traffic there made me want to jam a toothpick under my fingernails.

The library stood two levels, the bottom half made of brick, the upper half all glass to expose dozens of rows of books from my view in the parking lot. The sign above the automatic doors had three books layered on top of each other, *REDWOOD PUBLIC LIBRARY* in massive, bold letters to the right.

The amount of cars in the parking lot so early in the day surprised me. When I strolled in, I saw why.

At least thirty kids were making their way to the kids' area in the back of the library. It was summer break, after all, and the library had a calendar posted on the doors with the week's events. Today had a Dr. Seuss story time, a reptile exhibit, and something called Bubble Fun Run.

Glad I didn't have to be back there.

To my right was a long counter with a couple of librarians talking to visitors. They had a shelf behind them loaded with books with white receipts sticking out of each. That must have been the spot to check out books.

I moved forward and drew in a deep breath. The smell of old books never grew tired. It reminded me of the summers in Laredo. If I didn't have a sports activity during a summer day, my mom would drop me at the library in the morning and pick me up in the evening.

"You don't need a babysitter, mijo," she'd tell me. "Just read all day."

So I did. Plus, they had computers where I was happy to kill several hours playing solitaire and Minesweeper.

The signs in the library pointed me to a computer lab, non-fiction, fiction, and study lounge.

Another librarian sat at a wide desk in front of the non-fiction books, so I strolled up to her with a welcoming grin.

"Good morning," I said.

She looked up from her computer screen. She had short, curly hair and bright red lipstick to match her cat-eye glasses.

"Hello, sir," she said, holding an awkward eye contact with me. "How may I be of assistance?"

I planted my arms on her desk. "I was wondering if the library has archives for Redwood. Old newspaper articles. Stuff like that."

"We sure do," she replied. "Everything was digitized back in 2006, so all you need is to head into the computer lab, and you'll see a desktop icon called Preservica. All archives are stored in there."

"Great. Do I need a library card to access the computers?"

"No, sir. They are all open for public use."

"Thank you."

I spun and followed the signs toward the computer lab, opening the glass door to enter a quiet room with two rows of computers. Only a couple were occupied, so I took a spot in the back corner, as far away from the door as possible.

I still didn't trust whoever was out there watching me and didn't want to give them any type of advantage while I did my research.

The more I thought about it, the more I believed it may have been the police chief who left the note at my house. He had made a public statement after the first suicide, but had been silent since. I watched all the news coverage and had yet to hear him address anything about Timmy or Tyrell.

I opened an internet browser along with the program storing the archives. I first ran a search for *Mason Barker police chief.*

Tons of results came back, several online articles including interviews or quotes from the chief. After a few minutes of browsing, I learned Barker had been in his role for six years and had overseen an abnormally meager amount of crime during his tenure. He was plenty involved in the community, both as the chief and as a citizen. He once organized a Potluck for Police to increase the relationship between the police and the community. Several pictures showed him at various ribbon cutting events around town. One article gushed over his generous five hundred dollar donation made to Redwood's dog shelter.

I had to give Barker credit. He'd established quite the public persona. Man of the people. Donating to the dogs. People ate that shit up. Made me wonder if he had plans to run for mayor in the future. Or possibly even something bigger.

I found no mention of his time in high school or the championship team. Granted, there were fifty pages of search results, and I had no intention of clicking through them all.

I opened the archives program and read the prompt. It asked for a date range, topics, writer name, or zip code. Only one field was required to run a search, so I plugged in November 1999, since that's when high school football state championships were played.

The results brought back an assortment of scanned newspapers in their entirety, along with each individual article, to create a logjam of nine hundred published articles from the month of November alone.

Three different newspapers funneled into this archive system: *Redwood Bulletin*, *Central Oregon Daily*, and the *Redwood Source*. A bulk of the results came from the *Bulletin*, so I presumed they had more of the day-to-day coverage of happenings around Redwood.

The articles were sorted by date of publication, so I scrolled down the never-ending list toward the middle. I never got to play in a state championship game, but I attended it twice in Texas, remembering they always occurred in mid to late November.

I read headlines about the Redwood High School clinching the top seed, winning their first playoff game, second playoff game, and finally a third playoff game. After that, it seemed as if Redwood High School coverage overtook the entire media from this time period. Articles highlighting certain players, coaches, school officials.

Those old men at the diner hadn't exaggerated the mania surrounding the town's improbable run to glory. I counted thirty-two consecutive articles related to the school or football team. It truly was all they had cared about in Redwood at the time.

It somehow became even worse after the team won the championship. Articles about college prospects for the players. A parade downtown. Even the head coach was asked about moving up to collegiate ball. The entire second half of November in 1999 seemed like a party in Redwood.

I opened several articles in new tabs, lining up a dozen to start with. I was lucky enough to find an article that included a team portrait along with the names of every single player on the team.

Jackpot.

I sent that one to the printer immediately, grabbed the papers, and returned to read through more articles.

Practically all of them mentioned Tyrell Marshall playing out of his mind during his senior year. Jackson Green and Ethan Stokes, the team's top receiver and running back, respectively, were mentioned several times across the articles.

Coach Dan Bratten received tons of praise for leading a group of underdogs to the title.

The first batch of articles included recaps of the final game and season. As I opened a new dozen tabs, I came across articles with a slight shift in tone. One had a headline of "Trouble for the Champs?"

This one grabbed my attention, but when I clicked on it, the entire article was blacked out. It displayed the article and accompanying photo of Dan Bratten, but thick black bars covered every word on the page.

I returned to the list of articles and paid closer attention. The journalists in town had mastered the art of attention-grabbing headlines.

"Secrets in the Huddle."

"Locker Room Drama."

"What Happens When the Friday Night Lights Turn Off?"

I clicked into each of these articles and found them with the same black bars concealing all text.

"What the hell?" I asked my computer screen. There was no explanation anywhere on the page. I even looked around the walls in the computer lab to see if there was a sign explaining things.

Nothing.

It appeared the group of kids had settled into their back area of the library, leaving the rest of the building mostly empty. I turned off my computer's monitor and left the lab to return to the librarian.

She was deep into a romance book by Bernadette Marie and looked up with a great deal of angst.

"Have they gotten together yet?" I asked.

"I beg your pardon?" she replied.

"In the book. It's romance, right?"

The librarian let out a soft giggle. "Oh. Not yet, but it's coming soon. Is something wrong in the lab?"

I knew the tone. She was in the middle of a juicy part of the story and didn't want to be bothered with a trivial task like her job. I had plenty of reading sessions interrupted by the military, but they didn't give two shits if I was near the climax of a stressful book.

"I'm not sure," I said. "Found the archives you mentioned. Even found articles relevant to my search, but several of them are blacked out. Any idea what that means?"

She pulled a bookmark from the back cover and stuck it into her page—the ultimate sign of defeat. "Yes. It means one of two things. Either the original writer or publisher of an article requested to have the article pulled from the archives. Or there was a gag order from a judge. Were the entire articles blacked out, or just portions?"

"On the ones I saw, the whole thing was blacked out."

She nodded. "That's most likely a journalist or publisher request. If it's urgent, you could always go to the newspaper's offices to request a copy of the article. They may or may not grant the request. If they had it pulled from archives, it's not likely. But you never know."

"I see. Is that a common request for archives? I wouldn't think hiding an old article could prove beneficial, especially when there can be physical copies of it floating around somewhere."

"It's not too common," she said. "Usually means the writer could have gotten into some trouble. Maybe they were accused of fabricating stories. Or if the content was sensitive, the publisher could have received a request from the article's subject requesting it be taken down. The publishers are usually open to that if several years have passed since publication."

"Interesting," I said. "I don't suppose you know anything about the 1999 championship team from Redwood High. Any reason articles about that team may have been blacked out?"

She pursed her lips. "I'm afraid not. Moved here in '03, so that was just before my time."

Damn.

"Okay," I said. "Sorry to interrupt your book. I'll let you get back to it. Will do some more digging on my end."

"No need to apologize," she said, gracefully picking her book back up and returning to the story. She was definitely on a good part. Probably a steamy one, as they called it in the romance world.

I returned to the computer lab, printed three different articles with the censorship bars, and looked up a phone number for Carissa Summers. I typed it into my new cell phone, closed all my internet tabs, and bolted out of the library.

While I didn't find any useful information beyond the complete roster of names, I still uncovered a truth. Something was being hidden.

Now, I just had to find out what.

I dialed Carissa as I returned to my car, papers clutched in my free hand.

"Hello?" she answered.

"Hey," I said. "It's Jonny."

"Jonny?" she replied, a new energy sliding into her voice. "How did you get my number?"

"I'm at the library. Looked it up."

"Mr. Stalker," she said with a playful giggle. "What's up?"

"I need to talk to you," I said. "Are you free for dinner tonight?"

Chapter 13

To be fair, I never called dinner a date.

But Carissa did right before we hung open. She sounded overjoyed, and I chalked it up to her just needing some time away from the grief and drama surrounding her brother's death.

She suggested The Elkhorn for dinner, perhaps the finest dining one could find in Redwood. Her perceptions of the evening ahead might cause me difficulties in my hunt for the truth. But I had no choice. This was a date *and* an opportunity to uncover some dirt.

I didn't own anything nicer than a solid black t-shirt, so I slipped into that, a pair of jeans, and combed my hair before heading out. I had offered to pick Carissa up from her house and she agreed.

She was already waiting outside when I arrived, sitting in a chair on her front porch. Carissa rose as I stepped out of the car, and I had to control my thoughts and emotions upon seeing her.

She wore a form-fitting purple dress that perfectly highlighted every curve of her body. It was my first time seeing her done up, and I hoped it wouldn't be the last. Gone were the black bags under her eyes. She lit up with a wide smile as I approached her and stuck out my arm for her to grab. Her appearance, combined with a tantalizing scent of perfume, was truly breathtaking.

"Hello, Jonny," she said, giving me a couple of looks over.

We marched down the pathway, where I held open the passenger door for her to get situated. As I closed the door, I glimpsed her legs that drove me wild.

"Snap out of it," I said, circling the car for the driver's side door.

I suddenly found it difficult to focus. I was here to learn more about the championship team and what may have been left out of the news stories. But at the same time, Carissa seemed to have an interest in me. And it had been a while…

"I'm really excited for our night out," she said when I started the car and drove off.

"Me too," I replied. "Should be fun."

"Have you been to The Elkhorn before?" she asked.

I made a conscious effort to keep my eyes on the road, stealing a side glance of her smooth legs when it felt safe. "I haven't. Redwood is bigger than it seems. I try to eat somewhere new every week, but there are tons of restaurants around town. Besides, fancy steakhouses aren't really my thing."

"I assumed you'd like a big steak," she said. "We can go somewhere else if you really don't want to."

I grinned. "Look at us—well, you. Ready for the red carpet, I'd say. We're not gonna waste that and go anywhere else. Plus, I love steaks. Much prefer to grill them myself is all."

"Oh," Carissa said, fascinated by my last comment. "You'll have to cook for me sometime."

I reminded myself Carissa was an emotional mess right now. At least, I thought so. She seemed completely overrun with joy as we drove downtown. I avoided passing by the Royal Hotel, not wanting anything to spark a negative memory of her brother—which was probably a tall task in the town they had lived their whole lives.

"Certainly," I said, grateful to have reached downtown and would soon be parking.

"Warm night," Carissa said as we stopped at a red light one block away from the restaurant.

I rolled up the windows and cranked the air conditioning. Sweat dripped down my back, but I had thought it was just from nerves for the night ahead.

I parked in the lot next to The Elkhorn, a building with a gray stone facade and blacked-out windows making it impossible to see inside. A valet worker hovered at his stand, watching us with a blank expression as we got out of the car.

Carissa didn't wait for me to open her door, so I offered my arm once more before we strolled inside. The smell of seafood and sizzling beef clashed in the lobby. A man and woman stood behind the host stand, looking over the map of their restaurant while the waiting area piled up with at least a dozen people.

"Do you have a reservation?" the man asked as we approached.

"Yes," I said. "Party of two under Mendez."

The man had no change in expression as the glow from his computer screen splashed across his face. He scrolled with a long finger and eventually nodded. "Right this way, Mr. Mendez," he said, grabbing two menus and slipping out from behind the stand.

"You called ahead?" Carissa whispered as we followed the host through the dining area.

"As much as it pained me, yes, I did. All the reviews online said it's worth it, or else you can end up waiting for an hour most nights. I don't know about you, but I'd rather spend that time at a table instead of the lobby."

Carissa smiled as we reached our table, a cozy spot for two seated next to a glassed-off fireplace flickering in the middle of the dining room. A piano stood covered next to the fireplace, likely something they used on weekends.

We took our seats to find two glasses of water and a bread basket, complete with a small plate full of butter to spread.

The only music tonight was the soft hum of conversation and the clatter of silverware meeting plates.

"Good evening, folks," a young woman said, sliding over to the side of our table. "Can I get you anything to drink besides water?"

"Do you like wine, Jonny?" Carissa asked me.

"I prefer red," I said. "Unless we're having moscato."

"Red is fine," Carissa said. "Merlot?"

I nodded, turning my attention to the server. "Your finest merlot, please."

"I'll be right back with that," she said, vanishing from the table in a blur.

I took a sip of my water and grabbed a slice of bread.

"So," Carissa said, beaming at me from across the table. "What made you want to grab dinner tonight?"

Shit.

That was more direct of a question than I was expecting.

"A couple reasons," I said. "Both business and pleasure, I guess you could say."

Carissa arched an eyebrow, watching me with plenty of intrigue swimming behind her eyes. "What kind of business?"

"Well, I'm officially digging into these suicides. Now, with Tyrell as the third victim, it's blatantly obvious something is going on with that championship team. I tried speaking with the police, but they want nothing to do with my theory."

"And what is your theory, exactly?" she asked.

"I don't have a precise theory right now. Just that something is fishy about all three suicides and how they're linked. My initial guess is the players from that team made some sort of pact to take their lives all these years later. But the more I consider it, the less likely it seems."

"I agree," she said. "Not sure why they would do that."

"I assume you knew most of these guys, right?" I asked. "Even if not on a personal level, you went to school with them. Had a basic understanding of the type of people they were."

"Sure," Carissa said, as our server returned with wine and a fresh basket of bread. We placed our dinner orders. New York strip for Carissa, and a filet mignon for me.

"I spent my morning at the library today," I said. "Searching through the city's archives. I found plenty of coverage of the team leading up to the championship, and of course, after it. They were all fluff pieces. Then I came across some with more troubling headlines. Sounded like there was an issue. Maybe even a scandal. But I couldn't tell for sure because the articles themselves were all censored. Couldn't see anything besides the headlines and a picture of the head coach."

"And you want to know what the scandal was," Carissa said.

I sipped my wine. Merlot was dry, and I'd pay later with a headache. "Only if you know anything of significance. My only connection right now is that someone is trying to hide the truth—since they slipped that letter under my door. And the censorship looks like more hiding to me."

Carissa chewed on a piece of bread, then bit the inside of her lip while pondering. "I know the scandal. But first, you said this date is business and pleasure. If I tell you about the scandal, will you be able to let it go and truly enjoy the evening?"

I wanted to correct her about calling this a date. No such words ever came out of my mouth. But I still didn't raise the argument. Irrelevant at this point. My thoughts craved the information about the scandal. Something about it had to tie back to what was going on today.

"Okay," I said. "You tell me about the scandal—everything you know. Allow some questions. And I won't bring it up for the rest of the night."

Carissa grinned. "Deal." She drew a deep breath. "You ready? Because this story is truly fucked up."

Something about a woman cursing always made my heart skip a beat. "Try me."

"Okay. There was a member of the championship team you probably won't hear much about. Andrew Stone. He was the team's equipment manager."

"A fellow student?" I asked.

"Yes. Was one of the seniors that year. As the equipment manager, Andrew had a long list of responsibilities. Mostly matters behind the scenes to assist the coaches and players. He'd sort the equipment, sanitize it, prepare it all for road games. Our coaches even gave him an expanded role, with more involvement during the games themselves. He'd keep score and record videos of the games for coaches to review the following week. A few times, they even sent him to record future opponents."

"That's quite a lot for a high school student," I said.

Carissa nodded. "Perhaps. But Andrew loved his role. The more he got to do, the more he felt part of the team. He even received one of the formal placards each player received after winning the championship. The coaches loved him, as did most players. He kept the water jugs topped off at every practice and game. All Andrew ever did was make people's lives easier. He worked in the role all throughout high school. By senior year, he was thriving at it. Took on the same duties for the basketball and baseball teams. One of our teachers had a connection with the Trail Blazers in Portland and offered to set up a meeting between Andrew and the team to see if there was a clubhouse role he could fill after graduating."

"Did you ever interact with Andrew?" I asked.

"Sure did. He reserved a few rows at every football game for the family of the players. Not something any high school did, but he made it happen. He'd chat with us before and after the games. He was a good guy with a bright future."

"So, what happened?"

Carissa sighed. "Boys being bullies happened. Midway through the season, Andrew raised a concern to the coach. He said some players were picking on him. It started with minor incidents. They'd intentionally dirty a jersey right after he cleaned it. Dump a water jug down the drain so he'd have to fill it up again. What made him finally speak up was when a few players asked Andrew to join them on the field for drills. This wasn't unusual, either, because he often helped the coaches with the equipment during practice drills. They lured him out to the field, only to have the sprinklers go off and make him drenched."

"What did the coaches do?" I asked.

"They addressed the team and condemned the pranks. They emphasized Andrew's importance to the team and stressed the ways he made their lives easier to just show up and play. But the players at fault didn't appreciate Andrew going to the coaches, so they made things even more uncomfortable. There were stories of him finding dirty jockstraps in his backpack. Pulling them out in the middle of classes, only to get laughed at by everyone. Keep in mind he worked later than any other student in the building. The lights would often go out when he was working late, leaving him to close up in the dark. He insisted someone was doing it on purpose."

"But no one ever believed him?"

Carissa shook her head. "No one on the football team. Even the coaches dismissed it as the lights running on a timer. But everyone knew better. Especially once dead animals started appearing in the hallways late at night. Or in Andrew's locker the next morning. He kept bringing it up to the coaches, but Andrew had no proof tying anything to a player. They weren't taking his word without evidence. One coach even accused Andrew of setting these pranks up himself because he was jealous of the attention the football team was getting. But Andrew wasn't like that. He genuinely saw himself as part of the team. Not a player, of course, but someone with an important role that helped contribute."

"So he spoke with the coaches," I said. "Did he ever go to the faculty? Someone else who may have believed him?"

Carissa nodded. "Not up to this point, but he finally did after the first playoff game. That was the night everything changed. It was the first playoff game the football team had won in a decade, or something like that. After the game, a senior hosted a party to celebrate the victory. Parents out of town, older sibling with access to booze. You can see where this is going."

I nodded, having gone to plenty of similar parties in high school. A downfall of being popular.

"It was obviously a secret event they didn't want any adults hearing about, but everyone from the team was invited, including Andrew. Now, what happens next is exactly what I heard from my brother after it all went down. So I'm not sure how accurate these details are. This house had one of those walkout basements, and that's where they set up the booze and where most of everyone hung out. As you can imagine, the party got out of control. Furniture was damaged, holes appeared in the walls. Everything you'd expect from a group of drunk, unsupervised teen jocks. Even after everything those assholes on the team had done to Andrew, he still offered to help. Said he knew how to repair drywall and could make it look like no damage had occurred. After piecing together materials he found in the garage, he returned to the basement to fix the wall. By then, though, lots of kids had left already. There were maybe ten remaining, according to my brother, and that's when everything got *weird*. His words, not mine."

My stomach was twisting into knots. I'd seen plenty of times how cruel teenagers could be to each other. And by all accounts, Andrew Stone was as straight an arrow as they came. "What did they do?"

Carissa shook her head and lowered her voice. "They cornered him. Accused him of trying to throw off a miraculous season with his complaining to the coaches. Then they pulled their pants down and forced themselves onto Andrew."

"Are you fucking kidding me?" I asked, and my words came out louder than planned, drawing some curious stares from around the restaurant.

"Simmer down, Jonny," Carissa said, eyes wide from having become the center of attention. She kept her voice low. "That's as much detail as Timmy ever gave me. Said of the ten of them remaining at the party, five of the players cornered Andrew. Timmy said the others watched from the couch, not realizing what was actually going on. The guilt ate him alive for several years. Always said he should have stopped it."

"Jesus Christ," I said. "So, what happened after that?"

"A lot. Andrew went to the police with his parents and filed a report. Eventually charges were brought forward. Only three names were listed in the report: Tyrell Marshall, Jackson Green, and Kody Holt. The other two players were never mentioned. Everyone assumed they didn't actually perform a harassing act like the other three."

I rubbed my forehead. Our dinner arrived and I no longer felt like eating. "Two of those three names are dead. How is no one making the connection?"

"Remember how I mentioned Redwood likes to take care of its matters on its own? Well, our judicial system is no different. Everything was on course for this case to come to trial. The week before jury selection was to begin, the judge dismissed the case."

"*Dismissed*?" I asked, baffled.

Carissa nodded. "No one knows what happened besides that. The news stopped reporting on it. Andrew disappeared from Redwood. And the players moved on with their lives. It was like the whole thing never happened."

I blew out a long breath. "No justice system has ever been fair. Especially for rich, adolescent white boys. Makes me sick."

Carissa pressed her lips tightly together as she studied the steak in front of her. She grabbed her fork and knife and looked plenty eager to start dinner. "I can't exactly bad mouth the system here in Redwood. Not after what they did for me and Timmy. But yes, dismissing the case was the wrong move. It caused quite the uproar. People protesting in the streets. Taking sides and arguing with each other."

"Wait," I interrupted. "There were people siding with the sexual abusers?"

Carissa rolled her eyes. "You seem surprised. Of course, they had support. They had just won a championship and were about to graduate from high school. Some people chalked it up as a mistake teenagers make. Boys being boys. There was no reason to derail their lives because of a one-off mistake."

I shook my head. The world had no place for abusers of any form, shape, or age. My idea of justice for them would be a bullet to the dick. Unfortunately, I wasn't in charge of those decisions. "So the boys got off. How were they treated after that? And what happened to Andrew?"

Carissa swallowed her first bite of steak before replying, prompting me to dig in. No point in leaving a perfectly cooked steak on my plate. Filet mignon wasn't exactly something you wanted to reheat for lunch the next day. "Tensions remained high for about a month after the case was dropped. The boys and their families were shunned by most people in town. Tyrell went to college and had a fresh start. The others stayed in town, but no one really saw them out in public for at least a year."

"And Andrew?"

Carissa sighed. "The Stones left town. A couple of months after the case was dropped, a moving truck showed up. They left town and were never heard from again. I imagine they moved as far away as possible from Redwood after that. Naturally, rumors fly, but no one knows the truth. I like to think he had a happy ending. Living somewhere on the east coast, being an equipment manager for some college team at the least."

She shrugged.

We ate our dinner in mostly silence for the next fifteen minutes. My mind was occupied with this bombshell of a story, but I made a promise to not bring up the matter for the rest of the evening.

We finished our dinner along with a second round of wine, swapping stories from childhood to get to know each other. She spoke so highly of Timmy and did so without breaking down.

Once we finished at the restaurant, we strolled hand-in-hand to my car. Before getting in, Carissa stood on her tiptoes and planted a kiss on my cheek, whispering in my ear. "Why don't you come over for a nightcap?"

Chapter 14

I know what you're thinking. No, I didn't climb into the sack with Carissa.

But I can't lie—I really wanted to. She wanted me to.

Last night, I took her home after dinner, joined her inside for our third glass of wine of the night, and we both fell asleep on her couch watching *Crazy, Stupid, Love*. I was a sucker for Steve Carell and had no problem watching any movie he was in. Add in Emma Stone and Marisa Tomei, and I had no complaints about the movie selection. Carissa drooled over Ryan Gosling, so all was fair.

I woke up around six o'clock that Friday morning, Carissa's head resting on my chest. We may or may not have exchanged some saliva on that couch. But I'm not here to kiss and tell.

I had a slight headache—wine always dehydrated the shit out of me. When I got up from the couch, I kissed Carissa on the forehead and situated her to lie down completely now that she the couch to herself. I told her I had work to get to, and she mumbled inaudibly in response.

After a quick drive home with no traffic, I downed two glasses of water and sent a text message to Officer Santos outlining my findings from last night. I asked him to look up Andrew Stone, his trial, and the addresses of anyone from the football team who was still living in Oregon. I included a picture of the roster printout for his reference.

After making toast and bacon for breakfast, my headache cleared up, and I was back in business. I debated getting dressed to meet the guys for a day at work, but something told me to hang back and wait.

Carissa texted me when she woke up, a few minutes past nine, thanking me for a fun evening and asking when we could do it again.

I told her I also had a wonderful time, and we'd go out again really soon.

For now, my mind was fully consumed with the suicides plaguing Redwood.

We exchanged some flirtatious texts and went about our mornings. Right before ten o'clock, Santos messaged me back.

> *Meet me at the bowling alley. 30 minutes.*

There was only one bowling alley I knew of in Redwood. Miracle Lanes. I only knew it because it was next door to a Domino's Pizza, where I stopped in at least twice a month—if I was being good.

That left me about fifteen minutes to shower and get ready, so I wasted no time. When I stepped out of the house, the Walkers were tending to the flower beds spread about their front yard.

"Good morning, Jonny!" Rochelle greeted. "Everything going okay?"

Herb was further away, but tossed down his gardening gloves and shuffled over to join the conversation.

"Everything is going just fine," I said, which I thought was a rather accurate description of my past couple of days. "You'll be proud of me. I got a cell phone."

I reached into my pocket and waved it around for them to see. Now I could join the cool kids on the block with my updated technology.

"About time!" Herb cackled. "Welcome to society. We're happy to have you!"

Rochelle frowned and smacked her husband on the chest. "Stop your comments," she muttered under her breath.

I couldn't help but laugh. "It's no worry, Rochelle," I said, taking out my car keys to unlock the door. "Herb is just a jokester. I get it. It's our love language."

Herb grabbed his belly and laughed harder, his wife baffled by the exchange.

"See, I told you," Herb said. "Not everyone from the younger generation is weak. Some people can still take a joke!"

"You two have a good day," I said, opening my car door. "I'll see you later."

I drove off, leaving them to bicker as they loved to do.

At exactly 10:24, I pulled into the bowling alley parking lot. No police cruisers were in sight, but I saw the pickup truck from my house the other night.

I strolled into the bowling alley, greeted by the smell of hot dogs, nacho cheese, and popcorn. Way too early for any of that shit. Even worse, pop music blared through the speakers. Funny enough, no one was inside the bowling alley except for the employees and Officer Santos, who sat at a round table near the arcade area.

The workers continued on the concessions while a couple of others cleaned the lanes.

"Thanks for meeting me so soon," Santos said, standing up to shake my hand.

"Thank you," I responded. "I don't suppose you asked me here to play a game?"

Santos grinned. "I'm happy to break a hundred. Anything better than that is just a bonus."

"Good to know. I'd definitely smoke you."

Santos chuckled. He was in uniform, and I noticed a manila folder lying on the table.

"I had a slow morning today," he said. "Was able to look into those things you sent me right away. And wow. I'm blown away by what I found about Andrew Stone."

I nodded. "And I just learned about it last night. More about the trial and the town's reaction. Did you have access to any of the police records?"

"Sure did," he said. "Now, I didn't print those out to include in the folder—this is just all the names and addresses you requested. Everything about Stone was classified. But I did lots of reading."

"What did you find?"

"For starters, I have no idea why that case was thrown out. Mind you, the police records don't include information about the trial. But from what I read, that case was a slam dunk for any prosecutor. Definitely some corruption or a settlement."

I thought back to what Carissa mentioned about those siding with the abusers. They didn't want their futures ruined because of their horrific actions from one night of their high school careers. Perhaps these parents had money to throw at the matter. Made it go away, as rich people do. That seemed more likely to me than a corrupt judge.

"I've heard some theories," I said. "But it's all just speculation. No one knows for sure."

Santos shifted in his seat and leaned in. "There is something I found rather interesting." He looked around to make sure no one was listening. "Andrew Stone entered the witness protection program."

"Witness protection?" I repeated. "Was he in any sort of danger?"

"There were reports of phone calls to the Stones. Death threats. People were so pissed at the Stones, believing they caused all this drama in Redwood, and so soon after winning that championship. People weren't thinking straight. Blinded by the victory. That team was on a pedestal, and to have someone try to bring them down was simply out of line."

"Did the records show anything about where the family might have gone?" I asked.

Santos shook his head. "Afraid not. Once witness protection comes into play, that is fully in the hands of the U.S. Marshals Service. It literally creates a dead end in our records regarding Andrew Stone. His name is nowhere to be found."

I bit my bottom lip. There was something here, but I'm not sure what. Who was threatening the Stones all those years ago? Were they still in Redwood? And where did they send the Stone family?

"Do you know how any of that process works?" I asked. "I know the Stones moved away shortly after the case was dismissed. But for how long would the U.S. Marshall keep them in the program? Forever? A few years?"

"Sorry, Mr. Mendez, I have no knowledge of that."

"Me neither," I said. "I have some contacts in D.C. They might shed some insight on the program. And hopefully get me details—they owe me."

Santos chuckled. "You're not a man I would want to owe anything to."

I grinned. "I'm not a bad guy, Officer Santos. Just always found myself in fucked up scenarios—like this. Because of that, I've done lots of things to get people to safety. That's all. Save someone's life and they're willing to throw you a few favors. That's not something people forget about. By the way, why are we meeting in a bowling alley?"

Santos looked over his shoulder. "It's a safe place for me to meet for unofficial business. I love bowling. Play here once a week. And I've never seen another officer in here. And since I come here so often, I've become close with the owner and staff. If they have a rowdy customer, I take care of it. I told them this alley is my personal escape—which it is. They respect that, and won't ask questions. This is my first time doing something like this..."

"Something like *what*?" I asked. It was always good to understand how others perceived themselves.

Santos shrugged. "Well, I don't know what this is exactly. Sharing insider information with an outsider. Not even sure the legality of what we're doing."

"We're trying to solve a... problem? I don't know, either, I guess. Can't call it a case because there is no actual crime or suspects. But there is something going on. And it's not just people taking their lives for the hell of it."

"The bottom line is," Santos said. "Legal or not. If anything gets traced back to me and my colleagues come to the bowling alley to question the staff, I'm in the clear. No one here will say a single word about my presence—outside of playing in the Sunday night league and occasionally coming in on my lunch break to play a quick game."

"Glad you've thought this through," I said. "Many people overlook the importance of covering the tracks. Anticipating what *could* happen down the road. I have exit plans as well. Because you never know. That's why I travel so light. I can literally grab my backpack and leave town within a minute. No loose ends. No connections."

"What about that landscaping crew you work with?" Santos asked.

I raised an eyebrow. "How do you know about that?"

"Your name is swirling all over the station, Mr. Mendez. Officers are looking into you. Not sure why, but they want to know who you are and what you're doing in town. Do you trust the guys on that crew to have your back should they get questioned?"

I nodded. "You could call them my bowling alley."

"Good. Keep doing your work behind the scenes. Don't cause any issues, and I'm sure they'll eventually grow bored with you.

I shook my head. "So they'd rather waste time digging up dirt on me instead of finding out what the hell is going on."

"It appears so," Santos said, drawing circles on the table with his finger. "And I suspect it's coming from the chief."

"So you think he's involved somehow? Or at least has insight to what's going?"

Santos looked beyond me, thinking. "He must. But that's not something I can press him about. I have to play my role at the station. Take orders and act like I don't hear anything being said by the others."

"Do you think he's influenced the other cops regarding the suicides?"

"His words carry weight. Even if he's not intentionally reaching out to each cop and having closed-door conversations with them, what he says publicly is influencing the way they think of the matter. And right now, it's that these are all a coincidence. Anyone who suggests otherwise is looking for trouble. I should get going now."

Santos stood up and knocked on the table. I rose to join him and extended a hand. "Thank you for your help with all of this."

He shook my hand. "What are you going to do next?"

"I'm gonna go down that list of addresses and see what I can find out from any of these living players. I suspect it will be a whole lot of nothing, but it only takes one shred of information that can reveal something entirely new."

"Be careful out there," Santos said. "Stay out of the spotlight. Remember what I said—the chief genuinely believes anyone looking into these suicides is only looking to cause trouble."

I grinned as we started walking toward exit. "Lucky for him, trouble always seems to find me."

Chapter 15

I rang the doorbell for the home of Ethan Stokes.

He was the team's main running back during their glory years and still lived in Redwood. His house was in the northern outskirts of Redwood, in a newer development called the Northpointe Collective. They weren't quite mansions, but almost. Massive yards kept neighbors at least fifty yards away on either side. A black Rolls Royce sat in the driveway. I'd have loved to take that beast for a spin.

I waited at the front door and saw movement through the centered glass window. The figure approached and pulled the door open.

In front of me stood a short, pale man with red hair—a handful of grays peppered in. He looked up at me, brown eyes curious and cautious. "Hello," he said. "Can I help you?"

"Are you Ethan Stokes?" I asked.

A dog zipped by in the background too fast for me to make out what type.

Ethan looked around behind me. "Who wants to know?"

"Mr. Stokes," I said. "My name is Jonny Mendez, and I'm looking into the suicides of Jackson Green, Timmy Summers, and Tyrell Marshall. I understand you were all teammates during the town's championship run in 1999. I was hoping to ask you a few questions about them."

Ethan frowned. "So you're a cop?"

I could hear in his voice he didn't believe I was a cop. Good man. "No, sir. I'm a private investigator hired by the city. Suicides aren't exactly something police use their resources to investigate. But with so many happening so close to each other, they wanted an outside eye to see if there might be something going on. You are familiar with those three names and their recent deaths, correct?"

"Yes," he said. "Okay. Come in."

He shuffled aside and let me enter. The foyer had a spiral staircase leading up to a second level. To my right was a living room bigger than my entire main floor. A television at least one hundred twenty inches hung above a fireplace. The couch on the opposite wall was vast enough to swallow up even my massive body.

I noticed a deafening silence.

"I hope you don't mind me asking, Mr. Stokes. But do you live in this big house alone?"

Ethan laughed, shaking his head. "Goodness no. Although I wish that was the case sometimes—don't tell my wife I said that. We have four kids. They're all at summer camp today. My wife is in town doing who knows what. Spending all the money—I can tell you that much."

He laughed again, and I wasn't sure what to say. Me and this guy couldn't have any more opposite lives.

Ethan caught my discomfort and changed the subject. "So, do you want to chat out back? I have a shaded patio perfect for this weather. I can serve us some lemonade."

I smiled, not wanting to intimidate this wealthy man. "That sounds lovely."

Lovely? Who the fuck was I trying to be?

Ethan grinned and spun around to lead me through the living room and into a kitchen of every chef's dream. A center island stretching fifteen feet. Glass cabinets that spanned the entire length and height of the wall. Black stainless steel appliances with gold trim. Two sinks. Three wine racks. And six bar stools stationed around the island.

"Why don't you grab a seat out back?" Ethan said, shuffling over to the fridge. "I'll be right there."

He gestured to the open back door, a gentle breeze splashing across my face. I stepped out to see my fantasy backyard. Fire pit. A grill and smoker set. Putting green. And an assortment of lawn games piled in the corner: badminton, corn hole, horseshoes, and volleyball. The back porch was indeed shaded by the deck above, which I presumed was a walk out balcony of sorts from the bedroom upstairs. A ceiling fan hung above, along with surround sound speakers installed in each corner.

"What do you think?" Ethan asked from behind me. I turned to see him with a wide grin, holding a tray with two glasses and a canteen of lemonade.

"You have a beautiful home, Mr. Stokes," I said, following him to the table in the middle of the patio.

"It'll do," he said. "Care to splash any vodka in this lemonade?"

"Sounds good."

"My man!" Ethan reached into his pocket and pulled out a small bottle of Grey Goose. He poured in the equivalent of two shots into each of our glasses before topping them off with the lemonade. We settled into our seats as he passed over my glass, raising his in the air. "Cheers. To my old friends. May they live forever in our memories."

"Salud," I said, and we clinked our glasses.

"So, Mr. Mendez, what is it you wanted to talk about?"

I took a sip of my drink. The beauty of Grey Goose was that it virtually had no flavor. I'd be wise to not have any more after this serving. "Well, Mr. Stokes, I'm still in the early phases of this investigation—if we can even call it that. Three suicides within a week. All three were players from that championship team. The Redwood PD are calling the entire thing a coincidence, but there are plenty of people who think otherwise."

"What could it be?" Ethan asked, sliding forward in his seat.

"One theory is that some sort of suicide pact was made by the team."

"A pact?" Ethan shook his head. "I was as involved with that team as you could get. Never heard anything about a pact."

"Were you close with these three?"

"Of course! We formed a brotherhood. I'm sure winning strengthened our bonds, but we still would've been good friends had it never happened."

"When was the last time you spoke to any of them?"

Ethan's face soured at this question, and he leaned back, clasping his hands behind his head as he looked at the ceiling. "I don't know, Mr. Mendez. Maybe ten years. Fifteen? I haven't exactly been a good friend."

I scratched my chin. "Do you know if anyone stayed in touch all these years later?"

"We all stayed in touch," Ethan said. "We have an email thread with most of the team that we started a year after graduating. Whenever someone had life news—marriage, kids, that kind of stuff—we'd share about it in that thread. So while I haven't *spoken* to anyone on the team, I'm still aware of the things happening in their lives."

"And it's stayed in the email thread this whole time? You guys never upgraded to a group text, or maybe a Facebook group?"

Ethan waved off my suggestion. "I guess you can call us old school. Sure, we exchanged phone numbers and those who are on Facebook have all connected with each other. But our email thread was from the beginning and we like to keep it alive."

"I take it losing three of your teammates is a major life event you've been talking about."

Ethan nodded, then took a long swig from his glass. "Yes. The email thread is as busy as I've ever seen it. Not sure I'm even caught up on all the messages."

"And does anyone in there have theories about what's going on?"

Ethan's expression remained flat. He shifted, crossing his ankle over the opposite knee. "There are some theories. And they're not suicide pacts, either."

The shift in his voice told me he knew something he wasn't entirely comfortable sharing. I remained silent, waiting for him to continue. After ten seconds and another couple of drinks from our spiked lemonades, he spoke again.

"Winning comes at a cost, Mr. Mendez. Would you agree?"

I nodded. "Absolutely. Sacrifice. Hard work. You can't win without those."

Ethan's eyes fluttered as they focused on the table. "Sacrifice. Yes. Now, I can't call it intentional, but our coach may have sacrificed the well-being of every player on that team. Willful ignorance maybe?"

"How so?" I asked.

"Our coach, rest his soul, had no limits for how far he'd push us. He told us at the beginning of that season that we had the talent to win it all. That we lacked the discipline and guidance. But he vowed to lead us to the championship, and we believed him."

"So he was a new coach the year you won?"

"Yes. New coach. New athletic director. I'm not sure if someone at the school got sick of all the losing, but there was a concrete effort to turn things around. And it worked."

"At what cost?" I asked.

Ethan drew in a deep breath. "Like I said—willful ignorance. It was 1999. There were no concussion protocols or anything like that. Hell, I grew up watching the Cowboys. Troy Aikman had, what, ten concussions in his career? No one thought anything of it at the time. Getting hit in the head was part of football. He'd have his brains rattling around and they'd send him marching right back onto the field. Did you know he still doesn't remember playing in the 1994 NFC Championship? And he went out seven days later and won the Super Bowl."

I raised my brows. "I didn't know that, and I'm from Texas. Know plenty of Cowboys fans and never heard that story."

"My point exactly. Concussions were brushed under the rug. Dismissed like it was just a bruise on your leg."

"So what does this have to do with the Redwood High School team?" I asked, feeling a tad nauseous.

"I'm trying to paint the scene before I throw our coach under the bus. Like I said, he was relentless. That was my senior year and never had I seen kids throwing up during the summer practices. Coach pushed us beyond our limits. Ran us ragged. Are you familiar with the Oklahoma drill?"

"Yes." The drill had two players face off, getting a running start, essentially to see who could hit who the hardest.

"Well, Coach believed fiercely in the drill. Said it was what separated the men from the boys. And he didn't have us just run the drills. He encouraged us to hit each other in the head. Full helmet—to-helmet contact."

"I'm pretty sure that drill has been outlawed today," I said.

"Oh, it has," Ethan said, nodding. "But that didn't help us in '99. No, sir. We concluded every practice with that drill. Every damn day, hitting each other in the head. From June through November. And Coach loved it. He'd cheer and laugh and pump his fists in the air after the really monstrous hits. He'd scream to hit harder. Rattle their fucking brains, he shouted. I loved playing football, but I can look back today and see how barbaric that was."

"So you're suggesting all this head trauma has led to problems later in life?"

Ethan grinned. "Mr. Mendez, I'm not suggesting it. I *know* it. We all know it. Have you ever heard of CTE?"

I shook my head.

"Chronic traumatic encephalopathy," he said. "C-T-E. It's a brain disease and is linked to *repeated* trauma to the head."

"A disease?" I asked.

"Yes, sir. Football players. Boxers. Cage fighters. All those types of athletes are at high risk for developing CTE. Poundings to the head over and over again. Why do you think the NFL has implemented so many regulations today? It's because the lawsuits are coming. Junior Seau killed himself—remember him? He had CTE."

I raised a hand. "Hold on a minute. Forgive me because I don't keep up with too much sports news these days. You're saying CTE leads to suicide?"

"It's not always that drastic," Ethan explained. "But yes, it happens in the most severe cases. Many of us believe our three brothers took their lives because of CTE developing all these years later."

"CTE," I said to myself, burning the three letters into my memory. I wanted to learn whatever Ethan knew about this disease, but planned to do lots more research on my own.

"It's a bitch of a disease," Ethan continued. "Think of it as a parasite in your brain just slowly eating away."

"Is there a cure?"

Ethan chuckled. "A cure? There isn't even a way to officially diagnose the disease until you die and they take your brain out! They can run tests to narrow it down is a likely possibility, but that's as far as it goes. From there, they'll prescribe drugs to help ease the symptoms, but CTE is a runaway train. It takes your brain until it crashes and burns."

"Has anyone on the team been diagnosed?" I asked. "Or rather, *suspect* they have CTE."

Ethan nodded slowly, staring into the distance. "Oh yes. Most of us. I'd say eighty percent of the team have either received that diagnosis from a doctor, or believe they have the disease."

"Eighty?!" I slapped the table, not expecting such a high number. "So you're telling me this disease is plaguing the entire championship team? What is anyone doing about it?"

Ethan shrugged. "Not much we can do. Can't sue Coach—he's been dead for ten years. We could open a lawsuit against the high school, but what's the point? This happened a longtime ago. Most of the current school administration were just kids when we won the championship. No point in making their life hell. Most of us are just dealing with it. Understand some days will be better than others. I thought we had a strong support system in place, but after three suicides, I'm not sure."

"Is anyone else suicidal?" I asked, growing frustrated at how nonchalant Ethan was treating this matter.

"Not that they've said. But neither did the other three. Have you ever had a suicidal thought, Mr. Mendez?"

The question caught me off guard. "I... yes, actually. I have."

"And you're still here, so obviously you didn't go through with it. You'd be surprised how many people have suicidal thoughts. But for most of us, it's a line we can't cross. Even through all the trauma that can push someone to that point, it's still such a mountain to climb to convince yourself to do it. But that's the real bitch about CTE. That line of right and wrong gets blurred. It's like you fall into a trance and have no idea what you're actually doing. Harming yourself, harming others. Talking to the ceiling. It's all just chaos."

"Are you speaking from experience?" I asked.

Ethan closed his eyes and nodded. "I'm afraid so, Mr. Mendez. I've seen all sides of this disease, except for the ending. I've outrun many guys on the football field, but not even I can outrun the ending that awaits. It's coming. The average lifespan for a man with CTE is sixty years. If I'm lucky, I'll have a solid decade left in this world. All I do is try to make the most of it."

"What symptoms are you dealing with?" I slammed the rest of my drink. It was time to get to a library. Or perhaps to the next name on my list of people I needed to visit.

"Mood swings," Ethan said. "I can go from extremely happy one second to a raging asshole the next. I have meds to make these mood swings less frequent, but they still get me sometimes. Besides that, my short-term memory is going to shit. That's when I first had my suspicions. Drove to the grocery store one day a couple of years ago. Had no idea what I had gone there for. Walked the aisles to see if anything would jog my memory. Nothing. Returned home empty-handed, and that's the first time I felt scared in my own mind."

"And you told your teammates about it?"

Ethan nodded. "It's become like a milestone for us. Everyone shares the day they were diagnosed with CTE. Lots of condolences and well wishes to go around. But we all know we face the same fate. And can only hope we don't end up like these last three."

I stood up from the table. "I'm sorry, Mr. Stokes. It wasn't my intent to make you relive all this."

He waved me off, standing to join me. "It's not a big deal. Today is one of my good days, fortunately. If it wasn't, I'm not sure I'd have made it to the door to answer. Best to stay locked in a room during a downswing, as I call them."

"Thank you for all of this information today," I said, shaking his hand. "It's been a huge help and has given me some direction. I have some theories now, and I need to get to work on them."

He offered a polite smile as our hands parted. Then he pointed at me. "I'm not sure what you can do, but you better make it fast. It's only a matter of time before there's another suicide."

Chapter 16

I called Carissa on my way to the library and asked if she could meet me there. She was available and paced circles in front of the library entrance when I arrived.

We hugged before entering, and feeling her touch brought a rush of emotions back. It was always tempting to just run away from an issue and never look back. I had no ties to these men who had taken their lives. No obligation to the police department to find out the truth, especially since they insisted on keeping their heads in the sand.

But I knew what would happen if I skipped town. The situation would wear me down. I'd lose sleep knowing I left a loose end out there, especially when I was the only one who seemed to believe there was something far bigger at play than random suicides. As I'd been rewired from a young age, I never thought about the victims in these situations. Those men were gone and there was nothing anyone could do about it.

I thought about their kids. Their families.

Tyrell Marshall left behind his children, who would now deal with growing up without their father. That was me. A bastard child who had watched my mom get blown up by a car bomb not even intended for her.

I didn't need a shrink to tell me that's what pushed me every day of my life. If I could stop even just one more suicide from happening and spare a family the emotional whirlwind that came with the grief, then I could call my stay in Redwood a success.

"Do you usually bring a girl to the library for a second date?" Carissa asked, rubbing my arms as we pulled out of our embrace.

"I'm afraid this isn't a date," I said. "I just left Ethan Stokes. Do you remember him?"

"Ethan?" she repeated. Her eyes widened. "Wow. Yes, I remember him. Running back, right?"

"That's him."

"He became a real estate investor and got really rich," Carissa said. "That's the last I heard of him. Didn't realize he was even still in Redwood."

"Up in Northpointe with a big ass house. And a Rolls Royce."

Carissa grinned. "Good for him. He grew up in a trailer park. From nothing to something, right?"

"That's the American dream," I said. "Or so I'm told."

I never agreed with the statement *from nothing to something*. That implied that your net worth dictated your value to the world. There were plenty of wealthy individuals who could be deemed as nothing, and vice versa. I grew up poor, but never thought of myself as nothing. I just knew the life I lived and strived to make each day better than the prior. My drug lord father could deposit a million dollars into a bank account for me tomorrow and it wouldn't change anything about my value as a human being.

Fuck him, by the way.

"So, what does Ethan have to do with us being at the library?" Carissa asked as we started toward the front doors.

"Have you heard of CTE?" I asked.

She looked at the ground as we approached the door, mouth twisted with thought. "The brain disease?"

"Yes."

"I'm familiar with it, but don't know a ton. Why?"

"Good chance your brother suffered from it. Did you ever find out why he was seeing that doctor?"

Carissa's hand moved to her heart as we entered the library, the automatic doors swooshing open to allow the brisk gust of air conditioning to welcome us in. "No. He hasn't returned my calls. Figured he wouldn't. Unless Timmy gave him permission—even post death—the doctor doesn't have to tell me a thing."

"Well, after what Ethan just told me, it sounds like most of that team is suffering from CTE because of a particular drill the coach had them run every day. Head-to-head contact every day for about five months. I'm no expert in CTE either, but it sounds like that might be just enough damage to cause this disease."

"Timmy had CTE?" she asked. The tears made a comeback, welling in those hazel eyes.

I put my arm around her. "I know that's hard to hear. Your brother was suffering. We're getting closer to finding out what's going on."

She shook her head. "Jonny, I don't care what's going on. My brother is gone and he never gave me a chance to help him. That's what kills me. After relying on each other our entire lives, he chose to fight this battle in private. I'll never understand why."

Carissa broke into heavier sobs, burying her face into my chest. An elderly couple strolled out of the library, watching us with curiosity. I grinned and nodded to show them everything was fine.

"We can't bring your brother back," I said, running my hand up and down her back. "But we can try to understand what was going on in his head. Maybe give you some closure. From what I've heard so far, people with CTE struggle to think logically. Timmy must have convinced himself to not tell you what was going on."

Carissa peeled back from me, looking up. The sorrow plastered across her eyes was almost enough to make me break down. It was weird seeing someone grieve. It always triggered memories of my own sorrows.

"I don't want to be here, Jonny," Carissa said. "I'm sorry. It just doesn't feel right. Why can't we just go to my house and use the internet?"

Spoken like a true non-library person.

"I'm not here to use the internet," I said. "I have a phone now, remember? Let me grab a few books. At least I'll know what I'm reading in those has been peer-reviewed by actual scientists and not just some angry dipshit on the internet spewing their opinion."

This drew a laugh from Carissa. "Okay."

"But I do need you to come with me," I said. "I don't have a library card. Do you by chance?"

She nodded. "I don't have my physical card, but they should be able to pull me up through my driver's license."

"Perfect," I said. "Let me get some books and we can go back to my place to do this research."

We joined hands and walked deeper into the library. I noticed the couple of librarians working the checkout counter had been watching us during Carissa's emotional breakdown. But the place was rather empty, so I couldn't blame them for staying entertained by our drama.

Rather than confronting them, I sought the librarian who had helped me earlier. She was still seated at her post, but wasn't reading the romance book. Instead, she browsed the computer screen on her desk and looked up as we approached. She looked from me to Carissa, letting her gaze linger on my library date.

"You're back already?" the librarian said.

"Yes, ma'am," I replied. "Hoping you can tell me which books you have available about CTE."

"The brain disease?" she asked.

Did everyone know about this disease besides me? "Yes."

She pursed her lips and turned her attention back to the computer, typing quickly, looking up and down. After a quick nod to herself, she stood up and said, "We have a few you can check out today. Let me grab them for you."

She moved quicker than I expected as she vanished down the aisles of books. This was the non-fiction section of the library, her specialty.

Carissa remained silent as we stood at the desk waiting for five minutes. I'd rub her shoulders, then her back. And she'd lean her head against my arm.

The librarian returned with a short stack of books and placed them on the desk for me to review.

"*A Historical Foundation of CTE in Football Players* by Bennet Omalu," she said. "*Traumatic Brain Injury: A Clinician's Guide to Diagnosis, Management, and Rehabilitation.* Looks like a thesis from several doctors. *The Concussion Crisis* by Linda Carroll and David Rosner. *Play Hard, Die Young* by Bennet Omalu. And *Brainwashed: The Bad Science Behind CTE and the Plot to Destroy Football* by Merril Hoge. Sounds like one that might provide a different perspective. Always good to have some of that."

I flipped through the books, encouraged by what she had brought back. "I'll take them all. Thank you so much. This is a huge help."

"Of course," the librarian said, sitting back down and keeping her stare on me. "Are you doing a research project?"

I'm sure it wasn't every day she saw someone like me requesting such an odd set of books. "Yes. Research project. I go to RCC."

Redwood Community College. I drove by it at least once a week downtown.

The librarian nodded, accepting this as the truth.

Carissa slid her license across the desk, and the librarian checked us out. We exited the building and I asked, "You doing okay?"

"Sure. Just okay. Sorry, it's still eating me alive thinking about what Timmy might have been going through in his final days. I just don't get why he couldn't tell me. He went through the effort to find a doctor and everything, but never said a single word to me."

"I obviously can't speak for him," I said. "I didn't even know him. But from what I've heard about your relationship, Timmy thought the world of you. If I loved someone as much as he loved you, I'd have a hard time telling them I had an incurable disease. Why tell someone you're suffering when there's nothing they can do to help?"

Carissa shook her head. "He told the doctor."

"We don't know what he and the doctor said. He went in to the doctor and was given a diagnosis and meds. But even from what Ethan told me about CTE—which he has, by the way—the meds only do so much. The CTE always wins."

We approached my car. "Let me drive," I said. "You're in no shape to be driving right now. I can bring you back here to get your car later."

Carissa put up no argument and shuffled to the passenger side. I hurried around to open the door for her and closed it once she sat down.

I joined her, and she had tears streaking gently down her cheeks.

"I don't understand how my brother even got CTE," she said. "I know you can get it from playing football, but I thought it was something that only happened to the pros. You know, the people who play their entire lives. Timmy only played in middle school and high school. Could he have really taken that much damage to the head?"

I pulled out of the library parking lot and started the drive home. Carissa listened as I told her everything Ethan had told me about the savage practices their team went through the year of their championship run. She had never heard of Oklahoma drills. Now that she thought back to it, there were a few evenings when Timmy returned home in a bit of a daze.

"Like he wasn't really there," she explained.

Carissa recalled the same behavior from other players on the team. She spent time with many of them because of her brother and had always assumed they were simply focused on winning. It never occurred to her they were suffering through concussions as teenagers.

We pulled up to my house and I killed the engine. We sat in the car for a moment, Carissa studying the stack of books on her lap.

"I don't know, Jonny," she said.

"What's there to know?"

"What's the point of all this?" she asked. "Researching CTE. For what? It doesn't bring any of them back, and I'm not sure what it proves. Even if the others are suffering from CTE, what are you going to do about it? Knock on their doors and ask them to get their heads checked?"

I shrugged. "If that's what I have to do, then sure. If we can identify a clear reason people are taking their lives, then why wouldn't we try to stop more from happening?"

Carissa wiped her face clear and leaned across the center console to plant a kiss on my cheek. "You're a good man, Jonny. As pure hearted as anyone I've ever known. Let's go start on the research."

We filed out of the car and strolled up to the front door. Carissa carried the books with her arms crossed over them, and I considered it a glimpse of what she looked like in high school, walking the halls to get to her next class.

I stuck the key into the lock and pushed the front door open. Lying on the floor was a piece of paper, again with typed words. I bent down and picked it up to read six simple words.

NO MORE. BACK OFF. OR ELSE.

Chapter 17

Carissa begged me to call the police after I flipped the piece of paper over.

It contained another typed out message:

I'M WATCHING YOU, YOUR COP FRIEND, AND YOUR GIRLFRIEND.

I couldn't blame Carissa for her panic. She hadn't seen me in action and was oblivious to my capabilities to defend not just myself, but her.

"He knows who I am!" Carissa cried, pacing frantic circles around my living room. She had left the books on the kitchen counter, and I suspected we wouldn't be getting to those tonight. "And who the hell is your cop friend?"

"I've already texted him," I said, projecting all the calmness I felt. "And he's on his way over."

I really wasn't worried. This wasn't an actual threat. I was dealing with a classic keyboard warrior. They loved to sound big and tough, pick fights online, and apparently slip notes of paper under people's doors when they weren't home. Didn't you just want to punch these assholes in the face? I could only hope for the opportunity.

"I need you to relax," I said to Carissa.

She stopped, planted her hands on her hips, and gawked at me like I had just suggested she run naked down the street. "Relax?! There is some sick fuck out there who just called me out in that letter."

I raised a hand. "To be fair, that could be anyone. They didn't call you out by name."

"Cop friend and girlfriend," she repeated from the letter. "Are you telling me you have another girlfriend?"

"Another?" I asked. "We've only been out on one date, Carissa. I'm sorry, but that doesn't make you my girlfriend."

Carissa clenched her jaw, glaring at me. I raised a valid point and she knew it, but all her rage and worry tried to tug her in a different direction. "Okay. Let me rephrase that. Is there another woman you've been spending time with? Someone else this person might be confusing for your girlfriend?"

"No," I replied quickly. "Just you."

Carissa threw her hands in the air, rolled her eyes, and grunted. "So then it is me! We're just fighting over semantics that don't matter right now."

That was true, and I had to tip my cap to whoever left the note. If their intent was to spark an argument between Carissa and I—a *distraction*—then it was working.

"This is bullshit!" Carissa continued, still not relaxing. "I never asked to be a part of this. You can go play hero all you want—I'm just trying to move on with my life."

She started for the door.

"Where are you going?" I asked.

She stopped in front of the door, hand outstretched for the knob, and spun around to face me. Her eyes were red, fists clenched. "I will walk back to the damned library to get my car if I need to. Or you can give me a ride so I can return home where no one slips threats under my door."

"Carissa, please hear me out," I said. We stood six feet apart, and I was hesitant to step any closer. "You're safe here with me. I'd say safer than being at home on your own."

"I have a gun, Jonny," she fired back. "I don't need some macho man to protect me."

"Guns are great when you can easily identify the threat. But who-ever is leaving these letters doesn't want to be identified. That's why they've been typed and printed on common paper. Handwriting is like a fingerprint. Speaking of, we could try to get actual fingerprints off the paper, but they're not there. This person is too careful."

"And what does any of that have to do with me? The letter is for you. Slipped under *your* door."

"Yes. But they know who you are. And Officer Santos. And if they know who you are, there's a good chance they know where you live. Now, I highly doubt they'll come after a cop, which leaves you and I. And seeing as they are struggling with face-to-face confrontation, I don't think they'll be coming after me, either. Which leaves you."

"Leaves me for what?! What's even going on, Jonny? Just a few minutes ago, we were talking about CTE leading to these suicides. Now we're getting threats to stop looking into it."

"I know." Once Carissa lowered her arms to her sides, I took two steps forward and grabbed her gently by the shoulders. "Don't you see? Someone wants us to stop digging. That means we're on to some-thing. They wouldn't waste their time with these letters if we were looking in the wrong spots. We're getting closer. To what, I have no clue. But we've already done enough to make someone panic."

"Panic?" Carissa echoed.

I nodded. "There isn't even a clear threat in this letter. Back off or else? What the hell does that mean? Or else what?"

A knock came from the door, causing Carissa to shriek and jump back. I had to bite my lip to keep from laughing.

"It's Santos," I said, shuffling to the door and pulling it open. Carissa remained behind the couch as Santos entered. He had been off duty, arriving in black jeans and a button-up dress shirt. "You're looking mighty dapper. Big plans tonight?"

Santos grinned. "I *was* getting ready to go out tonight. Hit up a salsa club and see if I can meet my future ex-wife."

"And you still can," I said. "But I really need you to see something. First, I'd like you to meet Carissa Summers."

Carissa had been inching towards us, and I waved her over to come closer.

Santos extended a hand. "Nice to meet you, miss. My condolences for your brother."

"Thank you," Carissa said, offering a polite smile.

Santos turned his attention back to me. "What is it, Mendez?"

I had tossed the letter next to the books on the kitchen counter, and backpedaled to grab it. Santos wrinkled his nose as I handed it over and he started reading. He flipped it over and gulped as he read the back.

"This arrived today?" he finally asked.

"Yes," I said. "Slipped under the front door. Same as last time."

"Can you check it for fingerprints?" Carissa asked, rather eagerly.

"Fingerprints?" Santos asked. "For what?"

"To see who slipped it under the door," Carissa replied matter-of-factly.

I grinned, and Santos laughed. "I'm sorry, Ms. Summers, but that's not how any of that process works."

Carissa pursed her lips. "Why is no one else worried? He's calling out all three of us."

"Oh, I'm worried," Santos said. "I'm worried word might get back to the station that I've been seeing Mendez in private. That could provide me with some trouble. But that's about the most of my concerns. For all we know, some teenage punk could be slipping these notes under the door as a prank. Have either of you actually been threatened?"

Carissa looked at me, then shook her head.

"Okay then," Santos said. "Nothing here that requires police involvement. And certainly not fingerprinting. But use it as a reminder to stay alert when you're out and about."

Carissa jerked her head from side to side. "I can't believe you two. Jonny, you were the only person who believed there was more going on than suicides. And I assume you feel the same way, Officer, if you two have been meeting in private. After seeing this letter, now I'm fully onboard. Something is going on. And someone out there doesn't want us to know. But why?"

"Are we really doing this?" Santos asked me.

I shrugged. "We're all here. The only three people who believe there is more than meets the eye. According to the note, there's a good chance we're being watched right now."

Carissa glanced at the windows like she could spot their stalker that simply. "That's not funny, Jonny."

"No one's laughing," I said.

The living room fell silent. Santos scanned the books on the counter and handed the note back over to me. "Sorry, you two. I've had a shitty week at work and need to blow off some steam. If you want to play detective, go right ahead. But you'll have to count me out for this round."

"Thanks for stopping by," I said, shaking his hand.

"My pleasure. And thank you for calling me over. This *is* important. I don't want to discount that fact. We're unlikely in any physical danger, but still, be careful out there."

Santos left as quickly as he'd arrived, leaving me alone once more with Carissa.

"So that's it?" Carissa said. "We get this letter and the cop says fuck it, he wants to go dancing?"

"You're safe here," I reiterated. "I'm a trained killing machine. I've looked death square in its eyes and am still standing. If you think I'm afraid of whatever little coward is leaving these notes, you're grossly mistaken."

Carissa sat down on the couch, crossed her legs, and clenched her jaw. She glared at my coffee table before looking up at me. "So what, I'm supposed to live with you now? To keep me safe?"

"That's not what I'm saying. I just don't think you should go home right at this moment. If you'll hear me out, we can make a plan."

"And what plan would that be?" she asked, crossing her arms. This beautiful woman sat on my couch, yet was as closed off to me as she'd ever been.

"Let me clarify," I said. "Just because I don't think we're in danger doesn't mean I'm not concerned. Someone's watching us. I find that more exciting than anything."

"Exciting? What kind of sick response is that? How am I supposed to sleep in my bed tonight, Jonny?"

Her words felt like knives, each one attacking me like I had personally threatened her wellbeing.

"Two options," I said. "You can either sleep with a gun under your pillow. Or I can stay over and sleep on the couch."

Carissa scoffed. "I'm not sure I even want you near my house right now, Jonny. All this danger swirling around you. Maybe if you're out of the picture, I'll be fine."

I kept my distance, still standing near the front door. "Maybe you're right."

Carissa's eyes narrowed on me. "Excuse me?"

"Now that I think about it, that was just the first time the three of us were ever in the same room together. Whoever is out there is watching *me*. Luckily, I can retrace my steps to see where it might have been. That was only my fourth encounter with Santos. He brought me home from the police station, stopped by another night, met with me at the bowling alley, and then just now. You and I have spent time at your house, out at dinner, today at the library, and right now. That eliminates anyone *from* my neighborhood watching me, since this is your first time over."

"Can't it be someone simply following you around? Maybe they drove behind you on your way to different places."

I nodded. "That's most likely. There was no one at the bowling alley besides the staff. If it was one of them, they wouldn't know about you. It's got to be someone following me, and I'd bet they saw us out at dinner. Incredibly easy to blend into the background, less risky than parking outside my house. Or your house. It's me they want to stop."

Carissa stood from the couch and shuffled toward me. Our eyes locked. Her lips parted to speak, but I raised a finger to cut her off.

"We can't see each other," I said, letting the words linger. We held each other's gaze. I opened my arms and pulled her into an embrace. "If these were different circumstances, we'd probably spend every day together. But you don't deserve to be dragged into this mess. You're already dealing with it from a different perspective. You're still grieving. That should be your only concern right now. Dealing with your feelings, understanding how you'll move forward without your brother."

"But Jonny—"

I shook my head. "Trust me, I know how you're feeling. I don't want this either, but it's for your own safety. With all the sick people in the world, I'd never live with myself if something were to happen to you. This doesn't mean we can't talk. I have my phone now, remember? We can text, call, even do video chats. But we can *not* be seen together in Redwood, do you understand?"

"Yes," she said, disappointed.

"It's only going to get worse," I continued. "Because I'm not stopping. The closer I get, the more unhinged this person will become. Eventually, they'll panic even more. Make a mistake. If they're going through the trouble of typing these letters and delivering them to my house in broad daylight, they'll push the matter further. This is nothing new to me. I'm a disruptor. Bad people despise me because I ruin their plans. I've always come out alive, but one day my luck will run out. It's best if you're not there to witness it. Just in case."

I pulled her in tighter and she looked up at me, our faces inches apart. We kissed. My chest fluttered. I loved how her lips tasted on mine. I wanted more. More of her. But that would only further complicate whatever this relationship was. We pulled apart. Reluctant to do so. I wondered if I'd get to kiss those lips again.

Chapter 18

The next name on my list was Kody Holt.

I had it circled because it was perhaps the only one I felt anxiety about visiting. Carissa had mentioned his name was on the list of those accused of the sexual harrassment against the team's equipment manager, Andrew Stone.

The other two names listed, Jackson Green and Tyrell Marshall, were already dead by suicide.

I didn't have to drive far to get to Kody's house, maybe five minutes.

He lived in the next neighborhood over, a development of ranch-style homes similar to my own. I pulled up in front of his house shortly after ten o'clock on Sunday morning, finding a man sitting on the front porch, smoking a cigarette.

He watched me climb out of my car and take the short pathway to the porch. He didn't say a word, and kept puffing on the cigarette, eyes following my every movement.

"Good morning, sir," I said. "I'm looking for Kody Holt. Is he by chance here?"

The man, who had a buzz cut and several freckles across his face and arms, plucked the cigarette from his mouth and tilted his head to look me up and down. "You're talking to him," he said. "And who are you?"

"My name is Jonny Mendez, sir, and I'm helping investigate the suicides that have happened in Redwood over the past week."

I stuck out a hand, which he looked at for several seconds before returning a weak shake. He snorted. "Tough times for those folks and their families," Kody said, flicking his cigarette into the yard and reaching into his shirt pocket for a fresh one. He was the first person who didn't have further questions about my alleged role.

"Yes it is," I said. "I've spoken with several of the family members, along with others from your football team."

Kody lit his next cigarette and leaned back in his lawn seat. "So what brings you here, Jonny Mendez?"

"A couple reasons, Mr. Holt," I said, planting one foot on the porch so I could lean on my knee to converse in a relaxed manner. "It's no secret these three men all played together on that championship team. That's an interesting link between three men who took their lives within a week of each other. So I've started my investigation by speaking with others who were on that team. I actually met with Ethan Stokes yesterday at his home."

Kody laughed. "Stokesy? How's that rich motherfucker doing? I heard his toilet paper is made of money."

I chuckled. "Well, I didn't use his bathroom, so I can't say for sure."

Kody slapped his knee and cackled. "I'm just giving him shit. Stokesy's a good guy. Always was. What did he have to say?"

"We actually had a long conversation about CTE," I said. "Are you familiar?"

"I think we're all familiar," Kody replied. "Coach shook our brains out to win that trophy. Of course, we were just boys at the time and didn't realize what he'd done. We was just enjoying the moment. You ever been a king of a small town? Because that's what we all were. Free pies. Free sodas. Hell, if we weren't kids we coulda probably walked into any bar and got pumped full of alcohol. With no tab."

"I can't say I've ever gone through anything like that, but it sounds like every kid's dream."

Kody grinned, revealing yellowed teeth that had turned from the chain smoking. "Good times they were. Yes, indeed."

"Have you been checked for CTE?" I asked.

He took a drag before responding, blowing smoke above his head. "Checked for it? Nah. But I have it. Don't need a doctor to tell me that."

"How can you be so sure?"

Kody shrugged. "I'm forgetful. Get violent thoughts from time to time, and usually they come out of nowhere. Like I'll be mowing the lawn, say, and look over and see my neighbor. Then all the sudden I fantasize about taking my mower right over there and running them down. Sounds like fun in my head. But, shit, what a mess that would make, right?!"

I wasn't sure if I was supposed to laugh or not, so remained silent. "You know, Mr. Holt, if you get it checked out, you can get medication to help control the symptoms."

Kody cackled. "There's no cure. To hell with the symptoms. This is going to eat me alive with or without medicine."

"Is everything okay out there?" a hoarse voice called from the screen door.

I look over to see an older woman, hunch-backed with a sunken face, glaring at me from inside the house.

"We're good, Ma!" Kody barked, sounding frustrated. "Why don't you bring out my ring so I can show my friend?"

The old lady mumbled something about wetbacks as she vanished back into the house.

"I hope you don't mind me asking," I said. "But how has your mental health been? Any suicidal thoughts recently?"

Kody slapped his knee and shook his head. "Buddy, I've been having suicidal thoughts almost my whole life. Hasn't been the easiest of lives. After high school, I worked at a garage fixing diesels. You can actually make a lot of money doing that. Then Ma got sick. Couldn't work. So I helped her cover the bills. It's what you do when you got the money, right? Then her sickness got worse. And the hospital bills started piling up. She collects disability now, but it isn't much help paying off the three hundred thousand dollars of debt we have."

He looked at the ground and shook his head.

"I'm sorry to hear that, Mr. Holt."

Kody shrugged. "Nothing to be sorry for. That's life, right? I laugh at the people who think they're actually in control. We're all just one bad day away from living in hell."

I thought back to that car bomb taking my mother from me. "I suppose there's some truth to that."

He coughed and slapped his chest. "Don't get me wrong, I wouldn't say I'm suicidal. Not in the common meaning. I got no plans of blasting my head off. Definitely wouldn't jump off a building. Jackson always had big balls. Can't say I'm surprised he went out with such a bang."

Kody tipped his head back and laughed at the skies above. The screen door creaked open, and his mother appeared, a shiny ring held tight in her fingers.

"Thanks, Ma," Kody said, rising from his seat to grab the ring. His mother glared at me, remaining silent, before scurrying back into the house like a petrified cat. "Don't worry about her," he continued.

"Ma's all over the place. Happy when she can put her own shoes on in the morning."

"What ring is this?" I asked, knowing damn well what it was.

Kody raised it in front of his face. It was solid gold with a red diamond on each side. Emblazoned in the middle, however, was 1999 OREGON STATE CHAMPIONS. A lion's head was centered between the words.

"Hope you don't mind," Kody said. "But talking about those guys always makes me warm and fuzzy. I miss them."

It wasn't a leap for me to figure winning that championship was likely the biggest highlight of Kody's life. I'm not sure why else the ring would have been so easily accessible.

He slipped it onto his index finger and sat back down, admiring his achievement.

"You were saying you're not suicidal," I said.

Kody nodded. "Right—in the traditional sense."

He kept staring at the ring. This conversation was like pulling teeth—which he soon wouldn't have. "And what *is* the non-traditional sense?"

Kody's face soured. He licked his lips, which made disgusting sounds as his tongue ran over them. "Like smoking these cigarettes every day," he said. "It's not considered suicide when someone dies of lung cancer after smoking a pack a day. Sure, there are addictions people can't get over. But I'm not addicted. I choose to smoke these every day. Drink beer every night. I don't want to kill myself, but I don't want to be alive anymore, either. All the medical bills. All the lost hopes and dreams. And it's all because of something that happened out of my control. I would never turn my back on Ma. She's all I got. And I'm all she's got. Was always just the two of us. Daddy left us when I was three. Said he was going to fill the car with gas one night and never came back."

"I grew up without my father, too," I said.

"So you get it," Kody replied. "Sure, you can get used to it. But there's always that hole in your heart. Something missing. So you'll understand how you become the main man in your ma's life."

I nodded. "Sure did. Lost her at a young age, too."

Kody fidgeted with his ring. "I'd never wish Ma death. That's cruel. But I can wish it on myself. It would hurt Ma, but I can't take it no more. Just working to pay off the debt. It's an endless cycle. What's the point of living to pay off doctors until the day I die?"

I drew in a deep breath. "I can't lie, Mr. Holt. Your life is difficult. I wouldn't wish your circumstance on anyone. But is slowly killing yourself the best approach?"

He sucked on his cigarette longer than usual, perhaps trying to prove a point. "I call the hotline. Lots of us do. When the thoughts get dark."

"The hotline?"

"The suicide hotline," he repeated. "Just dial 988 when you're having the dark thoughts. They have the most incredible people over there. They have this way of sounding like they've been your friend your entire life. I've called them a few times and they always remind me the things worth living for. I wish I could calm myself down as good as them, but when you open past due envelopes every week, it gets hard."

"You said lots of you use it?" I asked. "From the team?"

"Oh yeah," Kody said. "Once all this CTE stuff got out, someone in our group shared about the hotline. Warned us it was only a matter of time before our thoughts took a turn. Sure as shit, it happened. I guess our three friends hadn't been calling the hotline."

"Not necessarily," I said. "But I can look into it. You said the number is just 988?"

"Yeah, buddy. 988 for those hard nights. The quiet ones."

I made a mental note to look more into the suicide hotline.

"I want to ask you one more thing," I said. "If you don't want to discuss, just say so and I'll leave."

Kody flicked his cigarette butt into the yard, but didn't pull out a new one. Not yet. His eyes studied me. I couldn't tell if he knew what I wanted to ask, or if he was just genuinely curious.

"Shoot," Kody said.

"I want to ask about Andrew Stone and the alleged events that happened."

Kody held his gaze and showed no emotion in his eyes. Maybe he hadn't heard that name in years. People could suppress negative memories and could become unhinged once reminded. My palms slickened with sweat, expecting some type of explosion from this down-on-his-luck former high school star.

But no such thing occurred, and we held an awkward silence for several seconds. Finally, Kody reached into his shirt pocket, pulled out a fresh cigarette, and pointed it at me.

"You can get the fuck off my property."

Chapter 19

My mind was rattled during my drive home. I indeed got the fuck off his property upon his rather calm request. There was no need to stick around and stir up shit with a man who felt he had nothing to lose. Those were always the most dangerous ones.

I had entered the 988 number into my phone, so I wouldn't risk forgetting it.

Kody's immediate shift in tone once I brought up Andrew Stone told me enough. It was still a sensitive matter all these years later. Considering it wasn't Kody who suffered through the trauma, his words led me to believe he had been involved. To what extent, I'd never know. But he was involved.

I wanted to call Carissa and see if she knew about the hotline or her brother using it. Maybe she could access his phone records to shed some light. I was also curious if the other deceased members of the team had used the hotline in the days leading up to their deaths. My time might be better spent questioning their families instead of other players from the team.

Still, through it all, my mind kept drifting back to Andrew Stone. Where was he? Was he even alive today? If anyone had an understandable reason to take their life, Andrew Stone had it.

I wasn't sure how much a conversation with Andrew Stone could help my cause today, but he was a missing piece of the puzzle.

I didn't want to call Carissa so soon. How shitty would it look for me to kick her out of my life, only to call her less than twenty-four hours later?

No.

But I had another call to make. One I had hoped to never need to place. But the time had come. Something deep in my thoughts kept pressing me to find Andrew Stone. One of the basic principles from my days in the CIA was to locate the common denominator.

I'd reached a dead end, which normally sparked a fresh wave of vigor within me. Work around the roadblock. But I had no such options. I couldn't Google my way into finding someone in witness protection.

I arrived home, poured myself a glass of water, and sat at the kitchen table, staring at my cell phone for five minutes.

There were four phone numbers stored in my mind. My childhood home phone—useless. My mom's cell phone—sentimental. The Bootheel—a bar in Texas where I worked during college. And Kayla Hernandez.

I met Kayla at the CIA. She worked in the D.C. offices and always provided me with any bit of information I needed to work on a case. Whether or not it was legal for her to do it. That was a perk of having work conversations while holding each other in bed.

Yes, our past was complicated.

We were in love once. So naturally, I had to run.

It wasn't just the CIA I left behind, but so much more. The life of stability most people dreamed of. I was aware of how much of a fool I was for leaving Kayla. She had even been willing to move with me when I didn't know where I was going.

I knew my mom was turning in her grave as she watched me throw away a life with a stunningly beautiful, smart, and motivated woman. We always pushed each other to be better. To make a bigger impact in the world.

My stomach felt like a wrung dishrag as I dialed her number. We hadn't spoken on the phone in about three years.

I left her digits dialed on my screen and stared at them longer, thinking of any other solutions to get the information I desperately needed.

I pressed dial and held my breath.

Part of me—my inner coward who lived *deep* in my fibers—prayed she wouldn't answer. Even better if the phone number no longer connected to her. That would bring me much needed closure I wasn't sure I even wanted.

I had plenty of moments where I imagined a future with Kayla. Big house in the suburbs. Two kids playing in the front yard while we watched them from—

"This is Hernandez," she said, her voice whipping my mind through the past, making me dizzy.

My chest fluttered. She was still Hernandez. Hadn't married yet. Not that it mattered, but still.

What the fuck was I even thinking?

"Hello?" she repeated.

I had to clear my throat that had clenched shut with tension. "Kayla," I said, more groggy than I'd hoped.

Silence for about five seconds. Or maybe five days. I wasn't sure.

"Jonny?" she whispered.

The only person in the CIA who called me by my first name. Hearing it come out of her mouth was borderline intoxicating.

"Yes," I replied. "I hope I didn't interrupt your day."

"No," she said. "Not at all."

We were both flustered. I could hear it in her voice. You never expected your past to come knocking on the door, but when it did...

"How are you?" I asked.

"I'm doing well," she replied, and I could hear the smile in her voice. That was a good sign. Hopefully, I wouldn't fuck it up. "And how are you? Where are you hiding out these days?"

She could have only known I was hiding if she had previously looked for me. The thought brought a grin to my lips. "I'm hanging in there," I said. "Hiding out in Oregon. Would rather not say the town."

"Classic Jonny," she said, and just like that, the joy had been zapped from her voice. Shit. "Always on the move. Running from his past and future. Somehow, at the same time. I take it you need something if you're calling me out of the blue and you're not in town to have a coffee."

"I don't drink coffee. You should know that."

She giggled, and the swing of her emotions put me on edge. Like I was handling a poisonous snake. "Of course. Sixteen ounces of water in the morning is all the body needs to energize itself for the day ahead. How could I ever forget all your lectures about proper hydration?"

"My only hope is you took the advice to heart," I said, imagining Kayla running her fingers along a water bottle on her desk. Along my chest and stomach.

Snap out of it, man.

"I stay hydrated," she said. "No need to worry about me. So, what is it you need? Who are you in trouble with now?"

"We don't have to get into all that right away. We can...catch up."

Now she laughed. "The Jonny Mendez I know despises small talk. Are you a changed man?"

"Not at all," I said. "Just being polite."

The truth was, I *did* hate small talk. I found it an incredible waste of time. But if there was one person I wanted to make small talk with, she was on the other end of the line. I could listen to her talk about anything under the sun.

She snorted gently through her nose.

"How are your parents?" I asked. Kayla came from a healthy household, something I knew nothing about. Her mom and dad had celebrated their twenty-fifth wedding anniversary shortly after we started dating.

"They're good," she replied. Joy back in her voice. "Dad's getting the itch to retire and spend his days on the golf course. Mom keeps telling him he should, but he insists on saving a little more. He's been saying this for a year now."

Kayla chuckled, ecstasy to my ears. I'd been all over the continent since leaving the CIA, but refused to step foot inside Washington. Kayla had a hold over me. She could make me melt with a glance across the room from those big brown eyes. If I wanted to maintain my current lifestyle, Washington would only complicate matters.

"Glad to hear they're still doing well," I said. The temptation to ask if she was dating anyone swelled to an all-time high. I bit my tongue, however, knowing that would open a can of worms neither of us wanted to deal with.

"You know, Jonny," Kayla said. "It's okay for you to call more than every few years. We agreed to stay in touch. Seeing as you're completely off the grid, it's kind of up to you to call me."

"How often do you look for me?" I asked, unsure if I actually wanted to know the answer.

I heard her sigh through the phone. "Does that matter? I've looked for you—I won't deny that. Why wouldn't I? I have a database of every single citizen in the United States at my fingertips. Even with your files scrubbed, it can always change if you make the tiniest of slip ups. But you don't."

"I'm flattered. I think about you, too. It's just…hard."

Silence.

"So, what do you need, Jonny?" she asked, her voice stern and unwavering.

"Well, that database you referenced… I'm looking for someone."

"Seems like a straightforward request," she replied. "You sure you didn't call me for another reason?"

"It's someone who entered witness protection in 1999," I explained. "I've found everything I could about him under his former name. But whatever happened after he entered the program is as off the grid as me."

"No shit, Sherlock. That's literally the point. Is this a good guy or bad guy you're looking for?" she asked.

"He was a victim of sexual abuse by a group of high school football players," I said. "I like to presume he turned out to be a good guy, but who really knows?"

"And you can't just leave him in peace?" Kayla replied. "Why stir up shit from the past?"

"It's a mess. Three of the players who were accused of the assault have all killed themselves within the past week. The townies are calling it a coincidence, but I call bullshit. The police chief played on the team. Almost all of them are suffering from CTE now. And there are so many questions swirling around Andrew Stone. I may or may not speak to him. Mainly, I just want to know where he is. If he's even alive."

"Andrew Stone," she repeated. "I'll need his last known location."

I hesitated, and she must have sensed it.

"Don't worry, Jonny," she said. "I'm not going to hop on a plane and fly to Oregon tonight to see you."

"And what about tomorrow?" I asked.

She giggled. I always could make her laugh.

"No. Not tomorrow."

"Fine," I said. "The city is called Redwood."

"Oh," she replied. "I know the city. Never been, but have heard of it. Isn't that kind of a bigger city for you? I thought you liked towns with populations under fifty?"

I laughed. "Well, yes. I prefer much smaller towns. But I mix things up every now and then. Even spent a few months in Los Angeles not too long ago. Just been traveling up the coast since then, staying places that seem peaceful."

"Hmm," she said. "I hope you can find that peace you've always been looking for, Jonny."

Having been on my own for so long and making zero contact with friends or family, Kayla provided a sense of nostalgia. She knew me. Everything. My past. My weaknesses and faults.

"And you said this all happened in 1999?" she asked.

"Yes. Timeline isn't entirely clear. Stone may have entered witness protection in either late 1999 or early 2000. It was him, along with his parents. They moved from Redwood, and that's where the information ends."

"I see," she replied. "Okay. Witness protection is one area I don't have direct access to. But I have some friends at the Marshal's office. They owe me. Give me a couple of days to see what I can find. Am I allowed to save this phone number and call you back?"

"Of course," I said. "But I'll be tossing it as soon as this is all done."

"I expect nothing less."

Silence lingered in the airwaves between us. I wanted to keep talking with her. Since we'd been on the phone, I had forgotten all about the suicides and Redwood. There was nothing else in the world worth focusing on.

"Thank you," I finally said. The words *I miss you* came to my lips, but I kept them in.

"It's no problem," she said. "We'll talk soon. And Jonny?"

"Yes?"

"Be careful out there."

Chapter 20

I spent the rest of the day and evening lost in my thoughts. Kayla kept slipping into my mind, distracting me as I tried to research the suicide hotline for a better understanding of how it all worked.

I quickly gave up, went to sleep, and headed to the library first thing the next morning, refreshed.

Being away from the house—and not having to use my cell phone for research—made me feel more at ease.

The librarian from my prior visits was not there. But it was Saturday, so I'm sure the staff had a rotation worked out so they could take turns enjoying a full weekend. The computer lab was buzzing. Six teens took up an entire row of computers, each one of them gawking at me as I slid through the narrow gap of the front row to sit at the lone open computer at the end.

The room was crowded, but everyone seemed locked in to what they were doing. The man in the seat next to me had an online course about investing pulled up on his screen. He had a bag of fast food on the desk, the scent of french fries filling up the entire space.

My mouth watered.

I settled in, slipped on my headphones connected to my old school iPod, and got to work while listening to a variety of nineties and early-2000s hip hop.

My search started with a high-level overview of the 988 Lifeline. The lifeline was a government service funded by the U.S. Substance Abuse and Mental Health Services Administration and the states in which they operate.

This was a new world to me, and the extent of their services surprised me. They provided more than intervention for suicidal folks. General mental health struggles, alcohol and drug abuse, emotional distress, or just a friendly voice to talk to. For us introverts, they even had options for online chat, text messaging, in addition to placing a phone call. Plus services in American Sign Language.

I knew some people who could have benefited from these services during our time in the military. But I couldn't recall ever hearing about such a resource. That was also a time when mental health had a nasty stigma. Certainly no soldier of the United States needed to get their mind checked out, right?

The deeper my research went, the more impressed I became. Services in multiple languages. Online material for those not feeling quite ready to get intimate with a stranger over the phone or web. And much more.

I clicked on the "Get Involved" option from the menu, finding both paid jobs and volunteer opportunities all across the country. The list was sorted in alphabetical order by state, so I scrolled down to Oregon, finding they had offices in Portland, Salem, and Redwood.

"Volunteer Opportunities at Crisis Center," I read gently under my breath. Each location had the same listing, but no paid positions available.

I followed the link to apply as a volunteer. The job description seemed reasonable enough. Answer calls for those suffering through a crisis or issue. Provide empathy. Document calls and follow up when appropriate. The available shifts were weeknights from six to ten.

I submitted my information and applied.

My only hope was the process moved quickly, which, judging by the gravity of their work, I assumed would be.

I wanted to get inside one of these centers. Talk to the existing employees and volunteers. If I could gain access to one of the computers in the Redwood office, I might find information about the dead men.

That was, if they had provided their personal information.

One tidbit I caught on the site's FAQ section was their commitment to privacy. Agents would ask for a caller's name, address, and phone number, but the caller had no obligation to provide any detail and could remain completely anonymous.

I needed the phone numbers of the dead men before I went into the crisis center. At the very least, they should have a log of the phone numbers that had called in. There might be similarities between all three men. If they had each called the hotline in the days leading up to their suicides, maybe something in the system would tell me who they had spoken with.

This all seemed like a desperate Hail Mary as I pieced together a plan in my mind. Especially considering I didn't clearly understand the processes for the crisis center. Maybe they *didn't* keep a log of phone numbers that had called in. At least, at the level of access I'd have as a volunteer.

But if I could just get inside the building, I trusted my ability to find out where such a secret might be stashed. One problem, however, was the center being open for twenty-four hours every day. If I could guarantee a time to have the place alone to myself, I'd absolutely get what I needed. But this was a complication I'd need to work around.

I closed my current search and looked up where exactly this crisis center was located. They were on the east side of town, in a nondescript brown building behind a Carl's Junior and a marijuana dispensary.

I'd been to the Carl's, and don't recall seeing the office.

Twelve minute drive from my house.

Looking at the satellite images, I saw the building had a large parking lot surrounding it. If push came to shove, I could go into full stealth mode and track a worker from the lot until I found an opportunity to snatch their badge and gain access to the building.

I had no interest in doing such a thing, especially to someone performing such a delicate job. The purest of work. But more lives were at stake, and Redwood needed answers.

After saving the address in my phone, I closed all my tabs and left the library. Kayla had vanished from my thoughts, but I knew she'd slip back in.

During my drove home, I thought about what Kody Holt had told me. Several players from the team knew about the hotline and used it. Just across town was a call center full of people who had likely spoken to these players. Helped them through a "dark day" with CTE, as Kody had put it.

Part of me wanted to drive to the center right now. Stroll in, schmooze the front desk worker into giving me a tour. Those things could work under the right circumstances in a corporate office. But this was the government. And I knew better than most how little of a shit they gave about my charm. Government workers were sticklers for following protocol. If I asked for a tour, they'd probably have security escort me right the fuck out.

No.

This was a long game. As long as it could be, considering the circumstances.

I pulled into my driveway and parked, re-energized by the possibilities lying ahead. Kayla didn't entirely hate me—yes, she crept back into my thoughts. Even though it didn't feel like I was making progress, the information I had gained over the past couple of days gave me hope.

Perhaps the puzzle unfolding was much bigger than I had realized. I had to remind myself that while the suicides were recent, the reasons behind them may be over two decades old. There were no social media profiles I could search through to piece together what exactly had happened in 1999. Three men were dead, and Andrew Stone may as well have vanished into outer space.

I prayed Kayla could find something for me. Who was I kidding? If Andrew Stone was alive, I would absolutely speak with him. While it would be difficult for him, as the victim, to recount the horrific events that happened, I knew he'd remember every single detail from that night.

Tragedy has a way of engraving the most obscure details into your memories. Like farmers branding a cow's ass with a hot iron. That shit wasn't going anywhere.

I knew this because of my own experience. The day that fucking car bomb went off and took my mother. Every minute detail stayed with me to this day. The woman shrieking down the block. The two squirrels sprinting up the nearby tree. A flock of pigeons fleeing from the same tree. The cherry sucker in my mouth, and how the flavor vanished instantly. Replaced by smoke and the dreadful stench of burning oil.

I couldn't even look at a red sucker without getting the urge to vomit.

Thinking of all this made me feel grimy. Like I needed a shower.

I zoned out and never saw Herb strolling over to my car.

He knocked on the glass and startled me.

"Shit!" I cried out, then immediately broke into laughter when I looked over and saw my elderly neighbor. He also laughed, clutching his stomach with his free hand. The other held a small brown box.

I opened the door and stepped out of the car.

Herb raised his bushy, white eyebrows. "Sorry about that, Jonny. Didn't mean to scare you. But that *was* funny!"

I chuckled, pointing at him. "You got me. Not many can say that."

"Well, call me honored. Got a package for you."

He handed it over, a box about four inches on each side. It had no shipping label, no markings.

I frowned at it. "Sorry, Herb, but who is this from?"

"Didn't get a look," he said. "Was watering the grass and saw the package on your doorstep. Your car wasn't here, so figured I'd grab it before the porch pirates. Can't believe that's something we have to worry about. If only you could shoot the assholes who steal packages. I mean, stealing mail is a felony, ain't it?"

"No idea," I said, unable to look away from the package now in my hands. Maybe I was paranoid, or perhaps the echoes of my past were still reverberating in my mind. But my stomach sank, expecting the box to explode. It was no secret someone out there wanted me to mind my business. And I wasn't stopping.

Leaving a bomb in a box seemed rather drastic, though. Especially for someone trying to keep a low profile. If a bomb went off right now, me and Herb would be dead. And *that* would spark an investigation.

No.

Whoever was behind the letters was too smart to get caught. This had to be another message, albeit a physical one.

"Well, thanks for bringing it over, Herb."

He waved me off. "No trouble at all. That's what neighbors are for. I gotta get back to the missus. We're watching our afternoon shows."

"Enjoy. And Thank you." I offered him a grin. We shook hands, and he returned to his house while humming an old Sinatra song under his breath. Might have been "Luck Be A Lady."

I didn't want to shake the box. Just in case. But I felt something rolling around inside. Not too heavy. If it was a bomb, it wasn't powerful enough to kill. Maybe take my hand off, at best. Maybe.

Once Herb disappeared into his house, I hurried inside my own, heart racing. I threw my keys on the kitchen counter before gently placing the box next to them. My hands seemed to move a thousand miles per minute as they fumbled with the tape across the box's seam. Yet my mind moved even faster.

I tore open the box to find a lone object glimmering beneath the lights. Growing more confused with each passing second, I studied the gold surface and red diamonds of the object.

Why would it be here in a box as if it was a delivery I was expecting?

I finally reached in and pulled it out to confirm what my mind was trying to convince me it was not. I held it up to see the truth.

The item in the box was Kody Holt's championship ring.

Chapter 21

I left the ring on my counter and raced back across the neighborhood to stop by Kody's house.

I parked along the curb and gazed at the home. He wasn't sitting out front smoking cigarettes like I imagined he did for several hours each day. But I could see through the screen door into what looked like a kitchen.

A figure was moving around. I couldn't tell if it was him or his racist mother.

It didn't happen often, but I had lost control of my thoughts. I wasn't even sure why I was sitting in front of Kody's house right now. Instead, I should have taken a moment to think. Now that I was here, that's exactly what I did.

Kody loved that ring. His pride and joy. His greatest accomplishment in what had been an otherwise fucked up life. Why would he leave it on my doorstep?

"*He* wouldn't," I said to my empty car.

Even if Kody was the man behind the earlier letters left at my house—which I highly doubted—what did he get out of leaving his prized championship ring?

"Nothing," I said, shaking my head.

So the ring had to have been stolen from Kody. And if it was stolen and given to me, that meant we were being watched the day of our chat on his front porch.

Fuck.

I had scanned the area, knowing the things to look for. Cars parked in odd places. Hell, maybe there was someone in a big black surveillance van. But I hadn't seen such a thing.

It's not even likely someone had followed me and just kept driving by. The ring was too specific. They would have seen it brought out in the middle of our conversation and thought of it as significant.

It wasn't to me, but clearly Kody had no problems busting it out to show a complete stranger.

Whoever had left the notes for me had to be the one who stole the ring and delivered it to my house.

But why?

I drew in a deep breath and got out of my car. The gloves were off. I needed information, and I needed it immediately.

I marched up to the screen door and knocked with authority.

"Who's there?" the crabby mother called out.

"Ms. Holt?" I replied. "I need to speak with Kody."

Kody's mother had been the one in the kitchen, and she labored toward the door, her eyes narrowed to see who I was.

She reached the door, paused, and took a step back, eyes flooded with terror.

"You," she said, pointing a wrinkly, bony finger at me from the other side of the door. "Get the hell off my property or I'm calling the police."

I raised my hands. "Ma'am, I just want a quick word with your son. Is he here?"

"Don't you dirty wetbacks listen?!" she replied. "I said to—"

"Enough!" I shouted. "Your son may be in danger. Where is he?"

I couldn't tell you the last time I raised my voice like that, especially toward an elder. But time was of the essence. And fuck this old hag.

She licked those crusty, sunken lips. "He went out with a friend last night," she said. "Told me he wouldn't be home until later tonight."

"Which friend?" I demanded.

She glared at me. Part of her wanted to keep insulting me, the other had concern for her boy. She shrugged. "I don't know. I was already in bed when he left. He came and gave me a kiss goodnight before going off."

"Did the friend meet him here?" I asked.

"Dunno. I didn't hear anyone, but my hearing's not the best these days."

"Have you tried his cell phone? Does he have a vehicle?"

"I haven't called him," she said, a waver in her voice. "I have no reason to. He told me he'd be home tonight. What's going on? What have you done to my son?"

Wow.

"Ma'am, I haven't done a thing. I'm not even sure he's in trouble, just that he *might* be. If you wouldn't mind, can you please call him? Just to make sure."

She held her gaze on me. She wanted to keep hating me, calling me names. I could see it in her eyes. Her lips pursed.

"Look," I said. "You can hate me for whatever archaic reason you may have. But I need you to push that all aside and call Kody. If he answers and says everything is fine, you'll never see me again."

The old woman nodded and reached into her pocket, pulling out an old flip-phone. I watched as she dialed and noticed the slightest tremble in her grip.

When she pressed the phone against her ear, I braced for the worst. Five seconds passed. Then ten.

I could hear the phone ringing and eventually stop as it went to the automated voice for Kody's voicemail box.

"No answer," she said, snapping the phone shut. She was no longer hiding her worry. Her eyes danced around, looking for answers. Or an explanation. But she had nothing.

"He always answers when you call, right?" I asked, knowing I'd be the same with my mother.

The woman nodded.

"Do you have any guesses who he might have gone out with?" I asked. "Man or woman? Friend from school, maybe work?"

She shrugged and dialed again. "I don't know. He didn't say. What should I do?"

Now she wanted my help. If only I could roll my eyes.

She snapped her phone closed again and shook her head.

"Did he drive himself to wherever he went?" I asked.

"I assume so. His truck's not here."

"What kind of truck?"

"An F-150. It's dark blue with some rust spots on the sides. Old truck, but he's kept it running."

"Okay," I said. "I don't want you to worry. Let me go find him. Keep trying his phone until he answers."

I turned and ran back to my car. The old woman shouted, "What the hell is going on?!"

But I couldn't waste any more time at this house. I was getting me nowhere in a hurry. I had to assume the ring was a taunt from whoever wanted me to stop looking into the suicides. If they had taken the ring, they must have known where Kody was.

I jumped in my car and drove off, Kody's mother still shouting desperately at me. I called Officer Santos as I kept my eyes peeled for an old F-150.

"Santos," he answered.

"It's me," I said. "Kody Holt is missing, and I'm hoping you can reverse lookup his license plate and put out a call to locate him."

"Whoa, pump the brakes," Santos said. "I can look him up, but I can't just put out a call without a good reason."

"He's in danger!"

"And how do you know that?"

"I was just speaking with his mother and she told me he left the house last night and hasn't been back. Then she tried calling him with no luck. She said he always answers her calls."

"He drives an F-150?" Santos asked.

"Yes. So you found him?"

I didn't want to mention the ring. At least, not over the phone. That would be better to discuss in person.

"Well, just in the system," Santos replied calmly. "Jonny, I can't put out a call. Especially for this guy. I'm looking at his record. He's been in bar fights all over town. Has even ended up in Tumalo and stirred up trouble there—that's the town about fifteen minutes north of Redwood. If I put out a call, no one's going to take it serious. It'll only raise suspicions about why I'm asking."

"Then frame it as the mother being worried," I said. "I'm telling you, he's in trouble."

Santos sighed through the phone. "You know something you're not telling me."

"I can't speak of it over the phone," I said. "Can you meet me in person?"

"Dammit, Jonny. No. I can't right now. I'm on patrol duty right now, clear on the other side of town from your house."

"I'll meet you," I said. "Just tell me where to go."

"I can't. Jonny, something's going on at the station. They're still talking about you. I can't risk being seen with you right now. Not if we're to keep this going."

"What the hell are they saying?"

"They know what you're doing," Santos said. "Ethan Stokes is still good friends with the chief. Told him about your visit. Chief is pissed about it. That's all I know. They're looking for ways to get you out of town. You need to play everything very carefully. You have a major target on your back."

The ring.

If the chief wanted me gone, could he have recruited all his ex-teammates to set me up somehow? Did Kody really want to show me the ring, or was it a ploy to make it look like I had stolen it?

"I have something," I said. "It would be ideal if I can show it to you and explain."

Santos sighed again. "This is getting too risky. Last time I'm going to your house, okay? But it's got to be late. I'll come by tonight. Let's say nine o'clock."

"Okay, fine," I said. "Then we can make arrangements for future meetings."

"We'll see."

I was losing Santos and couldn't blame him. He had his job and livelihood to look out for and wouldn't want to risk it all on me. Fair.

"Oh, Jonny," Santos said. "Seriously. Let me see what all I can find out at the station. Take a step back until then. Or things could get messy for you."

Chapter 22

I waited at my house for nine o'clock, oblivious to exactly how high the heat had been cranked up surrounding my name. I spent the afternoon driving around town, hoping to get lucky and spot Kody's car.

The thought at the front of my mind was Kody having gone off somewhere to take his life. He could have said anything to his mother to put her thoughts at ease before heading out last night.

Guilt crept into my thoughts. Could my visit have sparked something within Kody that pushed him to his final limit? Maybe no one had stolen the ring, after all. Maybe Kody dropped off the ring at my house. With no note or context, it was impossible to know the motive behind any of the actions. The more I thought about it, the less likely it seemed the ring was stolen. If it was, that implied someone had been inside his house. His mother hadn't mentioned any visitors, although she could have been hesitant to share details. Or even plain forgetful.

When Santos arrived, I hoped to give him the ring and let him deal with it. I had no reason to keep it in my possessions. And if he didn't take it, I'd just find a way to discretely take it back to Kody's house. Hell, I could put it back in the box and leave it on their doorstep. They didn't have a doorbell camera, so they'd never know it was me.

When the clock struck 9:15, I considered checking in with Santos. But I couldn't be too pushy. He was a police officer, after all, and I'd known plenty. He was likely caught up in a matter. Or paperwork. Bureaucracy required every damn detail to be written down and logged, even for something as simple as a speeding ticket.

At 9:30, I had my doubts if he would show, but trusted he'd communicate that in some form.

It wasn't until 10:15 when a patrol car pulled up in front of my house. Odd choice for him to come in his work vehicle.

"About damn time," I said, jumping off the couch and waiting by the door like an anxious puppy excited to see its owner.

When I pulled open the door, my stomach dropped to my knees. It wasn't Officer Santos.

It was two police officers, marching right up. Chambers and Roman.

What the fuck?

"Good evening, Mr. Mendez," Officer Roman said with a mocking grin.

The two officers stopped right in front of me and crossed their arms. Chambers looked queasy.

"Hello, officers," I said. "Is there something I can help you with?"

"You can start by telling us where you were last night," Roman said sternly.

"I was here."

"And can anyone vouch for that?" Roman asked.

"No, sir. I live here alone. You can ask my neighbors next door—the Walkers—they seem to know when I'm in and out."

Roman chuckled. "I wouldn't put much stock into that. I'd rather take your word, though. Do you mind if we come in and have a chat?"

Where was Santos? Clearly something was up. Was he *not* here because of it?

"I was actually getting ready to go to bed," I said. "Is it urgent, or can we talk tomorrow?"

Roman nodded to Chambers, who reached into his front pocket to pull out a paper. He unfolded it and held it up.

"Mr. Mendez," Chambers said. "We have a signed warrant to search this property. If you would please step aside and let us through so we can do our job."

I took a step back but didn't clear the doorway. "Excuse me? A warrant for what?"

"To search your house, jackass," Roman said, his hand falling to the baton on his utility belt.

"Let me see the warrant," I said, knowing my rights.

Chambers held it up again, allowing me to read it. It was real.

"Can I ask what this is about?" I asked.

"You can get the fuck out of our way," Roman said. "Or we can call back up."

His grip tightened on the baton. Dude felt empowered by having that little piece of paper to wave around. I wasn't going to try anything right now. Roman was too fired up and just might shoot me in the name of self defense.

I stepped aside and allowed the officers to enter my house.

They filed in, Chambers first, then Roman, who bumped his shoulder against my chest as he passed. Chambers stopped in my living room and placed his hands on his hips.

Roman shuffled next to him and they both scanned the area.

"Tell me," Roman said. "Where were you today?"

"I ran some errands around town this morning. Grabbed lunch. Stopped by Borders. Then came home. Been here all afternoon and evening."

I hated telling lies. But even more, I hated an asshole cop poking around my house when I had clearly done nothing illegal.

"Interesting story," Roman said, pacing around the living room, stopping to examine a bookshelf full of the owner's trinkets. "Not your house, right?"

"No, sir. Renting from a friend who's on an extended stay elsewhere."

I'm sure they already knew the information about the house's true owner if they went through the trouble of getting a warrant. But they wouldn't get a peep about him from me.

"You're sure there's nothing you want to tell us?" Roman asked, opening my bedroom door and sticking his head in.

I got the sense they were trying to get me to confess to something. "I wish I knew what you were talking about. Happy to oblige if you give me any idea."

But I knew. This was a chess game. The chief wanted me to stop snooping around his old teammates. Maybe I had been correct in the first place, suspecting he might be covering something up. But what did the chief have to gain by letting his friends die by suicide?

Roman flicked on the light switch in my bedroom and stepped all the way in. I glanced at the box sitting on my kitchen counter and wished I had tossed it. While I could explain its presence, having Kody's ring would raise more questions I didn't have answers for.

Since it was just me and Chambers in the living room, I said to him, "It feels like you're looking for something in particular. If you just say, I'm happy to help."

I knew Chambers liked me after our first encounter. But it was obvious he was now conflicted. He avoided eye contact and kept silent.

"Don't tell him shit," Roman said from my bedroom. "We already know he's a liar. Besides, this isn't official questioning. We'll save that for the station."

"A liar?" I said. "That's a heavy accusation to throw around."

"Is it, though?" Roman asked, stepping back into the living room. His eyes kept dancing, looking up and down. But for what? "You weren't running any errands. Maybe you went to lunch and the bookstore, but everything before that is a lie. We know where you were this morning."

Well, fuck.

That racist old bitch. She must have called the cops on me. But how would that lead to a warrant to search my house?

"Stop talking," Chambers warned his partner in a cautious tone. "You don't want potential evidence dismissed."

Roman snorted. "Please. We just need to find that one thing to lock his ass up. And I'm not leaving here until we get it. Tired of criminals thinking they can come into our town and bring their corruption. Not this time."

Roman entered the kitchen. I didn't know for sure what they were looking for, but I assumed it had to be what was in that box. All I could do was pray he wouldn't look inside. Maybe he'd dismiss it as random mail. If only I had a pile of actual mail. I was too off-the-grid to even receive spam. Roman studied my dining table, which had a couple of newspapers I had picked up in town a few weeks ago.

He lost interest and turned around, eyes immediately falling on the box on my counter. Roman took slow steps toward it, eyes widening as he approached.

Not good.

He separated the flaps and looked inside, a wide grin immediately coming across his face. "Well, well, well. What have we here?"

Roman reached into the box and pulled out the ring, raising it high in the air like a prized relic.

"You know what this is?" he asked. When no one answered, he continued. "Looks like a championship ring for the 1999 football team. Now, why would someone who just moved to town have this in their possession?"

"I actually have an explanation for that," I said.

"Save it, Mendez," Roman snapped. "And get your hands behind your back."

"You're going to arrest me because I have that ring?" I asked. "Seems drastic, don't you think? I'm happy to return it to its proper owner. Was about to, in fact—that's why it was in the box."

Roman clutched the ring tightly in his fist, an evil smirk plastered on his face. "Its owner...good one."

"Mr. Mendez," Chambers said from behind me. He had taken out a pair of handcuffs, which wavered in his grip. "Hands behind your back. You're under arrest for the murder of Kody Holt."

Chapter 23

I rode in the back of the patrol car in silence. Chambers had called ahead to the station to let them know of my arrest and pending arrival.

By the time we pulled into the police station, it seemed every cop car in town was there waiting for me, along with a half dozen news vans.

Roman preferred the theatrics, and walked me through the front entrance so all the cameras could snap pictures. The asshole had the audacity to throw up a fake smile. Anything to look good on the morning news that would air in a few hours.

They fully booked me, and I kept my mouth shut through the entire process. Fingerprints, mugshots, and the taking of my possessions—which was just my cell phone.

Kody Holt was dead.

I wish I could say I was surprised. I had expected as much. But *murdered*? That was the twist I hadn't seen coming. I was worried, sure. However, this wasn't my first time being arrested for murder. They had nothing to tie me to the murder besides speculation. I would be out of jail in no time once they heard my story.

They never put me in a jail cell, another good sign. Doing so would mean they had something concrete tying me to the murder. Instead, I was back in the interrogation room, hands cuffed behind my back as I sat in the same chair as last week. I was most likely detained, and my answers to their questions would determine if I spent the night in jail or got to go home.

With murder now in the picture, these guys were done playing nice. They left me in the interrogation room for over an hour. Might have been closer to two. They were likely trying to piece together their story for why I was in the interrogation room. Or were trying to make me sweat it out. Make me exhausted. It was almost one o'clock in the morning.

My thoughts tried racing, but I kept them at bay, along with my heart rate. I knew I hadn't killed Kody—quite the opposite, in fact. But god knows what his mother had told the police about my presence at their house.

All I had were the facts about how that ring ended up at my house—which I didn't actually know. It was time to come clean about my involvement with asking around about the suicides. The police wouldn't like it, but I didn't believe anything I had done violated any laws. Maybe this had to be the end of my time in Redwood. No more prodding around. Leave town and be left alone.

These assholes didn't even give me any water. It had been a long day with little water, and my kidneys were tight with protest.

It was almost two o'clock when both officers entered the room with another man. He wore a raggedy suit, his gray hair disheveled, bags under his eyes.

"Good morning, Mr. Mendez," the man said, sitting at the table across from me. He had a file that he opened and spread across the table. Dozens of sheets of writing that I couldn't make out from my angle. "I'm Detective James Parker, and I'm leading the investigation into the murder of Kody Holt."

"Wish we were meeting under different circumstances," I said, but offered a polite nod.

The detective's eyes fluttered as he studied me. "I'm familiar with your background, Mr. Mendez."

The two officers filed out of the room and were presumably watching from the other side of the two-way mirror.

"So you'll know I'm not a murderer," I said.

Detective Parker raised a hand. He had thick fingers, the golden wedding ring appearing too tight as his flesh puffed around its edges. "Just because you've served your country with great honor doesn't get you off the hook. There have been plenty of ex-military who become abusers, and sometimes worse."

"Of course," I said. "But that's not me. I'd love to hear exactly what evidence you have connecting me to Kody's murder."

The detective sighed. "First off, Mr. Mendez, I'm not the one who brought you in here. I'm still getting caught up on everything—that's what's been going on outside this room for the past two hours. I want to get into formal questioning, and it appears you haven't even been read your Miranda rights."

He shuffled through his files with one hand, the other rubbing his forehead. Good to know I wasn't the only one fed up with the Redwood police department's bullshit. He read my rights, and I declined a defense attorney at this point.

"Let's start with the ring," he said, sitting back and crossing his arms. "Why was it in your house?"

"Wish I knew. I arrived home from the library and my next-door neighbor brought me a package he saw left on my doorstep while I was out. The box had no postage or markings. Inside was the ring."

"And did you know what the ring was?"

I nodded. "State championship ring from 1999."

"So you'd seen one before. Why?"

"I met Kody Holt at his home yesterday—well, two days ago now. We chatted about his glory days in high school, and he had his mother grab his ring to show me. I found it odd he wanted to show me, a stranger, the first time we met."

The detective's eyebrows shot up. "So you met his mother?"

"Not formally. She didn't seem too pleased to have me at their house. She handed Kody the ring, called me a wetback, then returned inside. Didn't see her the rest of that visit."

"And why were you there?" he asked. "Seems like an odd encounter."

"I've been looking into the suicides plaguing Redwood. Something is off about them. So I've been going around to all the players from that championship team—the ones still in town—and asking general questions."

"And you found something?"

I liked the way this detective talked. Straight to the point. No bullshit. I even got the sense he could read me. No easy feat.

"Nothing concrete," I replied. "Lots of those players are now suffering from CTE. Apparently, that coach inflicted a lot of damage to their brains through brutal practice drills. Do that every day for an extended period, and your brain develops a disease. These poor men never had a chance."

"Interesting," the detective said, frowning at his notes. "When did you last see Kody Holt?"

"That was my only encounter with him," I said. "Ended on bad terms. I asked him about a sexual assault matter he was reported to be involved in during that championship run. He got pissed off and asked me not-so-kindly to leave."

"And why did you return to his house earlier today?"

"Because of the ring. I've been getting messages left under my front door while I'm out. Threats for me to stop snooping around the suicides. Naturally, that only confirms something bigger *is* at play, and these men didn't take their lives as some coincidence."

"What kind of threats?"

"Nothing concrete. Things like 'stop, or else.' Can't say any of it bothered me. But when I saw the ring, I knew it was a taunt. Someone's been watching me and knows who I've been visiting. No other explanation for that ring to end up on my doorstep. And now Kody is murdered, so I'm calling it a frame job. How was he killed anyway?"

The detective pointed at me. "I'm asking the questions. So you went back to Kody's house. What happened?"

"I really just wanted to see if he was okay. I assumed it was his ring because he had shown it to me the day before. Sure enough, he wasn't there. I had to speak with his lovely mother—she's just the sweetest thing—and she told me he went out the night before with word he'd be back the following evening. She didn't like when I suggested he might be in danger, so she called his cell phone and got no answer. I found her mostly useless to my cause of trying to find him, so I left."

Detective Parker leaned forward, pulled out a sheet of blank paper from his files, and pushed it across the table. "I need you to write your name. Print and cursive."

I stared at it and shrugged. "You know I'm handcuffed, right?"

He bit his bottom lip as he rose from his seat and circled the table to take the handcuffs off my wrists. I wished they had used zip ties instead. Those usually had more give and didn't cut off the circulation to my fingers.

I wiggled my fingers to bring them back to life. Detective Parker returned to his seat across the table, pushing across a black pen. I did as instructed and moved the paper back.

The detective nodded, snatched the paper, and stood up. After collecting his files, he started for the door and said, "Hang tight, Mr. Mendez."

And he vanished, leaving me alone in the interrogation room for another hour without water. At least I wasn't handcuffed any more. I gazed at the two-way mirror, wondering if my cop friends were still there. Hopefully, they heard how ridiculous their reasoning was for not just arresting me, but going through the trouble of securing that warrant to search my house. All because of the jaded story from Kody's racist mother.

I pushed that shit out of my thoughts. The most important thing from this fucked up night was confirming I was right. I found it impossible Kody's murder was random. How could it be after someone went through the trouble of stealing his ring and delivering to my house? Find who stole that ring and we had our killer. But it would not be that simple.

I wondered if Kody had plans to discuss matters further with me. Spill some relevant details about all these suicides that might unravel what was happening behind the curtain. I wasn't quite ready to call the suicides staged, but it was obvious there was some sort of mastermind behind their orchestration. If someone was in enough of a manic state, they could have been pushed into suicide by someone convincing enough.

When I got out of here, I needed to narrow my focus even further on those families of the deceased. I wasn't sure talking to other players from the team would bring me any closer to finding the truth. Most of them had CTE, which made them vulnerable to all sorts of mind games. But who? And why?

When Detective Parker finally returned to the interrogation room, my brain itched with fatigue. I had so much to do, but would need at least four hours of sleep.

"You're cleared, Mr. Mendez," he said, no files in his grasp. "We spoke with your neighbor, and he confirmed the package being left on your doorstep. Also clarified Ms. Holt's story about your two visits to her house. We were under the impression you had entered the house at some point, but now understand that is false. Since this is an active murder investigation, we must ask you to leave Ms. Holt alone. We'll be checking the ring for fingerprints and will return it to her once that's complete."

"You've kept me here as an innocent man, detective. The least you can do is tell me what happened to Kody Holt."

Detective Parker sighed and nodded. "That's another reason you're cleared, Mendez. Your writing sample doesn't match the suicide note we found with Mr. Holt."

"Suicide note? You said he was murdered."

"The note isn't a match to his handwriting. Not even close. Nor does it match yours."

"Someone faked a suicide note?"

"It appears so," the detective said. "And that's the only mistake they left behind. Otherwise, we'd never have guessed it *wasn't* a suicide. Mr. Holt was found in his truck with his wrists slit. The note was resting on the passenger seat."

The image made my stomach turn. A staged suicide. This was it.

"Where did you find his truck?" I asked, wondering where I had missed during my parade across Redwood.

The detective pressed his lips tightly together, likely debating if he should keep telling me this information. He finally did.

"We found him in the parking lot at Redwood High School."

Chapter 24

They called an Uber to take me home.

Apparently, when the police make a wrongful arrest and fuck up your night by falsely accusing you of murder, they don't have the stones to face the music and take an innocent man home.

I wouldn't have done, or even said, anything to them during the short drive to my house. Awkward silence was my favorite music, and I enjoyed watching those less comfortable with it squirm around.

The fuckers.

I saw several officers during my walk out of the station. They all avoided eye contact, especially Roman. Two failed attempts now for him. He just might have to accept I'm not a dangerous man.

When I returned home, the box remained open on the kitchen counter. I threw it down and stomped until it was completely flattened. After I threw it in the trash bin, my head spun to the point of needing to grab hold of the counter to not fall over.

Fuck me, I couldn't remember the last time I'd been this exhausted.

It was approaching four o'clock in the morning. I'd been awake for twenty hours straight.

So much to do, but I needed rest. I crashed into my bed, not bothering to take off my clothes, and didn't move an inch for the next seven hours.

I woke at eleven; the sun pouring into my bedroom, as I hadn't closed the curtains. I still couldn't believe I had spent most of the night at the police station. This had become trend I hated. Why did crimes always get blamed on me?

I took a quick shower and dressed for the day, my usual jeans with a solid t-shirt. On the rarest of occasions, I'd use product in my hair to give me an extra dazzle. Today was that day.

My stomach grumbled, so I toasted a bagel, spread cream cheese, and slammed it within a minute. Time was of the essence.

I knew the police department wanted me to stay put, maybe go to work and come home in the evenings like a normal person. But we were beyond that point. I wouldn't go near Kody Holt's home. Hell, I wasn't even going to visit any of the families of the deceased.

Not yet.

Things needed to cool off first. I still hadn't heard from Officer Santos. He had been off the clock since I got arrested last night, and I'm sure had already been caught up on the details by now. If I wanted to keep my only insider within the department, we'd have to go our separate ways for the time being. He'd be there when I needed him.

Rested, fed, and cleaned, I chugged a glass of water before heading out.

Herb and Rochelle were both out front, tending to their garden.

"Good morning, Jonny!" Rochelle called over.

I reached my car door and stopped to wave. "Good morning. Busy day ahead."

"Of course," she replied, her husband joining her side.

"We can always use the help in the garden," Herb said, cracking a grin. "We can pay in lemonade and freshly baked cookies."

Rochelle threw an elbow into Herb's side, earning a hearty cackle from her husband.

"You don't need to do any such thing," Rochelle said, waving at me to get in my car. "Enjoy your day, Jonny!"

Herb pulled his wife in for a squeeze and they returned to their garden.

I wondered if they had seen anything last night, but apparently not. The patrol car had arrived without the lights on. No sirens. The last thing I needed was my neighbors thinking I had any association with murder.

As long as I had people on my side—the Walkers, Officer Santos, and Carissa?—then I'd eventually uncover the truth behind these suicides.

I hopped in my car and drove across town, tuning into the local news radio station in search of updates about Kody Holt's murder. All they mentioned was a murder had occurred last night, and they currently had no suspects. Somewhere in Redwood, Officer Roman was screaming at the skies above.

The thought made me smile.

I pulled into the parking lot for the Redwood office of the National Suicide and Crisis Hotline. A couple days had passed, granted over the weekend, since I applied to be a volunteer. Maybe they were more accepting of those who took initiative.

The lot had a scattering of cars and I figured the lunch break had started for those who worked the more traditional shifts. I checked my face one last time in the rear-view mirror before stepping out and marching up to the office building.

It had automatic, sliding doors that parted as I approached, a gust of cool air escaping from inside. I entered the lobby, finding it much more zen than the usual government offices I'd been in. Plants stood in every corner of the lobby. A diffuser puffed some sort of scented steam into the air. And the sounds of a flowing river played softly through the speakers in the ceiling.

A lone desk stood against the back wall, occupied by a skinny woman with her gray hair pulled back into a ponytail.

"Good morning, sir," she said, looking up from her computer screen. "Can I help you?"

"Good morning," I replied. "I was hoping to speak with someone about an application I sent in last week. To volunteer. I didn't see a phone number or email address to reach out to, and was in the area. Figure I'd swing by."

Her eyes perked up, and she promptly returned her attention to her computer. "Let me see which supervisor is here right now. Can't make any promises they'll meet with you, but I'll ask."

"Thank you," I said, shuffling toward the desk.

The woman slipped on a headset and clicked around frantically on her computer.

"Ron?" she said into the headset. "I've got a man here regarding an application, hoping to speak with someone."

She nodded three times before saying, "Okay." Then took off the headset.

"Ron will be with you in just a moment if you'd like to take a seat."

Chairs lined the walls, and I grabbed one facing the only other visible door, where I presumed the call center was.

Five minutes passed, a couple of people going in and out of the door. Finally, a man dressed in khakis and a red polo shirt stepped out, looking around until his eyes fell on me.

He had wavy brown hair, glasses, and a thick mustache. "Hello, sir," he said in a deep baritone. "You submitted a volunteer application?"

I stood up and extended my hand, the man's eyes moving higher and higher, as if he couldn't believe how tall I was. "Nice to meet you. I'm Jonny Mendez."

"Ah, yes," the man replied, shaking my hand. "Mr. Mendez. My name is Ron Hartman. I saw your application, but admit I haven't reviewed anything yet. Please, come with me."

He turned around and started for the door he had just stepped out of.

My senses immediately kicked into high gear. I wasn't expecting to go into the belly of these offices so soon.

"Can I get you a bottle of water?" Ron asked as we passed through the door and it whooshed shut behind us.

"That would be great," I said, and Ron started down a long hallway that opened to the bullpen. At least twenty cubicles were set up across the floor, each with towering dividers to give each desk solitude and peace. This wasn't like calling into some company's customer service department where you hear all the other chatter in the background as you struggled to cancel your internet service.

These calls were intimate and needed to provide the sense of complete privacy for those calling in.

Ron took a sharp right through an open doorway into a break room and kitchen. He opened the lone refrigerator and pulled out a bottle of water, handing it to me as we returned to the hallway.

"Let's have a word in my office, Mr. Mendez," Ron said, leading me past the bullpen.

Half of the desks in the bullpen were vacant, and of the other ten people sitting around, only one was on a phone call.

We filed into his office, a crooked sign hanging on the door that read SUPERVISOR.

The office had three different desks, each positioned against a different wall and with their own sets of computers and family pictures on display.

Ron took the desk to our immediate right and rolled over another chair for me to sit.

"So you want to volunteer," Ron said, sitting down in his creaky chair and jiggling his mouse to bring his computer back to life. "Have you volunteered before?"

Ron's desk was a shitshow. Mountains of paperwork in many colors. Magazines, newspapers, mail—both important and junk—spread all about. His arms even rested on a stack of papers while he typed on his keyboard.

"I have not," I said, shifting in my seat.

"What gave you the itch?" Ron asked, pulling up my application on his screen, then leaning back in his seat and clasping his hands over his belly.

"All the suicides happening around town have opened my eyes," I said. "I'd never really given thought to mental health struggles—at least not to this extreme. Happy to help any way I can."

Ron nodded, pleased with my response. "Well, Mr. Mendez, you have an impressive background. If I had read this before you came in, I probably would've thought it was fake. Not every day we get a former SEAL or CIA agent. And here you are, both wrapped up into one."

I smiled, knowing I needed to show my soft side if I wanted this job. "I've always been driven by service. Making the world a better place. It's been a struggle to do that as a citizen, but volunteering here seems like a perfect opportunity."

Ron narrowed his eyes on me, searching my soul for something. "How's *your* mental health, Mr. Mendez?"

"I like to think it's solid. I've had my struggles in the past, seen plenty of things I wished I hadn't, but I take care of myself."

"What outlets do you have?" Ron asked. His voice shifted to complete seriousness. We were now in a full-on interview.

"Reading," I said. "And shooting."

"I see. This is heavy work, Mr. Mendez, especially for someone doing it for free. Your days will be spent talking to people giving serious consideration to ending their lives. And if it's not that, it could be a woman just beaten by her husband or boyfriend. Maybe a gay teenager getting bullied at school *and* at home. The biggest misconception about our work is that we only handle suicide calls. But that couldn't be any further from the truth."

"How does the call distribution work?" I asked. "Is it random? Or are there specialists within the call center based on the type of caller?"

"We absolutely have specialists," Ron said, scratching his head. "We have reps who work best with abuse victims, teens, women, you name it. If we hire you on, we'd probably ask you to specialize in military calls. It's always an added benefit to the caller if they're speaking to someone who's had similar experiences."

"Makes sense."

Ron raised a finger. "However, there are times when it's busy and everyone is on a call. You may not have the chance to transfer the caller to someone specific, and you have to handle it yourself. Times like these can take a toll on everyone in this building. We do our best to staff based on historical trends—higher calls in the spring and summer, weekends—but it's not always enough. You *will* have a call where you have to talk a sixteen-year-old girl through a tough time. Maybe she was just abused by a relative. Or raped. And our teenage specialists will all be on calls, so it falls to you. How would you handle a call like that, Mr. Mendez?"

"If a young lady was raped, do we not inform the police?" I asked.

Ron shook his head. "Unless she asks that, we cannot. The only time we get the police involved is if we believe someone is truly a danger to themselves or society. Happens less than one percent of all calls. Back to my question, then. Young lady calls in, she's just been raped. Feels awful. Guilty. She's considering taking her life because of it, but hasn't committed to the idea. What do you tell her?"

I closed my eyes, needing to give this serious thought. This wasn't some corporate interview where you could blurt out whatever the hiring managers wanted to hear. I didn't have to reach deep into my thoughts. During a deployment in Afghanistan, we bombed an entire village that housed ten members of one of the most dangerous terrorist groups in the region. We had calculated eighteen people living in the village and planned the attacks during a time when the three children were away.

After the bombings, a few of us hung around to ensure no other terrorists arrived later. None did. Instead, a twelve-year-old girl returned home after school to find her home destroyed. Her family dead. With an eerily calm calculation, she sifted through the damage and dug out a hand grenade.

In a thick accent, she faced our direction where we were perched a quarter-mile away and started shouting. I'd never forget how far her youthful voice traveled in the deathly silence of that demolished village, but we heard her plain as day.

"You forgot me!" she had shouted, waving the grenade. "You killed my family. Just kill me!"

I was surprised how well her English sounded, but later learned most kids in Afghanistan take English classes as a second language.

Even the girls, who were forbidden from attending school after the sixth grade.

She marched down the dirt road toward us, and we all drew our rifles. The initial debate among our squad was when to shoot the girl. There had been instances where these kids tossed the grenades in our direction, having been taught from a young age how to use them.

But I looked at her through my scope. Tears ran down her face. She walked with her eyes closed. The girl didn't want to die—she had been brainwashed into believing that was her only option if she ever returned home to find her terrorist father slaughtered.

I told my squad to lower their rifles and started on the road to meet the girl, much to their disapproval.

The girl never threw the grenade at me, and I thought of our brief conversation as I mulled this question from Ron.

"I would tell her that today is as bad as it will ever be. That what happened today will not define her life. The coming days will have their difficulties, but that's no excuse to not push through and see how beautiful life can be on the other end."

A small grin touched Ron's lips. "That's not a bad start at all."

When I had spoken these same words to that young girl, I was also speaking to my younger self. To us soldiers, we had done our job of removing terrorists from existence. We made the world a safer place. But for that girl, she had lost her family.

"I may have nothing in common with a teenage girl," I said, focused on Ron's curious gaze. "But I can always relate to trauma."

Ron stood up from his seat. "Well, Mr. Mendez, I guess that leaves me with one more question. When can you start?"

Chapter 25

I was in, but not to the extent I had hoped.

The call center hired in classes, and the next class wasn't scheduled to start for another three weeks. And from there, the complete training lasted four to six weeks, depending if the rep was deemed ready to hit the phones.

None of this worked for me, but I couldn't tell Ron. No point in burning a bridge before I got to cross it. I took the volunteer opportunity as a ticket into the building at a future date.

For now, I returned to my car and called Carissa. A few days had passed since we last saw each other at my house, and I didn't expect her to answer.

But she did.

"How are things?" I asked.

"I'm making it through the days well enough," she said, her voice tired. Distant. "Are you still being followed?" Her question sounded mocking, like I had made the whole thing up.

"Actually yes," I said. "They arrested me for Kody Holt's murder, so that was a fun few hours in jail."

"You *what*?!" Now she was back to life.

I chuckled. "Don't worry. It wasn't really me. Total frame job. Our friend with the love notes upped their game and left a package with Kody's championship ring on my doorstep. Combine that with Kody's mother thinking the world of me, and it all came crashing down. They had no actual evidence, of course, considering I've never stepped foot in Redwood High School."

"Jesus, Jonny. Are you okay?"

"Totally fine. Nothing I haven't handled before."

"I thought of you the second I heard about Kody," she said. Her disgust toward me seemed to have evaporated. "Picked up my phone to call you several times, but decided against it. In the off chance you were right about being watched. I've been incredibly paranoid since I left your house that night."

"You have nothing to worry about," I said. "Whoever is watching, their entire focus is on me. It's only going to get worse now, too, now that they've murdered Kody."

"You think it's the same person? How can you be so sure?"

"Well, I wouldn't say I'm a hundred percent sure, but framing me for a murder paints an obvious picture, don't you think?"

"You have a point," she said, chuckling. "So what made you call me today?"

"Well, I've been digging deeper and was wondering if you've received your brother's cell phone back yet?"

"I actually got it a couple of days ago," she said. "Why?"

"And you could get in?"

"Took me a few guesses on his password," she said. "But yes, I got it."

Every part of me wanted to drive to her house right now and look through the phone. But I couldn't. Not with eyes on me. The heat had been cranked up and bringing Carissa back into the loop would only prove disastrous.

"I need to know if he ever contacted the suicide hotline," I said. "If you wouldn't mind going through his past calls and texts. The phone number is 9-8-8. There could be outbound calls to that number, or text messages to it. If you can let me know the timestamps of each call he made to that number. Or, if he was texting with them, you can send me pictures of the conversation."

"What's this all about?" she asked.

"I'm not entirely sure yet. Several players from the team have been using the hotline. It may be nothing, but I'm curious to see how recently they called the hotline before taking their lives—if at all."

"Let me see," Carissa said, and I heard the whoosh of movement through the phone. "I can look real quick. I went through his text messages already and didn't see anything out of the ordinary. Also checked his emails—was really hoping to find any communication with Doctor Sowerby. Nothing."

"And you haven't reached out to the doctor?" I asked.

"I've called and emailed," she said, letting out a frustrated sigh. "No responses, and I've followed up multiple times. It's like Doctor Sowerby is ignoring me. One of his assistants confirmed my brother hadn't checked the right boxes for their office to share any information about his health history. It's a dead end. And HIPAA doesn't expire until fifty years after a person's death... unless it can be proven their death resulted from foul play, which suicide is not."

"I see."

"Okay, his phone is on," she said, and her voice lowered, followed by distorted sobbing.

"Carissa?" I said. "Is everything okay?"

"Sorry," she said. "His phone background is a picture of him and I as kids. Hard to look at still. Okay, let me pull up his call history."

I waited as the line went silent for the next thirty seconds.

"Jonny," Carissa finally said, and I heard plenty of worry in her voice. "There are *tons* of calls to that 988 number. He called them almost every day for the last couple weeks of his life, including the day before."

My gut twisted into knots. Daily calls? He couldn't have been toying with suicidal thoughts every day—Carissa would've caught on, considering they also spoke on a near daily basis.

"Okay," I said. "Text me a list of all the calls he made. Dates and times. I want to see if there was a pattern. Is there anything else you're noticing from his call log?"

"Yes, actually," she said. "Lots of inbound calls from a restricted number during his final days. Looks like the last week or so."

"How many?"

"Let me count," she said, and I waited once more. "Fifteen calls from the restricted number. Five were from the night before he died."

I hadn't even started my car yet, and kept staring at the office building in my rearview. "Send me those calls, and I'll see what I can find."

"Okay," Carissa said, sounding focused. "Check for a text message in about five minutes. And please let me know what you find."

"Of course," I said. "And Carissa."

"Yes?"

"Thank you. For believing me. For trusting me. I miss spending time with you."

I could hear the smile in her voice as she responded. "I miss you too, Jonny."

She hung up, and I threw my head back against my seat. I looked at the office building, it's many answers just waiting inside to be discovered. After a few minutes of devising a plan, and receiving the text message with a breakdown of Timmy's calls to the hotline, I stepped out of my car and faced the building. It became obvious what I had to do next, so I started marching to the entrance.

I had to go back in.

Chapter 26

The woman working the reception desk was named Patricia Henault. I knew this because I had to approach her desk once more, this time paying more attention to the smaller details surrounding her rather than the entire lobby.

"Did you forget something, Mr. Mendez?" she asked.

Her name plate sat on the ledge of her desk, and I traced the letters of her name with my finger. "Nothing in particular, but I was hoping for another quick word with Ron. Just thought of a question as I was pulling away."

"Oh, certainly. Let me call him."

I waited again for this routine, and was pleased at how much quicker it went the second time.

"He'll be right out," she said, shooting me a friendly grin.

I didn't even make it to a seat before the door flew open and Ron strolled out.

"Hey, Jonny," he said. "Back so soon? What can I do for you?"

I cleared my throat. "I'll be honest, Ron. When I got back to my car, I started having second thoughts."

Ron frowned at my suggestion, but gestured for me to keep talking.

"What you said about these calls taking a toll on the reps. I'm not sure I'm ready for that. Was hoping you might allow me to shadow some calls before I decide."

"Oh, Mr. Mendez, I'm afraid you can't begin listening to calls until you've started training. Lots of privacy violations if we were to let you sit next to one of our reps before you've even officially started. I don't always encourage this, but check out YouTube. There are lots of volunteers who post videos about what their typical day looks like. Now, it won't give you a concrete example of a live phone call, but you'll get the gist."

"Is there no one here that can chat with me about that?" I asked. "I'm sorry to bother, but I don't want to waste your time if this ends up not being a good fit for me."

Ron nodded. "I understand and appreciate that. Let me see if anyone is available. Be right back."

I waited near the door for five minutes. Patricia had lost all interest in speaking with me, tending to her computer instead. I didn't blame her. The workday was almost over—at least, I assumed it was for her. Almost four o'clock.

Ron opened the door and stepped back out with a young Asian woman trailing behind him.

"Mr. Mendez," Ron said. "This is Avery. She's been working here as a full-time employee for six months now and has a solid understanding of how everything works in our corner of the world. She's agreed to take you through the call center and show you around the office. Granted, that won't include listening to calls. But ask her any questions you have. I'd do it myself, but I have to get on a call."

Avery stuck out her hand, and we shook. She had a wide smile. "Nice to meet you, Mr. Mendez."

"The pleasure's all mine," I replied.

"I'll leave you to it," Ron said, nodding before spinning around and disappearing back into the office, holding the door open for me and Avery.

"Shall we?" she said, leading us back into the call center.

I followed her through the bullpen and into the kitchen where Ron had stopped earlier. The tables were tall, requiring barstools for sitting. We each pulled one out and sat facing each other.

"So," Avery said, drumming the table with long fingernails. "What kind of questions did you have?"

"Well, Avery, I really want to make sure I'm not getting in over my head. Are the calls as bad as I'm making them in my head?"

Avery shook her head, black hair whipping back and forth. "For the most part, no. I'd say ninety percent of the calls are people looking for guidance through a tough time. That's not to discount their issues, but most can be handled by offering an ear for them to vent. We deal with tons of lonely callers, so it's best to keep that in mind. They just want someone to talk to."

I nodded. "And the other ten percent of calls?"

"I won't sugarcoat it. Those other calls will be difficult. It's not always talking someone off the ledge, but it's close. I'd say I have at least two calls a day where I need to go for a walk afterward. They weigh you down. We're trained to first talk people out of hurting themselves, and second, to seek professional help. We're not trained therapists, which some callers believe. They think this is a free way to get therapy. But you'll see our training is actually focused on immediate crisis relief. Sure, there is psychology that goes into it, but what we learn isn't to perform long-term therapy."

I rubbed my forehead. "What if someone were to call in everyday? It may not be formal therapy, but if they speak with you daily, is that not therapy? And are there any procedures in place if you believe someone is abusing the hotline?"

Avery studied me. I must have asked questions out of her comfort zone. These certainly weren't typical questions for a new hire, and I needed to use more caution with how I phrased things. Didn't want to seem too suspicious.

She finally answered. "We *do* have people call in multiple times. Those callers are usually working through a bigger issue. Maybe a series of bullying or abuse. Again, even us walking these folks through hard times is far from therapy. I'd compare us more to guidance counselors than actual therapists. As for people abusing the hotline, we don't really get that outside of occasional prank callers. We just hang up on those."

"And do you ever have a reason to make an outbound call?" I asked, hoping with each question I wasn't crossing any boundaries.

"Oh, definitely," Avery said, lighting up at the question. "Those calls are actually my favorite to make. It's a personal choice, not part of our formal procedures, to ask if the caller would like a followup call. That can be the next day, next week, whatever they request. Most accept the offer."

"Why are they your favorite calls?"

"Because we are proactively reaching out to someone dealing with life issues. They are always so appreciative when we make those calls, like it was the best part of their day. Remember, some of these people are simply dealing with loneliness. Something as simple as receiving a call in the middle of the day to check on them makes an enormous difference for their mental wellbeing."

"And that fits into your schedule?" I asked.

"Mostly. We try to schedule these outbound calls during our typical slower times, like the middle of weekdays. We don't give the outbound calls a priority if we're busy with incoming calls. In a typical shift, I can usually expect a thirty-minute block of no incoming calls, and that's when I'll make my outbounds."

"I see. I'm curious about scheduling. Ron told me there are lots of volunteers, and that I'm applying for a set shift time, but what does that look like further down the road? If someone's a volunteer, does that mean they can just not show up and face no consequences?"

Avery shook her head. "There are consequences, and you can absolutely be 'fired' as a volunteer. That's rarely an issue, though. People who volunteer for work like this typically have a firm commitment to the cause. They only volunteer because they genuinely want to help those in crisis. It can get hectic, as a full-time employee. Many faces cycle through here daily. Most volunteers work sporadically—random days of the week, shifts several weeks apart. One of Ron's initiatives with this position is to find more consistency with a volunteer position. He's testing it out to see how it goes. If you end up getting this job, just be aware of that."

"Can a volunteer come as often as they want?" I asked. "They're not getting paid, so it's not like they're owed overtime."

Avery nodded. "Absolutely. Some of the more senior volunteers have a really light schedule—like one or two shifts per month—but they come in much more than that. It gives them flexibility. But you can only reach that type of status if you've been a volunteer with strong performance and two years of service."

If people could come as they pleased, there was no saying if any of the football players always called in and had the same rep. Unlikely, in fact.

"I believe I have one last question," I said, leaning forward in my seat. "How are calls logged? Is there a database with each rep's call history? And are any of the calls monitored or recorded?"

"We log all our calls in our internal system," Avery replied. "But it's nothing too formal. Callers don't need to provide us any information and can remain completely anonymous. As reps, we don't even see the names or phone numbers of the inbound calls. If the caller provides us with any information, we add that to the notes when logging the call. Privacy is the most important thing for the hotline, so we can't even access our notes or prior calls. When we make notes to call someone back for a check in, that's all based on physical notes we take in our notebooks. The call center is fine with that practice, as long as the notebook stays within the building."

"So, do any calls get monitored?" I asked.

"Yes, they do. Managers have access to download old calls. I'm not sure what all information they have access to see, but they'll spot check calls to make sure everyone is carrying out good practices."

I wanted to ask how long managers had access to calls for, the wheels already turning in my mind. But that was too specific of a question.

"Okay," I said, looking around the kitchen. I hadn't studied the space this entire time, now noticing the fully stocked snacks and see-through fridge. Sodas, flavored waters, and a carousel of various cereals made this my kind of place.

"Do you have any more questions, Mr. Mendez?" Avery asked, folding her hands on the table and giving me a warm smile.

"I can't say I do. You've been an incredible help."

"Glad I could clarify some things for you," she said. "I'll say, your questions seemed specific, like you've done this line of work before."

"I've worked in call centers before," I lied. "So I have plenty of experience there. I've just never done anything like this specifically."

Avery stood up, and I followed suit. "Well, I can say it's been the most rewarding work of my life. No one does it for the money. But if we each give a bit of time to a cause bigger than us, we help make the world a better place."

My eyes scanned the kitchen for a public schedule, or even names on lunchboxes in the fridge. But I found nothing of relevance. If I could just get a list of names of people who worked here, I might get to cross reference them in the future. I'd eventually get back to questioning the football players, and knowing who they might have spoken to in the past could prove beneficial.

I thanked Avery for her time, and she guided me out to the main lobby. Patricia had indeed left for the day, the lights now dim as the call center entered its evening shifts.

"Hope I didn't keep you too long," I said to Avery.

She checked her watch. "Not at all, Mr. Mendez. I only have ten minutes left before I can clock out, so you brought me right to the end of my day."

We shook hands and went our separate ways.

I climbed into my car and wasted no time firing up the engine. I'd need to find the best time to let Ron know I wouldn't be taking the job. Three weeks was simply out of the question. How many more "suicides" would happen within that time frame?

Considering what happened to Kody, I now doubted the validity of each of the prior suicides. But it was currently impossible to prove them as anything else. I had seen with my own eyes as Jackson Green jumped off the hotel roof. No one had pushed him.

But could Jackson have been having an episode from his CTE? The disease I could only *assume* he had suffered based on the testimony of others from his team.

My head throbbed, a rarity. But this was all growing too messy to keep sorted out. I pulled out of the parking lot and drove home, unaware of the pair of eyes watching me from a distance.

Chapter 27

I lay in bed, consumed by a million thoughts flooding my mind for the rest of the night. Sometimes I got too much into the thick of a matter and could no longer tell up from down.

It was these instances when the most logical next step evaded me.

So I slept it off. If you count tossing and turning until midnight as sleep. I eventually dozed and woke up at eight o'clock the next morning with a renewed energy. While my two discussions at the call center seemed useless on the surface, they had provided me with a bedrock of knowledge that would eventually pay off.

First thing I needed to do today was call Officer Santos. I appreciated his need to keep away while I was arrested for murder, but he had access to information that would help move my investigation along.

I called, and he answered after one ring.

"I was wondering when I'd hear from you," he said.

"You can call me, too, you know," I replied. "Kind of hurts my feelings you didn't check on me after that arrest." Santos chuckled. His background was filled with silence. "Are you at home?"

"Yes," he said. "Don't start my shift until four today."

"Good, because we need to talk. First off, what's the word around the station about me?"

Santos sounded on the verge of laughter as he responded. "Roman is livid. That man absolutely hates you. He's been reprimanded for bringing you in so soon without any concrete evidence. The whole thing with the championship ring wasn't valid. No grounds for arrest. I think he saw the ring and jumped to the conclusion that best fit his narrative."

"What about Chambers?" I asked.

"He took a good shouting from the chief, but no official reprimand. Roman actually stood up for him and took the fall for asking Chambers to arrest you. He's off the hook, but tensions are high right now."

"The chief was upset? I'm surprised to hear that."

"As was I," Santos said. "This is completely my theory with no actual basis, but I think it may have been a show the chief put on. I'd guess he was just as upset about you getting let go so soon after being in custody. It makes more sense if he was pissed about *that* and channeled that anger toward Roman."

"You must have some reason for this theory," I pressed the young officer.

"The chief has been having lots of closed-door meetings with Roman. Now, that can all be part of this debacle, but I'm not sure what they'd need to discuss further about it."

"Is my name still being floated out there as a suspect?"

Santos laughed. "Your name is forbidden from being spoken right now inside that building. That was an order from the chief, which only adds to my suspicions about his involvement. I figure he wants to play matters close to the chest now. No more mistakes with you. Be careful out there. I don't doubt they're still watching you, just waiting for an actual, valid reason to arrest you."

"So I'm being watched by multiple parties? Great."

"It's possible. Unless it's the same person. We still don't know."

"What are the odds of you pulling phone records for a particular agency?" I asked.

"Agency? Who are we talking about?"

"The suicide and crisis hotline. Good chance all of our deceased made calls to the hotline before taking their lives."

"Oh, Jonny, I don't know," Santos said, the enthusiasm fleeing his voice. "It's already a tall task to get a warrant for an individual's call history. For a government agency that has so many privacy restrictions in place, the judge would need solid evidence a crime was committed to grant this warrant. I can try, but don't get your hopes up."

My phone chimed to alert me another call was coming through. This one from a restricted number.

My heart raced.

"Okay," I said. "You do that and let me know. I'll have to call you back later."

"Okay, Jonny, but—"

I ended the call with Santos, my curiosity growing as I answered the second call.

"Hello?"

"Jonny. Surprised you answered."

I breathed a sigh of relief, as I often did after hearing this voice.

"Kayla," I said. "You had to call from a restricted number?"

Kayla laughed. "I know how much stress that causes you. Think I forgot how quickly you'd Google an unknown number before deciding to answer or not? Restricted numbers may as well be your biggest weakness."

I laughed back. She was right. I found phone calls inconvenient, especially in the era of cell phones. Whoever thought it was a good idea to grant around-the-clock access to each other? Phone calls were the worst, as you had to drop whatever you were doing to answer them. Sometimes I missed life before cell phones. Back when people had to call your landline at home. And if you weren't there to pick up? Tough shit. Leave a message.

"Well, I'm glad I answered," I said. "How are you?"

"I'm fine, Jonny. I have some information you may find useful."

My senses heightened. I wasn't expecting anything substantial to come from my last call to Kayla. Just nostalgia and regret. I was happy to be proven wrong. "Oh? And what would that be?"

"Like I had said, I couldn't promise much. My contact at the Marshal's office is a tight ass, but they gave me the name. It's William Barnes."

"They changed Andrew Stone's name to William Barnes," I said to myself. "Poor guy. Doesn't sound anywhere as cool as Andrew Stone."

Kayla laughed. "I agree, but that's what they did. And that's all the information I could extract. They wouldn't give me the names of his parents or the location they moved to. So you're stuck with William Barnes."

I sighed. "I appreciate it, Kayla. Thank you. Afraid I've never heard that name mentioned in Redwood, but I'll see if I can find anything out."

"Not sure why you would," she said. "Why would anyone return to the site of a horrific crime they lived through? I suppose it's possible some people might visit. Get closure. But move back there and build a life. Unlikely."

She raised a fair point. Not that I expected Andrew Stone—sorry, William Barnes—to have returned to Redwood.

"I don't suppose you can do one more favor?" I asked, bracing myself for a sassy response. But none came.

"What do you need?" she asked.

"These men who have killed themselves were likely all calling into the suicide hotline. The 988 number. That's run through the government. Do you know who?"

"Department of Health and Human Services," Kayla replied with confidence.

"I'm curious about getting a copy of those phone records. For the Redwood office. I'm interested in how many times, and when, these men called in before ending their lives. Not sure how specific you can get, but if I can find out who specifically they had spoken with from that call center, I could track them down and question them."

Kayla blew out a long breath from her lips. "Jonny, that's a tall request. I don't have a trustworthy contact in that department for something like this. I might have better luck if you can get me the phone numbers belonging to the deceased. At least from there, I'm not violating any living person's privacy."

"I can get you one to start, and will work on the others."

"Great. That I can do. I am in the CIA after all, and have plenty of friends happy to assist with a side task. Pulling phone records doesn't even take much effort. So what's the number?"

"I don't have it, but I'll get it. Just a quick phone call away."

"Wow," Kayla said. "Jonny Mendez making a second phone call before lunch time? You really are a changed man."

I laughed, recognizing her sarcasm I always loved. "Actually, this will be my *third* call of the morning."

I heard Kayla slap her desk, and we both started laughing. We'd always worked so well together. It was a relief knowing we could jump right back into being ourselves. The thought tugged my heartstrings, but I wouldn't let it pull me all the way back to D.C.

"Alright, I'll be waiting for your call with that phone number. And Jonny, I looked. There are over three hundred people with the name of William Barnes living in Oregon alone. Please don't punch the first one you meet."

I grinned. "I promise. Call you back soon. Thanks again, Kayla."

We hung up. Dammit, I missed that woman. She was the only person who made me feel alive after my mother's death. Why did I have to run from her?

I immediately called Carissa to get Timmy's phone number. The call went straight to voicemail.

Strange.

I called again with the same response.

Fucking A. I just needed that phone number and I could finally make some serious progress on this investigation.

Third attempt yielded nothing different.

She could have been sleeping and turned her phone off. Lord knows I had done that plenty of times. I didn't think anything negative about our last phone call, but it was always possible she reconsidered and never wanted to speak to me again.

I hurried next door and asked if the Walkers could try calling her. The call also went directly to voicemail without ringing.

"Is everything okay?" Rochelle asked, dialing a second time to receive no response.

"I don't know," I said, rushing out of their house.

"Where are you going?" Herb called after me.

I was nearly in a full sprint, and could only look over my shoulder as I shouted back. "To her house!"

Maybe I was paranoid. I hadn't thought much about Carissa today until receiving that call from Kayla. Even still, Kayla was all I could think about.

That was shitty to kick Carissa to the back corner of my thoughts. I enjoyed the time we had spent together and hoped I'd get to again. But as I jumped into my car and sped out of the neighborhood, I realized maybe Kayla was the reason I could never get close to other women. At least, not in the sense of developing a serious, long-term relationship. Could my subconscious be holding me back? Saving that special spot for Kayla. *Only* Kayla.

I wasn't one to analyze my own deepest thoughts. Not that anyone could perform such a task on themselves. It's called a subconscious for a reason. Those thoughts you kicked under the bed like dirty laundry before company came over to visit. After a couple of days, you forget all about the laundry and move on with your life. Until months later, when you have to come to terms with your hastened actions all those days in the past.

It was the middle of the day, traffic non-existent. I may have run a couple of red lights and stop signs. Redwood's finest never caught me, so no harm done.

Perhaps allowing my mind to shift back to Carissa allowed the rest of my body to synchronize. I'd always had a strong sense of intuition for those in my life. My stomach felt hollowed out as I drove, now two minutes away from her house. Whoever was trying to stop my involvement in this vigilant investigation had become completely un-predictable after delivering that ring to my house in broad daylight.

It was a ballsy move, one I wasn't sure happened out of confidence, fear, or desperation. Ultimately, it didn't matter.

As I screeched to a halt in front of Carissa's house, my stomach sunk further. Her front door was wide open. That alone wasn't a reason to panic. Maybe she was on her way out or in. Her car was in the driveway, after all.

But still.

I hopped out and dashed up the pathway, stopping when I reached the front door. The doorframe stood in shattered ruins, splinters sticking out from the edges where the door had been kicked in. A dusty shoe print remained on the door's surface. It wasn't a fingerprint, but good police work could identify the size and make of the shoe. Then we'd at least have an idea about the size of person I should look for.

Seeing the shoe print immediately eliminated Chief Barker from my internal list of suspects. No way in hell the leading member of the police force would be stupid enough to not only break into someone's house, but to leave an obvious mark like the shoe print. Even if he was the ringleader of whatever the fuck this operation was, he'd never get his officers tied up in a scenario that left so much evidence behind. If the shoe print was here, there could be other clues inside.

"Carissa?" I called into the house.

No response. Fuck.

I spun around and hustled back to my car. When I first got it, I placed a gun under the driver's seat. I arrived in Redwood with two firearms. A Glock 48 and a Beretta APX. The Beretta stayed in the car while the Glock was my preferred weapon of choice for home, sitting snugly in the top drawer of my nightstand.

I grabbed the Beretta, confirmed all thirteen rounds were loaded, and returned to the front door.

"Carissa?" I called out once more, getting only my echo in response.

I looked around at the neighborhood behind me. Not a soul in sight, minus a couple of cars cruising by without a care in the world. The air felt still.

Carissa was either inside and unconscious. Or not here at all.

Either way, it was time to go in.

Chapter 28

The house looked no different compared to the last time I'd been inside. A faint scent of bacon lingered in the air. My kind of woman.

Aside from the bashed in door, I saw no signs of a struggle. The messy stack of papers remained on the kitchen table. A few dirty dishes piled in the sink. I didn't take Carissa as someone to roll over if someone broke into her house. She would fight.

I held the Beretta in front of me, cocked and ready to blast.

"Carissa!" I shouted, louder. "Give me a sign you're okay."

My voice bounced around the walls of the living room and kitchen. I drew a deep breath. I had no choice but to check the house room by room.

I started in the living room, checking first the coffee table for any clues. A cup of tea sat on a coaster, the bag still steeped. She liked to start her mornings with either coffee or tea. The cup was cold. How long could her front door have been hanging open on busted hinges before any of these useless neighbors noticed? If the cup had gone cold already, it could have been two hours. Or even an entire day.

The thought made me sick.

The house was too still. I didn't think anyone was inside, but I needed to make sure.

Right when I started down the hallway to Carissa's bedroom, my cell phone buzzed in my pocket.

"The fuck?"

I pulled out my phone and saw Carissa's number.

"Hello?" I answered, trying to not sound too panicked.

"Ah," said a man's voice. It was an awkward baritone, like he was forcing it to be deeper than it actually was. "Jonathan Mendez. We chat at last."

"Where's Carissa?"

"Don't worry about your little girlfriend, Jonny. She's alive and well. For now."

"Why are you doing this?" I demanded. Having taken lessons on bomb threats, I'd learned if dealing with someone making such a threat called, they were always equipped to answer the who, what, when, and where. But never the why.

This asshole on the other end of the line was better prepared, however. Or perhaps had a few screws loose.

After a brief pause, he responded, "Why not, Jonny? You fuck around with my world, so I fuck around with yours. It's only fair. Would you not agree?"

"I agree with the logic, but Carissa has nothing to do with this. Why not come for me?"

The man laughed, a tone lighter than his forced speech. "Oh, Jonny, I hear you! I never thought the letters would actually scare you off, but they were worth a shot. I thought for sure the ring would have landed you in jail for that dumb hick's murder. But I underestimated the competence of our police department. They are much stupider than I thought. Makes sense, I suppose, considering the chief is a raging narcissist. Why do people like that get put into power? Only looking out for themselves. And that attitude trickles down to everyone who works under them."

"Are you throwing your name in the hat, then?" I asked. "You've certainly got my vote."

The man chuckled. "I've heard you're a jokester."

"What we playing at here?" I asked. "And are you ever going to tell me who you are?"

"Well, that would take the fun out of my life. C'mon, Jonny. Don't you enjoy the chase? Not that you'll actually find me. I'm always one step ahead. Plus, you're still a newbie in this town. I've been here forever. I know every back alley, every hiding spot. You have no way of finding me."

"If you hurt Carissa, it will be the last thing you do. You have my word on that."

The man laughed. "I hear you, Jonny. All that tough talk from a tough guy. But you don't even know where to look. You might as well shout your silly threats to the sky. Maybe then, these good-for-nothing police will lock you up."

"Your involved with the suicides," I said. "How? And why are you so desperate for me to stop looking into them?"

"What are you suggesting, Jonathan? That I brainwashed people into killing themselves? Do you *really* think that's possible?"

"I didn't suggest that, so now I'm thinking that's exactly what happened."

The man giggled like a giddy teenage girl. "God, I wish. Would've made my life a whole lot easier. Let's not worry about the details, okay? All you have to do is leave town. Never come back. And I'll let your girlfriend go. It's that simple."

"Simple, huh? I'm just supposed to take the word of a coward who won't even tell me his name. Do you take me for a fool?"

"Please, Jonny. Who's the fool? Your slick talk won't get you anywhere with me. I have your woman. I'm in control. You answer to me. Are we clear? Just leave Redwood and I'll set her free. She hasn't seen my face, so I'm not worried about her reporting me. She's still blindfolded, in fact, and has no idea where she is."

"And if I don't leave?" I asked.

"I wouldn't advise that, Jonny. If you stay in Redwood, your girl stays with me. And you won't like the things I have planned for her. She smells so good. I wonder how she tastes."

"You're a sick fuck."

"Ah! That I am. Consider this your last warning, Jonny. I'm not interested in discussing the matter any further."

I shuffled to the front door. This asshole had to be watching me. How else would he have known to call shortly after I arrived? But I saw no one as I scanned the neighborhood once more.

"Do we have a deal?" the man asked, sounding like he was thoroughly enjoying himself.

"No deal," I said. "Put her on the phone. I need to hear she's okay."

"I hear you," he said. "Give me just a moment."

I heard footsteps walking along a hardwood floor. Ten seconds later, Carissa was speaking to me.

"Jonny!" she cried. "Please help. He keeps *touching* me."

"Where are you?" I demanded, hoping she might give away any clue.

"I don't know. I've been blindfolded the whole time. Please, Jonny. Just come help me!"

Carissa's fear radiated through the phone.

"Shut up, you dumb bitch!" the man said, and moments later, he was back on the phone. "So, do we have a deal?"

"How will either of us know if the other is holding up their end of the bargain?" I asked. "I still don't trust you to let her go. And how can you prove I actually left town?"

"It's a two and a half hour drive to the California border," the man said. "Go there, take a selfie with the sign welcoming you to California, send the picture to your girl's phone number, then keep on driving."

I drew in a deep breath. If I went along with this plan, I could be back in Redwood in a little over five hours. It wasn't even ten o'clock. I could be back by three, not that I'd announce my arrival.

"And if I do this," I said. "How will I know you've let her go?"

"She'll have her phone back, Jonny," the man said calmly. "I'll keep her blindfolded until I release her. Once she's free, I'll make sure she calls you to confirm she's safe."

"And if I don't get that call?"

The man laughed. "Not even I'm that stupid, Jonny. If you don't get that call, I know you'll turn right around and come back here. And that's *not* what I want. You'll get the call."

My mind raced. I stepped back into the house so he couldn't see me—I just assumed he was watching me somehow. Switching the call to speaker phone, I pulled up the maps app and typed in the destination for the California border. One hundred and fifty-three miles. With a full tank, I could get there and back without stopping. Aside from snapping the picture, of course.

"Do we have a deal, Jonny?"

My body tensed with rage. I had to force myself to loosen my grip on the cell phone before it exploded into plastic shards all over Carissa's living room.

"Deal," I said, and hung up.

Chapter 29

I drove like an absolute lunatic down Highway 97. Sixty miles per hour when passing by a town. Ninety when I found myself in the middle of nowhere. I may have touched three digits twice, but Camry's just weren't built to sustain such a high speed for long stretches.

When I passed the town of La Pine, I called Officer Santos.

"Mendez," he said, almost cheerily. "What trouble are you stirring up now?"

"Cut the shit," I said. "We have a serious problem."

He indeed cut the shit, and his voice shifted immediately. "What's wrong?"

"Carissa was kidnapped from her home. If you go over there, you'll see her door busted open."

"What?!"

"Calm down," I said. "She's okay. The kidnapper called me and let me speak with her. All he wanted was for me to leave town, so that's what I'm doing."

"Hold on. You're gone?"

"Just for a bit. He wants proof of me gone, so I'm driving to the California border to take a picture, and will turn right back around. Should get back to Redwood around three."

"Jesus, Mendez, do you know where she is?"

"I don't. And she didn't either. She was blindfolded from the moment they left her house. This guy says he knows Redwood inside and out and that I'll never find him."

"And this is the same guy?" Santos asked. I could hear the intrigue rising in his voice. Young cop with a shot to bring down a psychopath. An opportunity that could change the trajectory of his career.

"Yes. He admitted as much. Left the letters under my door. And Kody's ring. His goal was to frame me for the murder just so I could stop looking into the suicides. I was supposed to be locked up in jail, but obviously it didn't play out that way."

"Christ, Mendez, what are you planning to do when you get back?"

"I don't know yet. I have some time to figure that out. Assuming he follows through on his word, we need to keep Carissa safe. She can't stay at her house. Or mine."

"She can stay at my place," Santos said. "It's your typical messy bachelor pad, but it'll be safe."

"Good," I said. "I was thinking of asking the Walkers if she could stay there."

"Right next door to you? Seems risky, Mendez."

"Doesn't really matter as long as she stays inside," I said. "Which she'll have to, regardless of where she stays. This guy won't have any reason to think she's staying at the Walkers. Now that I think about, it makes more sense for her to stay there since he knows you've been involved."

Santos sighed. "Good point. What can I help with?"

"I need a list of all the volunteers who have worked at the suicide hotline during the last six months."

"Okay?" Santos replied. "You're still hung up on the hotline, I see."

"CTE is the only common denominator across the deceased, aside from being on that championship team."

Shit. I just realized I never sent Timmy's phone number to Kayla. Well, I hadn't gotten it.

"Actually, if you can get me the cell phone numbers for the four deceased men and text them to me. I may have something in the works with those."

"That I can do," Santos said. "Pretty straightforward. The list of volunteers, though, I'm not sure that's something they'll just hand over because I'm a cop."

"Just try, Santos. If not, I'll go in there and get it myself."

"Slow down, Mendez. I said I'll try."

"We're beyond needing effort right now," I said. "We just need results. I need that list of names and those phone numbers. I'm convinced there is a connection in there, and we just need to find it."

"And do you know anything about this guy who called you?"

"His shoe print is on Carissa's door," I said. "Why don't you examine it and see what you can find from that? Probably not much, but you never know. Ask neighbors if they saw or heard anything. I would have, but ran out of time when this jackass called me. Need to play his little game, then I'll be back in town to end him."

"Are you planning on returning to your house?" Santos asked. "It can't possibly be safe."

"I'm not worried about this guy," I said. "He's afraid to confront me face to face. That's why he's been hiding behind letters and half-assed frame jobs."

"But he's a murderer," Santos said. "Right? He would have killed Kody Holt as part of this scheme. No one else would have done it."

"That's true. But I'm still not worried. Why go through all that trouble if he could have just killed *me*? Kody wasn't exactly a threatening type of guy. Besides, whoever this is knew Kody on a personal level. At least, if what his mom said was true."

"Yes," Santos said, like a lightbulb had just gone on. "You're right. She said Kody told her he was going out with a friend. But she didn't know who. And that was the last time anyone heard from Kody Holt."

"I'm not intending to be mean," I said. "But I don't imagine Kody Holt had a big circle of friends. Maybe see what you can find out there?"

"You're throwing a lot at me, Mendez," Santos said. "I need to go to Carissa's house and file a report. We can get our entire force on this."

"Don't do that. We can handle this."

"Sorry, Mendez, it's not a question. You can't report a kidnapping to a police officer and expect me to do nothing. I'm heading out right now—guess it's an early start to my day."

"Officer Santos, please. If the police are hunting for this man, he'll act out. And we still don't know what we're dealing with. He could hurt Carissa. Or even other people in Redwood."

Santos sighed. "I'll buy you some time, okay? I'll head over to her house in about twenty minutes. Take my time looking around. Will even go door-to-door down her block to chat with the neighbors. Then I'll start filing my report, which will take some time. We're looking at two hours before word gets to the station about Carissa missing. From there, it's out of my hands. But you have to let us do our job, Mendez. I still take orders from the chief, not you."

I punched my steering wheel out of frustration. "Okay, fine. I'll take it."

Two negotiations that didn't go my way within the last hour. Not my best performance. But I'd make everything right when I returned to Redwood.

"Are you going to let me know when you get back in town?" Santos asked.

"No," I snapped back. "Now that you're getting the rest of the police involved, I'll be staying out of touch. I'm not returning to my house. I'll have Carissa call you to pick her up and take her to the Walkers. Make sure no one is following you."

"Mendez," Santos said, irritation slipping into his voice. "You can't take this guy on yourself. Like you said, we don't even know what we're dealing with."

I laughed. "I've taken on more dangerous men than this clown. By myself. You need to understand, it's not a matter of trusting the police to do their job. It's that I can do things better. I don't have to follow protocol or worry about reports. Definitely don't need warrants or permission from anyone. I will simply eliminate the threat as I know best."

Santos let out a long sigh. "And if you kill this man, before the police can get proof he kidnapped Carissa, then you're out there wanted for murder."

"It's never my intent to kill," I said. "I'll only do that if my life is in danger—which is called self defense, in case you're not aware. As for proving all that, I guess that's not up to me. If I have to kill this man, I'll be gone from Redwood before anyone realizes what happened. And unlike him, you'll actually never find me. So, kill all the time you need at Carissa's house. Follow your procedures. I'll be back this afternoon. And if I don't hear from you, I'll get that list of volunteers myself."

"Don't fuck anything up, Mendez," Santos said. "Or it'll be your ass. If anyone asks, I dropped you off at home that first day we met and never saw you again."

"That's a cute thought," I replied. "But our friend saw us together after that. Could've been at the bowling alley or my house—it doesn't matter. He saw us and he'll bring both of us down if it comes to it. Get me the list."

I hung up, done with this call, and kept speeding down the freeway.

My mind drifted in and out of a variety of thoughts, as it does when alone for a long period. I thought about Kayla. Carissa. Redwood. How did I end up tangled in this mess?

My mother had always encouraged me to mind my own business, but I found it impossible. Especially with my skills and body. No one in the world frightened me. And if I saw someone in duress, I had to help. More importantly, my mother raised me to be a light in the world—something continued by my aunt. Help those less fortunate. And that's what I did.

People were dying in Redwood. Innocent men. Family men. Nothing pained me more than to see families shattered by an unexpected death.

Ninety minutes later, I arrived at the California/Oregon border and pulled to the side of the road. There it stood, a rectangular, solid blue sign that read *WELCOME TO CALIFORNIA*. Three flowers decorated the right side of the sign. I didn't know shit about flowers, so couldn't tell you what kind they were. Below this sign was a smaller, green one that read *SISKIYOU COUNTY LINE*.

There wasn't shit around me. Some green hills in the distance if I kept driving into the Golden State. Tumbleweed blew across the highway. A couple of semi-trucks zoomed by. Feeling like a tourist out on a road trip, I pulled out my cell phone, walked up to the base of the sign, and took a selfie with the sign as a backdrop. I flipped up my middle finger on my free hand as I took the picture.

I rushed back to my car, sent the picture to Carissa's phone, made a U-turn, and crossed the border back into Oregon.

During the drive back, I could only think of the voice on the other end of the phone. That man. That piece of shit. I couldn't wait to slip my hands around his throat and squeeze until he begged for mercy.

As if reading my thoughts, the man responded from Carissa's phone fifteen minutes after I left the border.

Thank you. Enjoy California. Your girl will call you within the hour.

Forty-five minutes later, my phone rang.

"Carissa?" I answered.

"Jonny!" she cried. "Oh, thank God."

"Are you okay?" I asked, relief flooding my entire body.

"Yes. I'm fine, and I'm free. He dropped me four blocks from my house. Told me to get out of the car and not take off my blindfold until I counted to twenty or else he'd shoot."

"Did he harm you at all?" I asked, driving faster now that I knew she really had been set free.

"No. He kept touching me, though. Running his fingers up and down my legs. My back. Said he hoped you would stay in town so he can take me for a spin. Oh, Jonny, I don't know how I can ever repay you. Will I even get to see you again?"

"Santos should be at your house right now. Or at least in your neighborhood. I'll send you his number because you need to call him immediately. He's going to take you to the Walkers' house, and you have to stay there—inside—until this is all over."

"Over? Is it not?" Carissa asked, her relief giving way to worry.

"Far from it, I'm afraid. You're not safe until this dick head is locked up. Call Santos, and make sure he calls off any investigation into your kidnapping immediately. The less the police know, the better I can handle this."

"Jonny, you can't be serious. You heard him. If you come back to Redwood—"

"I don't give a shit what he said," I cut her off. "Do you really think you'll be safe as long as he's roaming Redwood? He knows where you live. Has seen the inside of your house. We need him behind bars. Plus, he has answers. He knows something—a lot, I'm guessing—about these suicides. Don't you want to know what really happened to your brother?"

"My brother shot himself, Jonny," Carissa said with a harsh undertone. "In the head. There's no conspiracy behind it. He was mentally ill and snapped. I've come to terms with that. And I wish you would too."

"It's not that simple, Carissa. This man kidnapped you to get me to stop looking into the suicides. He murdered Kody Holt and tried to make it look like a suicide. When that failed, his fallback was to frame me for the murder. Who's to say he didn't do the same thing to your brother?"

Silence filled the line, but I knew the call hadn't ended. I could hear the faint sound of traffic driving by through the phone.

"I know part of you—a big part, I hope—knows your brother wouldn't have taken his own life. Now that we know this man is capable of murder and framing it as suicide, we owe it to your brother to confirm his death was his choice. Because if it wasn't, your brother needs justice."

"Okay," she said, deflated. "Only because of what he did to Kody. But the second you find out Timmy really took his life, I don't want to hear a word about any of this again. Are we clear?"

"Crystal," I said.

"Good. So when will you be back?"

"Today. I don't know when we can see each other. I won't be returning home, not on the off chance this guy drives by my house. Stay with the Walkers, and don't step foot outside until you hear we're in the clear. For now, call Santos and let him drive you to the Walkers. Oh, and can you text me Timmy's phone number?"

"For what?" she asked, and I could hear the annoyance in her voice boiling over.

"I'm working on something. With a CIA friend. Just making sure we didn't miss anything."

Following a long pause, she finally responded with a forced, "Okay."

"Thanks, Carissa. Maybe we can grab dinner when this is all done?"

She laughed. A light-hearted sound. "You just saved me from that sicko. I'm buying dinner, and you can't stop me."

Hearing her playfulness brought a smile to my face. "Deal."

We hung up, and I continued blazing down the freeway. I didn't think it was possible to drive for two and a half hours with a complete laser focus, but I did. I'd become possessed by an external force willing me back to Redwood.

It was 3:05 in the afternoon when I passed the sign welcoming me to Redwood, a Purple Heart City. I never noticed that when I'd first arrived in town. Having two Purple Hearts, I wondered what that meant. I'd have to look that up after I captured this asshole.

I never heard from Santos, and could only assume he was busy taking care of matters with Carissa. With no list of call center volunteers and employees, I drove straight for the offices of the suicide hotline.

I parked there a few minutes before 3:30, with no plans of entering the building until the receptionist, Patricia, left for the day. With an hour to kill, I forwarded the text message Carissa had sent me with Timmy's number to Kayla.

Santos was supposed to get me the rest of the numbers belonging to the deceased, but I'd yet to see anything.

This was exactly why I tried to never rely on others.

With an hour to go, I sat in my car, waiting for my moment to go inside.

Chapter 30

I sent a second text message to Kayla with the names of the other deceased. Told her I wouldn't be getting their numbers anytime soon, and asked if she might have any way of looking those up for me.

My hour waiting outside the call center made me wonder if I had grown too obsessed with this list of workers inside. The list itself wouldn't provide any clues, but I'd need it to cross reference if, and hopefully when, Kayla replied with information about who the deceased may have spoken to.

If I could pin down who exactly these men had spoken with, they might provide more insight into the final moments of their lives.

When the clock struck 4:34, Patricia strolled out of the building, purse slung over her shoulder, lunchbox gripped tightly in hand.

I watched her get into a battered Nissan Altima and drive off into the evening.

I stepped out of the car, stretched my arms and rolled my neck, and started for the office building.

The front doors weren't locked yet, so I entered the dimly lit lobby and scanned the area. I shuffled to Patricia's desk and sat down behind it, powering on the computer and waiting a minute while the machine hummed back to life.

Password protected.

"Shit."

I tried the typical basic password guesses, but none of them worked. Then I noticed a sticky note hanging from the bottom of the monitor with a random sequence of letters, numbers, and symbols.

I typed in the sequence, and sure enough, it let me into her computer. People put more effort into their personal passwords instead of their work ones, and Patricia had just fallen victim of the same trap.

She kept a rather clear desktop. The only icons were to her email inbox, Google Chrome, and everyone's favorite, Solitaire.

Even her desk was cleared of noise. Pens, staplers, sticky notes (minus the one that got me into her computer) were all in their proper positions in the desk organizer tucked behind her computer screen.

I opened her email software and waited for it to load. The archaic system of Microsoft Outlook. Jesus. We were using Outlook during my time in the SEALs...fifteen years ago. And it still looked mostly the same. I found an inbox with only five emails remaining. All marked as read. Patricia ran a tight ship. No clutter. No bullshit.

I spotted a *Contacts* tab along the top and clicked on it. A list populated with hundreds of names. My heart raced. This was something. Good enough. The list didn't differentiate who was who, but if I could export it and print it out—Patricia had her own printer on the floor beneath her desk—this could provide me with enough to cross reference later on.

The door into the call center swung open, and out stepped Ron Hartman. His eyes immediately found me, and his brows shot high up.

"Jonny Mendez?" he said in that tone people use when they were about eighty percent sure of your name.

I closed all the tabs and powered off the computer before he started toward me.

"What are you doing here?" he asked, his head cocked to the side. He scanned Patricia's desk for any signs of what I'd been up to.

I stood up. "I need some information."

"Okay?" Ron replied, now inching slower toward me. He was afraid. He had every right to question me, but I could tell he didn't want to challenge someone twice his size. "You don't start work here for another two weeks. What exactly were you thinking you could find on Patricia's computer?"

"Well, I was hoping to find *you*," I said, forcing a laugh I hoped didn't sound too fake. "I came in and no one was here. Obviously, the door is locked to the call center. Tried knocking, but no luck. Thought maybe I could find your phone number or email on this computer, but I couldn't even get past the password screen."

"I see," Ron said, blinking rapidly as he stared into me. He didn't believe a word I said.

"Can we have a word in your office?" I asked.

"Actually, Mr. Mendez, I'm more inclined to call security. This is not at all how we handle matters at this call center. I believe I stressed to you the importance of privacy in our work. Discretion is everything. And whatever you just tried doing goes against everything we stand for. Hacking an employee's computer, no matter your reason, is absolutely forbidden."

I raised my hands. "Technically, I didn't hack anything. No password."

"I'm not here to discuss the finer details of whatever you were doing," Ron said in the sharpest tone I'd heard from him yet. He reached into his pocket and pulled out a cell phone, immediately dialing.

"Wait, Ron," I said. "Put the phone away, and I'll come clean."

"Come clean?" he asked. "So you admit to wrongdoing?"

I nodded. "I haven't done anything wrong, but intended to."

"Consider your future employment here terminated. I will not discuss the matter."

"Please, Ron," I said, extending my hand like I was urging him to put down a loaded gun instead. "Let me explain. There's a major issue you can help me with."

Ron considered, looked at his phone, then pressed the red button to hang up the call. "Start talking."

"Thank you," I said, circling around the desk to stand face to face with Ron. "First off, I'm sorry, but I never intended to work here. Well, not in three weeks from now. I only applied to gain access to the building. Someone in your call center may have information about the recent suicides in Redwood, and I've just been trying to figure out who, so I can ask them questions."

"Excuse me," Ron said. "But I'm afraid that information is way out of bounds. Our job is to protect the privacy of our callers, first and foremost. After that, my job is to protect our employees and volunteers. They have the same right to privacy as our callers."

"And I agree with that," I said. "I'm hoping you can take me at my word."

"Is this some sort of covert operation from the CIA?" Ron asked. "I can't imagine the CIA would care about a few suicides in a smaller city like Redwood."

"No," I said. "I'm no longer affiliated with the CIA. This has been something I've investigated on my own. Aside from the four deceased men having a shared bond of playing on that championship team all those years, they also shared troubling cases of CTE. I've learned from other members of the team that they all use the hotline when dealing with bouts of CTE. I'm only assuming those four men called in to here, but when, or who, they spoke with, I don't know. That's where I'm hoping you can help."

Ron laughed. "I can't share that information, Mr. Mendez. That would be career suicide for me. If word ever got out that I allowed such a thing, I'd be shunned from this industry forever."

"No word will get out," I said. "If you have any way of tracking down who spoke with those men, it can go a long way in figuring out what actually happened."

Ron frowned. "I'm sorry, but what do you mean? Those men took their own lives."

"That's the assumption," I said. "But with what just happened to Kody Holt, we're not so sure. He was murdered, and the scene was framed as a suicide. It wasn't until a forensics team concluded the handwriting on the note was no match to Kody's."

"I haven't seen that in the news," Ron said, scratching his head.

"I can't speak for the news, but that's the truth. And trust me when I tell you this, because they arrested me first for the murder. The handwriting sample set me free, along with the fact I didn't do it."

"It's still too risky," Ron said. "Even if this is all true, I can't justify handing over confidential information. That's assuming I can even find anything. If these men called in anonymously, we won't have a trace of their names, numbers, or anything."

"But you *can* look it up?" I asked, seeing the dials turning in Ron's head. Managing a call center couldn't have been a fun job. Especially one dealing with the calls they received on the hotline. Sometimes you just had to sell people on excitement. Throw in a splash of hope, and you could convince them to do anything.

"Well, yes," he said.

"Okay. What if we try this instead? You take me back, look up these potential calls—again, I don't even know for sure if they called in to here—and you provide me with whatever information you have. Verbally. I won't write anything down. Nothing needs to be printed. I'll mentally file away the information in my head and keep it at that. No paper trail. That way, you're at no risk of getting caught, *and* you'll have helped move this investigation forward. Win-win."

I crossed my arms and waited for him to consider this option. He liked it. I could see it in his wide eyes.

"And if we find something," he said. "Like who these men had spoken with, what do you plan on doing?"

"I'll need to question them," I said. "But it won't be here. I'll find them out in public, or at home to ask my questions. Nothing threatening. Just trying to paint a picture of what happened in the last moments of these men's lives. And even that may end up being nothing. But we owe it to the deceased to make sure they didn't have the same fate as Kody Holt."

Ron stared at me, his eyes studying mine. I could see it. He was convinced, but was still looking for any way out.

"Okay," he said. "Here's what we'll do. I'll take you back to my office—if anyone asks, it's strictly follow-up from your interview. You can give me names, numbers, or whatever you have. I'll enter them into my database and see what comes up. From there, I'll decide if I want to share the information or not."

"Okay," I said. I just needed to get inside the office. I had Ron on the ropes. He could create whatever parameters he thought necessary in his head. If there was information to be had, I'd talk him into it.

Ron drew in a deep breath and blew it out slowly.

"You have my word, Ron," I assured him. "I'll never speak of this to anyone."

He nodded and turned around. I followed him through the door into the call center.

The phones were much more lively compared to my last visit. As we passed the bullpen, I saw at least a dozen agents, all on the phone.

"I'm sorry to hear that," one agent said.

"Have you tried talking to your mother about it?" asked another.

"I hear you," said a third.

Their chatter overlapped, creating a steady hum. But I heard that phrase again.

"I hear you."

They were all saying it.

The man on the phone had said those same words to me. Multiple times.

I followed Ron into his office, and he closed the door behind me.

"Have a seat," he said, extending his arm toward the open chair across his messy desk.

I noticed a slight tremble in his arm. He was nervous. Doing something he shouldn't have been, but too engrossed by the thrill. I wondered why he had agreed so easily. I didn't have to persuade him as much as I had thought. Maybe his dedication to the company's values was only lip service. Like the drone-like employees who could rehearse an entire company handbook, yet got caught smoking cigarettes in the server room.

I had an English teacher in high school who loved to profess, "You have to know the rules to break the rules."

While I understood how that quote applied to writing, I carried those words with me for the rest of my life. The saying applied to everything, not just writing. Understanding a rule book meant you also understood the loopholes. Maybe that was all running through Ron's mind. He *knew* the loopholes and saw the opportunity to test the waters.

Most people, no matter how pure of heart, couldn't resist the temptation of seeing what they could get away with. That's how we end up with con artists and bank robbers. And politicians.

Ron smacked the space bar on his keyboard and waited for his screen to come back to life.

"I hear you," I said.

"Excuse me?" Ron replied, his eyes still focused on his computer.

"That phrase. *I hear you*. Everyone was saying it on the phones."

"Oh. Yes, that's part of our training. Using those three words tells the caller we're actively listening and engaged."

"I see. Makes sense."

"Alright, let's look," Ron said, his tongue pinched between his two lips as he gave his computer his entire focus. "Do you have a phone number? That's the easiest way to find anything."

"Yes," I said, and pulled out my cell phone. The text from Carissa was still the most recent in my inbox, so I read off Timmy's number.

Ron typed it in, clicked three times, and sat back and waited. "Takes about fifteen seconds to load results."

He drummed his fingers on the edge of his desk while waiting, then leaned forward and squinted at the screen. "Well, that's odd."

I leaned forward, planting my hands on Ron's desk. "What is it?"

Ron clicked around a few more times, then shook his head. "So, normally when I search a phone number, it will populate a list of all the inbound calls. But it's pulling up an error message I've never seen before. Says the records are restricted."

He typed something else and rubbed his forehead.

"Just tried my phone number," he said. "We use it as a test during training. Everything pulls up as normal. Let me try that number again."

He did and slapped the top of his desk when it returned the same error message.

"Who can restrict records?" I asked.

"I have no idea," Ron said, shaking his head in more disbelief. "I didn't even know that was a thing. My guess would be someone at the main office in D.C. But I don't know *why* a record would be restricted."

"Do you want to try searching the other names?" I asked. "Sorry, I don't have the phone numbers for them yet."

Ron tossed up his hands. "Okay, sure. What are they?"

"Jackson Green, Tyrell Marshall, and Kody Holt."

I watched as Ron typed furiously. Clearly, this guy had just encountered something he didn't know for the first time at his job.

"We have fifty-seven different accounts for Jackson Green," Ron said. "Six within Redwood. None have a home address listed, so I can't know for sure which one we need. Let me click into each of them."

I waited while he clicked, his eyes jumping from the top of the screen to the bottom. After a minute, he leaned back in his seat and crossed his arms, glaring at the computer like it had just told him to fuck off. Which, I suppose, it had.

"Just clicked through all six," he said. "Five don't have any additional details. And one has that same restriction on it."

Ron didn't have to say it out loud. We both assumed the restricted one was the one we wanted.

"Is there anyone you can call to ask about it?" I asked.

Ron shrugged. "I could call the regional director, but you know how it is. The higher ups spend less time using these systems. I doubt

she'd actually know. Plus, she'll have questions why this is so important."

"Good point," I said, sitting back and stroking my chin. "We can't
loop anyone else in. Maybe the restriction is a clue. But not a helpful
one, if we don't know who did it."

"I'm going to dig into this more," Ron said, turning his attention
away from the computer. "I'll look through our handbooks and see
what they say about restricted accounts. It must mean *something* if it
exists in our system."

I stood up and extended my hand. "I'll let myself out. Sorry to have
wasted your time today. If you come across anything, let me know."

Ron shook my hand and didn't offer to follow me out of the building. When I left his office, he immediately returned to his computer
and spoke to himself. Poor guy. This discovery would probably have
him up all night now, trying to figure it out.

As tempting as it was to snoop around the call center, I couldn't
betray Ron's trust. Not so soon. I still hoped I'd get a list of volunteers.
And maybe he'd be the one to help me with that.

As I strolled through the bullpen toward the exit, I stopped and
looked over the cubicles housing the agents, who all still appeared to
be on calls. I couldn't see many of them, but their voices carried above
the dividers. And that phrase kept hitting me. No, *slapping* me across
the face.

"I hear you."

"I hear you."

"I hear you."

I needed that list of volunteers and employees. Even the information about the inbound calls from the deceased seemed less important
as that three-word phrase kept filling my ears, shedding light on a
disturbing truth:

Whoever had killed Kody Holt and kidnapped Carissa worked in this call center.

Chapter 31

The thought of a murderer working in the call center occupied my thoughts for the rest of the evening. I couldn't tell Ron my theory, either. The last thing I needed was him acting suspiciously around his employees and colleagues. The less he knew, the better.

I returned to my neighborhood, but drove around to the block behind mine. If I parked my car in the driveway, the man on the phone would know I was back. As would the Walkers and Carissa.

If I was going to catch this guy, it was best everyone thought I was actually out of town.

So I parked on Juniper Street and waited for the sun to go down. My stomach growled, but I paid it no attention. The thought of shoving food into my mouth seemed irrelevant right now. My life was in danger, along with others.

Especially others.

If the man I spoke with earlier believed I had left Redwood for good, I presumed he planned to return to whatever his involvement was with the suicides. I was assuming he was killing these men and framing their deaths as suicides. Or at the least, forcing them to take their own lives. That seemed more complex, but anything could be accomplished with some blackmail and a loaded gun.

When the sun finally went down, I used the cover of darkness to hurry along the side of my backyard neighbor's house. I hopped a low fence separating their front from the back, and found a backyard full of kid toys, bicycles, and a trampoline I'd never seen used during my time living right behind them.

A motion light flicked on from the back porch, so I sprinted across the yard and vanished into the thick shrubs that grew over the fence dividing our properties. Crickets chirped while cicadas buzzed high in the trees. My arms burned with the meager scratches earned during my venture through the shrubs.

After pushing through, I felt the fence and climbed over it, feet landing on my side of the property line.

I had spent limited time in my backyard. Maybe a couple of nights enjoying a rum and Coke while the sun set. Eddie and his crew stopped by once a week to mow the lawn, pull weeds, and spray pesticides on the flowers lining the yard's perimeter. This was all arranged before I'd moved in, and I had no complaints about not needing to tend to those matters myself, although I usually helped them, anyway.

From my view along the back fence, I could see through the Walkers' rear window that looked into their kitchen. My heart raced at the sight of Carissa sitting at their dining table, sipping from a cup of tea while conversing with Herb and Rochelle.

She was safe.

As long as she stayed in that house until I captured this lunatic, she'd remain safe, too.

My cell phone buzzed in my pocket. A text from Officer Santos.

Keep a low profile. Neighbors saw you enter Carissa's house. Police are looking for you.

"God dammit," I said, stuffing the phone back into my pocket. It obviously wasn't Santos's fault, considering he just sent me a warning. A neighbor could have seen me and called the police before Santos even arrived to investigate. Carissa might have been safe, but I wasn't.

As if a killer stalking me around town wasn't enough. Now I had to deal with this incompetent police department.

Shrouded by the night, I ran across my backyard to the rear door. No motion lights for me—I had turned those off. I never locked the backdoor, not sensing a reason to. Not in Redwood.

I let myself in and had to move through the darkness. I wouldn't turn a single light on as long as I was here, just needing a place to rest and, hopefully, sleep.

Closing the door behind me—and now locking it—I shuffled through the house and peered through the front window. Sure enough, a couple of cop cars sat toward the end of the block, facing my direction.

These motherfuckers.

It had to be Chambers and Roman. Led by Roman, of course. He just couldn't let me go.

Hell, I couldn't blame him. I *did* have ties to the two most recent crimes in Redwood. And now he had an eyewitness who I'm sure spoke all about the six-and-a-half-foot tall Mexican man who had walked out of Carissa's busted front door.

Cooking in the dark was out of the question. Not even the dim light above the stove would be used during my stay. Instead, I lowered myself into a crouched position and crawled into the kitchen like a child trying to sneak a cookie in the middle of the night. I fished around the counter where I kept a bowl of fruit and helped myself to a banana. Once I finished that, I felt around the snack cupboard until finding a chocolate chip and peanut butter granola bar. The best.

With some food in my stomach, the rumblings stopped.

Thirty minutes passed as I sat on the kitchen floor, my back against the cupboards. I couldn't recall the last time I hid like this—probably in the Middle East during a tour—but if the police knew I was home, my hopes of catching Kody's killer would die out.

And the asshole on the phone admitted as much. The police keeping me detained allowed *him* to roam freely.

I crawled back to the living room and peeked through the window. Both police cars had left.

I was home free and could enjoy a night in peace. And darkness.

The only decision in front of me for the night was to sleep on the couch or in my bed. After confirming both the front and back doors were locked, I chose my bed and climbed in. I kept my clothes and shoes on, just in case.

Checking it under the covers, my phone told me it was nearing eleven o'clock. I'd have to spend tomorrow getting that list of names from the call center. If it meant another awkward visit to Ron, so be it. But I was convinced Kody's killer worked in that building.

An hour passed before I started drifting. I didn't quite go all the way under. Too many thoughts pounded around my head. My stomach rumbled again, not satisfied with a banana and granola bar for dinner.

It was almost 12:30 when I heard a motor outside. Not too loud, but enough to announce its presence. I thought nothing of it, my mind half asleep, until the sound of glass shattering in the living room startled me out of bed.

I rolled off the side, pulled open my nightstand drawer, and snatched the Glock 48 I kept loaded.

I was about to stand up when a barrage of gunfire rained down on the house. More glass shattered as I heard bullets bouncing off the siding outside. Others made it inside, through the broken windows, and splintered the living room's drywall.

The shooting stopped. My heart pounded in my ears as I climbed to my feet, tumbling into the living room in a daze. I still refused to turn the lights on, but once I heard burning rubber as the car sped off down the street, I used the flashlight on my cell phone to examine the living room.

Shards of glass lay scattered across the hardwood floor. The center pane of the window behind the TV was completely blasted. A brick lay in front of the coffee table between the couch and TV. It had a piece of paper attached to it with a rubber band.

I crunched glass as I stepped toward it, noticing bullet holes in the TV, the screen now splintered in several directions. The couch absorbed a couple of shots, feathers from the stuffing having floated to the floor.

A quick browse of the area told me at least thirty shots had been fired. Probably more. The shooter would've had a semi-automatic firearm, if not fully-automatic.

My cell phone rang. Carissa.

"Hello?" I answered.

"Jonny! Oh my God, you're okay!"

"Why wouldn't I be?"

"Your house was just attacked by a drive-by shooter," she cried. "It sounded awful."

"I told you I'm not staying at my house," I lied.

"But you are in Redwood, right?"

"Yes, I came back. Not going to say where I'm staying. The less you know, the safer you'll be. Obviously, your friend is out to get me."

"Don't call him that, Jonny," she replied in a stern voice.

I let out a light-hearted laugh. "I'm just teasing. And don't worry. He won't be laughing once I find him. Are you feeling safe at the Walkers?"

"I was," she said. "Until what just happened. Can't say I've ever been that close to gun shots. They sounded like they were coming from just down the hall—that's how loud they were."

I knew. My head still rang after the tsunami of bullets that had torn apart my temporary house.

"You'll be fine there," I said. "Even if they come back every night to shoot my house. They don't want to get anyone else involved. As long as you keep a low profile, they'll have no reason to attack the Walkers' house."

"How much longer of this, Jonny?" Carissa asked. I heard the desperation in her voice. The last two weeks of her life had been tumultuous, to say the least.

"I'm hoping to make some progress in the next couple of days," I said. "I should get going, though. Long day ahead for me tomorrow. Are you sure you're okay?"

"I'm fine, Jonny," she said in a caring tone. "I just wanted to make sure you hadn't come home after all. Can't imagine you'd have survived what just happened to your house."

I looked at the bullet holes in the drywall behind me. "Sounds like I got lucky tonight. Thanks for checking on me. Always good to know someone's thinking about me."

"Of course. Rochelle already called the police, so I'm sure they'll be over soon."

"She *what*?!" I asked, not trying to sound as panicked as I actually was.

"Jonny," Carissa said. "It sounded like a war zone outside. Did you think no one was going to call the cops? I'm sure Rochelle wasn't the only one. I'm looking out the front window now and see at least four other houses with lights on. If anyone on the block actually stayed asleep through that, I'd be surprised. I'm telling you, it was like someone lit an entire basket of fireworks right outside my window."

Hearing this news started an instant countdown in my head. How far was it to the police station? Six minutes?

Three had already passed since Carissa called. I'd need to make quick work of getting out before the police arrived.

"I really need to get back to sleep, Carissa," I said. "We'll talk soon, okay? I'm looking forward to our dinner."

We hung up, and I immediately squatted down to pick up the brick. The paper tucked under the rubber band was folded in half to conceal the message inside, so I plucked it out and unfolded it, reading the typed text in a wavering hand.

YOU LIAR!

DO YOU KNOW WHAT I DO TO LIARS, JONNY BOY?

I KILL THEM AND EVERYONE IN THEIR LIFE.

YOU GET ONE MORE CHANCE.

LEAVE TOWN.

OR DIE!

"All this rage," I said to the brick, folding up the note and tucking it into my pocket. I tossed the brick onto the couch, preparing to dash out of the backdoor and return to my car on Juniper Street. "One of us is going to die alright."

Chapter 32

I slept the rest of the night in my car.

After driving out of the neighborhood and going a mile west, I found a church parking lot that wrapped around the building. St. Thomas Catholic Church, somewhere I probably should have visited at least once during the past few months.

I used to go to mass every Sunday with my mother as a kid. My brother would join us when able. And every week after mass, she'd take us to a cafe called Ricardo's. It became our favorite breakfast spot in Laredo. The owner was an immigrant from Mexico and always offered my mom a job. She would take on just about any job under the sun, but always refused to work in the food industry.

"Cocino para relajarme, no para trabajar," she'd tell me every time I asked her why she didn't want to work at our favorite restaurant. She cooked to relax, not for work.

These memories kept me company as I drifted to sleep in my reclined driver's seat.

I slept until the sun rose moments before six o'clock. A couple of pigeons had landed on the hood of my car, staring at me with curiosity. I honked the horn and laughed when they flew away in a panic.

My head was cloudy with fatigue, breath sour from overnight and no way to brush my teeth. That shit pissed me off. I had a handful of those red and white peppermint candies in my backpack, and popped one into my mouth to freshen up.

I rolled my neck until it cracked in several places. Sleeping in a car wasn't ideal for a body over forty years old, my back offering plenty of protest as I twisted around to stretch my limbs.

With a new day ahead of me, I needed to get the list of names from the call center. Kody's killer would be on that list. Considering I could cross off all the women, that would hopefully leave me with a reduced workload of finding which man was behind the orchestrated murder.

I pulled out my cell phone and dialed 9-8-8. I couldn't just show up at the call center again. Eventually, Ron would place that call to security and I'd be banned from the building forever.

I listened as the phone worked through an automated recording informing me the first available agent would be with me in less than one minute. Ten seconds later, a woman answered in a friendly voice.

"Good morning, my name is Michelle," she said. "Are you comfortable sharing your name with me?"

"Good morning, Michelle," I said. "My name is Jonny."

"Thanks for sharing, Jonny. What would you like to chat about today?"

I was expecting more of a business feel to the call, considering it was a call center with agents handling dozens of similar calls throughout the day. If I hadn't known better, Michelle could have been a friend I was catching up with on the phone.

"Did I lose you, Jonny?" she asked after I failed to respond.

"Sorry," I said. "I was actually hoping you could help connect me with someone I had spoken with last week. I don't remember his name, but he told me he liked to help athletes. Do you know who that might be?"

"Hmm," Michelle said. "Let me check through our directory. I'm not familiar with anyone who specializes in athletes. Keep in mind, we do all have the same training experience."

"I understand, Michelle," I said. "And I'm not currently having a crisis, but wanted to follow up with the gentleman I had spoken with. He really helped me get out of a pickle, and I just wanted to thank him."

"Oh," Michelle said, her voice becoming even cheerier now that she knew I wasn't having an issue. "I'm not showing anyone on my list notated for athletes. Do you remember what his name started with?"

I smacked my forehead with the palm of my hand. Michelle was more than willing to give me the name of an agent at the call center. If only I had the slightest clue of where to start.

"I'm afraid not," I said. "I'm so mad at myself for not remembering his name."

"I wish I could be of more help," Michelle said. "We have a roster of almost one hundred agents who handle calls for the Redwood region."

"I understand. Thank you anyway for your help. I'll call back if I can remember his name."

"Sounds great, Jonny. I'm glad to hear you're doing better. And remember, we're always a phone call away if you need us."

"Thank you," I said, and hung up.

I felt like shit after placing that call. Michelle was ready to help someone in need. Not only had I lied to her, but I had taken up valuable time on a phone line that could've helped someone truly in need. Even with my justification of trying to catch a killer, the matter didn't sit right with me.

I fucked up. My judgement clouded by my personal greed to succeed. I'd never dial that number again unless I needed it.

Unfortunately, it was too late to do anything about it. But dammit, I needed that list of volunteers. And Michelle had one. She referenced checking a directory with all the agents who worked in the call center. And it wasn't just a list of names and numbers, either. She had checked notes to see if anyone was marked as specializing in helping athletes.

I rubbed my forehead, banging the back of my head against the car seat. The list was likely digital. I doubted the agents would reference a printout, especially considering how often the roster of their colleagues was surely changing.

If I could get back inside the office and through the door leading to the call center bullpen, that still wouldn't guarantee me anything. I'd need to get lucky. First, with not being spotted by Ron. Second, with finding an unlocked computer when an agent stepped away. Considering their dedication to privacy, the agents had to be trained to lock their computers every time they stepped away.

But what if there was a diversion? Perhaps a pulled fire alarm that sent people into a panic.

"No, dumbass," I said, looking myself in the rear-view mirror. "That pulls everyone off the phones. Not the point."

Fuck.

The exhaustion was getting to me. I never really felt when it crept in, but could tell when my ideas became absurd and messy. Like I could walk into that building, pull a fire alarm, and go against the herd of employees filing out of the call center to hopefully find an unlocked computer. All without being spotted. Not to mention the police just waiting to pounce on me.

I had to laugh at myself. If only I had the tools to scale the building and sneak in through the roof. Crawling through vents like some expert ninja. As much as I wanted to be Batman, I simply wasn't.

That left me with two options.

Either wait to start working at the call center. Or wait for Michelle outside the building and intimidate her into producing the list for me.

My stomach twisted from starvation and anxiety. Both options were shit. The first allowed too much time. How much more would this psychopath crank up the heat during a three-week stretch? Burning down my house didn't seem out of the question at this point. And it wasn't even my house. And while intimidating Michelle could yield the fastest results, it wasn't guaranteed to work.

I couldn't leave anything to chance or luck. Not this close. The margins for errors this late in the game had all but vanished. One slip up could land me in jail—again. Or dead. Neither appealed to me.

I could always try Ron again, but felt one more rattle of his cage would end our relationship for good. I had to keep my upcoming job in the back of my pocket in case the horrific scenario of waiting three weeks with no results actually came true. That was now my very last resort. Right next to barging into the call center with my gun and demanding the list.

I fired up the engine and left the church behind. All I wanted was some breakfast and couldn't go to my house—or even my neighbors—for a quick bite. I drove until finding a Mexican restaurant called Sol Verde. They had a bright sign in the window advertising breakfast burritos served until eleven o'clock every morning.

They had them pre-made, so I grabbed two bacon burritos and scarfed them down in my car, pondering my next move. I had nowhere to actually spend the day. The cops would lurk around my neighborhood today. If Redwood hadn't had a suicide in several years, I wondered when the last time they had a drive-by shooting. I only hoped the Walkers didn't get dragged into anything for being the next-door neighbors, although I could see Herb completely on board with giving an interview to the local news. All while Rochelle rolled her eyes and smacked him across the arm.

I drove to the call center. It seemed the only logical place to go. I constantly looked in my rearview while passing through town. No signs of anyone following me.

The brick was too deliberate. How did the killer know I had returned to Redwood?

It was a thought I hadn't given serious consideration after being forced from my house. Highly unlikely he waited around to see if I drove back into town. If he had let Carissa go, he trusted I wasn't coming back. No point in throwing away what he surely saw as his only bargaining chip with me.

I had only visited the call center after returning to town. Even there, I only encountered Ron. Besides him, the only people who knew I was coming back were Officer Santos and Carissa. And I'm sure the Walkers knew because of Carissa.

But the only person who had physically seen me was Ron.

Nothing about him screamed out murderer. But that was how they were sometimes. Ron would be in any company directory they could produce. Naturally, he wouldn't have wanted to hand that over. Now that I thought back, I'd never actually seen his computer display when I was in his office. Could he have made up the entire story about restricted accounts to throw me off? His desire to look into the matter and find answers fabricated?

That fib would buy him time to come up with a new story. Even lead us to a dead end. I pulled into the call center parking lot, my thoughts on fire. Thinking back to common denominators, what did the four deceased have in common?

CTE. Calls to the suicide hotline. Championship rings.

Which left one link between those men. A second common denominator tying the deceased to the call center.

Ronald Hartman, manager of the Redwood branch for the National Suicide and Crisis Hotline.

And he had my address from when I applied for a volunteer position. I'd handed it to him on a silver fucking platter.

Ron Hartman was the only person who could confirm I was back in Redwood after driving all the way to the California border and back.

My heart raced as I pulled into the lot and parked so I'd have a clear view of the building's only entrance and exit. There were other details to iron out, but Ron was my primary target now. But I needed more proof. Something to tie him to the murder or the kidnapping.

Until then, it was my word against his. And the way the police trusted me right now left me no chance. This left me with one obvious choice.

I needed to follow Ron.

Chapter 33

At eight o'clock sharp, I strolled through the doors of the office building.

I had seen Patricia enter ten minutes prior, and wanted to let her get settled for her day before questioning her.

She was typing on her computer, sipping from a tumbler full of coffee, when I entered the lobby. She did a double take, recognizing me.

"Good morning," she said, raising a brow. "I didn't think the new class was starting for another couple of weeks."

"I'm not here for that," I said. "Was hoping to speak with Ron."

Patricia let out a relieved laugh. "Oh, thank goodness! Because I haven't started on the new hires badges yet. That would have been bad."

I echoed her laugh, hoping to build her trust. But she didn't seem to care either way.

"Ron?" she repeated, returning her attention to the computer. "Ron is out today. Actually, he's out for the next three days, it appears."

"Oh," I said, forcing my disappointment that wasn't all that fake. "Is he on vacation?"

Patricia pursed her lips as she stared at the screen again, slowly shaking her head. "I don't believe so. He hadn't mentioned anything earlier this week. Looks like he just submitted the time off before he left the office last night. Could be sick, I guess."

Yeah. Sick of having me around and trying to bring him down.

"Well, dang," I said, giving a friendly pat on the top of her desk. "I'll have to try back in a few days, I guess."

"You can always call him and leave a message," Patricia said. "Or I can take a message and put it on his desk for you."

"That's okay," I said. "It's nothing too pressing. I'll just swing by in a few days."

"Works for me," Patricia said, shrugging. "I guess I'll be seeing you soon, then."

"Absolutely. Have a great rest of your day. Looking forward to starting work here."

I shot her a grin before leaving the building.

When I returned to my car, I called Santos.

He answered after two rings, speaking in a hushed tone. "Where are you?"

"Good morning to you, too, sunshine," I replied.

"Seriously, what's going on? I'm at your house right now."

He lowered his voice even more to say that last part. Santos was at my house on official police business, along with other officers.

"Funny," I said. "I don't recall inviting you over."

"Enough with the jokes," Santos snapped. "Do you even know what happened here?"

"Of course. I was sleeping in my bed last night when I was woken by a brick being thrown through my window, followed by thirty rounds. Lucky for me, he only wanted to shoot into the living room."

"Did you see anyone?" Santos asked. "A car?"

"Afraid not. I was lying on the floor, making sure I didn't die. Didn't get up until I heard the car speed away."

Santos sighed. "You're causing quite the headache for our department."

"Sorry I'm inconveniencing you all. It's not like I called you guys. I'm happy to handle this matter myself."

"Enough of the tough talk, Mendez. This is getting out of hand. I was fine letting you catch this guy on your own, but now we're dealing with drive-by shootings in the middle of the night. What if someone had gotten hurt? We may have been lucky this time, but luck runs out. Always."

I didn't believe in luck, but was happy to let Santos think whatever he pleased. People used luck as a crutch. They cried bad luck when things didn't go their way. Good luck when things turned out better than expected. It was all an illusion. Bullshit.

"What exactly do you want me to do?" I asked. "Come home and share the story of what happened? You can clearly see what happened."

"No," Santos replied. "Keep under cover as you've been. If they bring you in for questioning, there's no knowing what that will turn into."

"Comforting. I didn't call to chat about any of this, though. I need an address, and was hoping you can help me get it."

"You know who the killer is?" Santos asked, taken aback.

"I have a lead. No proof. But I just want to keep eyes on this guy. Name is Ronald Hartman."

I spelled the name for Santos and waited, as it sounded like he'd placed his phone in his pocket and started walking.

The rustle stopped and his voice came back on. "Ronald Hartman. I'm in my car now. Let me see if I can find anything real quick. If not, you'll have to wait until later this afternoon."

"No problem."

I heard the car door slam, followed by the clatter of keys from his laptop. Santos whistled to himself while completing the search. It reminded me of my grandfather. He was a handyman who loved to whistle the tunes of popular songs from Mexico while repairing drywall, laying out new flooring, or painting a wall.

"I have two Ronald Hartmans," Santos said. "One is seventy-six years old, the other is forty-two."

"It's the younger one," I said.

"Alright, his address is 6221 Clearwater Drive. Looks like he has a clean record. Never had so much as a speeding ticket. You sure that's our guy?"

"No murderer wants any encounter with the police," I said. "You'd be surprised how many killers had a clean record before getting caught."

"Good point," Santos said. "I can't stay out here too long. Anything else you need?"

"No, that was all. Thanks, by the way, for taking care of Carissa. I'm sure she'd be in danger again since this guy knows I'm back in town."

"It was my pleasure," Santos said. "She was surprisingly calm when I picked her up. I'd have expected her to be in plenty of distress after being kidnapped. I asked her about it, and you know what she said?"

"Enlighten me."

"She said she knew you'd get her out safely. Had complete faith in you, and you delivered. I can't lie, Mendez. I've been hesitant about what I share with you. But after talking with Carissa for just those ten minutes during our drive to your neighborhood, she convinced me you're as pure as they come. Part of me wanted to believe you were the killer. But I know better now, and I apologize."

"I'm not sure what you want me to say," I replied. "Thanks, I guess."

"Nothing to say, Mendez. Just wanted to let you know. Whatever you need, just say the word. I haven't been able to get that list of volunteers. Not even sure the best way to go about that, if I'm being honest."

"Leave the list to me," I said. "And thanks for your help."

We hung up, and I immediately typed the address into my phone's map software. When it pulled up the results, I checked the address to make sure I'd entered it correctly.

"Six, two, two, one, Clearwater Drive," I said, reading it aloud to make I wasn't mistaken.

It was correct, and the red pin showing the location on the map may as well have been the devil's eye staring me down.

I'd been in the neighborhood before. Knew it well, in fact. And that only added to my growing confusion that seemed to spiral beyond control now. I didn't know if this address was an answer to my questions, or just another question to remain unanswered. Or maybe it was all a joke.

I turned my car back on and prepared for another drive across town.

Ron Hartman lived one block over from Carissa's house.

Chapter 34

I couldn't stop thinking about how easy it was for Ron to keep eyes on Carissa throughout this entire affair.

It was hardly even stalking. He could have just been a normal guy out for a walk in his neighborhood, glancing into Carissa's house each time he made a lap around the block. He would've seen my car parked out front during one of my visits, and followed me home one night.

The thought of him watching Carissa this entire time made me sick. I wanted to call her and tell what I'd discovered, but there was no point right now.

I just needed to find Ron and crank up the pressure until he confessed what he'd done. Or if he wasn't home, break in and find a clue.

During my race across town, I grew antsy knowing what awaited. The last thing Ron would expect was me to arrive on his doorstep. He'd be caught completely off guard, and that's when liars slipped up. Everything could run smoothly as long as they had time to plan their every move and word. He thought quick on his feet that day I showed up to the call center. But he'd have less time to react once I rang his doorbell.

I pulled into the neighborhood ten minutes later, driving past Carissa's house first. The door was still damaged, but it was closed and wouldn't look suspicious to anyone driving by. You had to really look at it to see the destruction.

I kept driving and turned right at the end of the block. The next cross street was Clearwater Drive, where I turned left and crept down the road. I stopped three houses short of Ron's. He lived in a two-level home with light yellow siding and a chain-link fence surrounding the front yard. A red Toyota Tacoma sat beneath a car port constructed over the end of the driveway.

After parking along the sidewalk, I killed the engine and planned my next move. I retrieved my gun from the glove box and tucked it into the back of my waistband. I didn't think I'd need it for Ron, but it was better to be safe.

The doorbell looked like one of those camera ones from a distance. If I strolled up and rang it, he'd be able to see it was me and refuse to answer. Hell, he might even sprint out the back door. Because if I'm knocking on his front door, he'd have to assume I found him out. May as well take a chance running instead of entering a fist fight with me.

I got out of the car, mind made up for what I wanted to do.

Sure enough, I strolled right up to the front door, passing through the gate that had a *WELCOME* sign hanging from it. I stood directly in front of the doorbell. Close enough where he'd only be able to see my shirt through the camera. I pressed the button and waited.

A chime rang out from inside, and I listened for any thudding that might signal movement from within. I heard none after thirty seconds and pressed the doorbell again. The front door was under a portico, so he wouldn't see me from a window above. The windows on either side of the door had curtains drawn shut. Possible he had peeked through them. I was at a reliable angle where he shouldn't have been able to completely tell who I was.

I knocked instead of ringing the doorbell a third time. Why would Ron have called out sick the morning after my house was shot up? And for three days. He had something else planned.

"Fuck," I muttered under my breath, stepping back from the door. I couldn't just keep pounding away at the front door. Eventually, a neighbor would see me and raise suspicions I didn't need.

I shuffled along the house and into the carport, looking over my shoulder to ensure no one was watching. In front of the parked truck was another fence with a gate leading into the backyard.

I let myself through, the low-hanging gate screeching as it dragged along the concrete. The backyard was riddled with weeds and a scattering of rocks. Bags of mulch and soil stood in a lopsided pile in the back corner. Some bags were busted open, their contents spilling out like lava from the heap of landscaping material Ron clearly never intended to use.

A dog barked at me from across the yard, charging at me full steam. It was a white Yorkshire Terrier. A little guy with a yapping bark as he bounced around my ankles in energetic circles.

"Come here, you," I said, squatting down and picking him up. He licked my forearms in delight, and I read the tag on his collar. "What the fuck?"

The dog's name was Kody. Spelled exactly the same way as Kody Holt, with a K. Coincidence, or another sign of some strange obsession with the championship team?

I placed the dog back on the ground and watched him speed away toward his dog house on the opposite side of the yard.

I trudged up to the backdoor and pulled open the creaky storm door. Ron was apparently as trusting as I had been and left his door unlocked. The hinges whined as the door slowly swung open, revealing a kitchen table with an abandoned bowl of cereal.

Fruit Loops. One of my favorites.

"Ron?" I called out. "It's Jonny Mendez. I just wanted to check on you."

The less confrontational I sounded, the better chances I had of getting Ron to cooperate. Unless he knew I was on to him. Then it didn't matter what I had to say.

"Ron? I know you're here. I see your cereal. And your truck. Give me a sign you're okay."

I held my breath and listened, only hearing the sounds of my heartbeat from within. I reached back and pulled out my Glock. The air was too still in the house. Too silent. Ron wasn't going to reveal himself, which meant he knew exactly why I was at his house.

I cocked the Glock, the sound echoing throughout the kitchen as I moved through it with slow, gentle steps. Aside from a sink full of dishes, the kitchen was in good shape. Clear counter tops, polished appliances, and no clutter beyond a stack of mail sitting center on the table.

For this game of hide and seek, my only option was to remain silent. If Ron knew where I was, he could make a move on me. If my presence in the kitchen was my last known location to him, I could make my way through the house. As long as there were no creaky boards, he'd have no way of knowing where I was.

I passed the kitchen and entered a hallway that split in both directions. Straight ahead was the foyer and living room, along with a staircase leading up. I walked with the Glock held in front, taking spaced out breaths to help listen to my surroundings. I entered the living room and spotted a grandfather clock ticking away. The TV was off, a couple of blankets and pillows in neat order on one end of the couch.

The main level was entirely hardwood flooring, making it more difficult to conceal the sound of my footsteps, no matter how delicately I took them. The stairs, however, were all carpet, and I presumed that continued on the second floor.

I started up them. If I could eliminate the entire floor as a possible hiding spot, I'd feel much better about snooping around the main level. Sure enough, the hallway on the second level was all carpet, as were the three bedrooms. Only the bathroom had tile flooring. All four doors were open, sunlight splashing through the bathroom window and into the hallway. The bedrooms were all dimmer, thanks to closed curtains.

The bathroom was the door directly in front of me from the second floor landing, so I poked my head in there first. Nothing to see. The shower doors were all glass, so no one hiding in there.

I pulled back and took a left down the hallway where only one door awaited. The other two were at the opposite end. I stepped in and studied the room. It appeared to be the one Ron slept in. A queen-sized bed sat in the center, the sheets a tangled mess. A glass of water stood on the nightstand next to empty candy wrappers and a box of tissues.

As I approached the edge of the bed for a closer look at the nightstand, I never heard the whisper of another set of footsteps approaching me from behind.

What I did hear was the cracking of an elbow joint. When I spun around, it was already too late. The last thing I saw was Ron's horrified face. He clutched a wooden baseball bat in both hands, the barrel soaring through the air until it connected with the side of my head, knocking me out cold.

Chapter 35

I woke in the same room, propped up in a seated position on the floor at the foot of the bed.

Ropes bound my legs together and my arms against my torso.

It felt like a stake had been driven into the side of my head, throbbing with heat all the way to my brain's innermost core. My scalp around the area of impact pulsed. Without even feeling it, I knew a massive bump had formed.

The room was empty only for a few seconds after I woke. Ron appeared in the doorway moments later.

"You son of a bitch!" he shouted at me. "Look what you've made me do."

The room moved around me. I was still dizzy. Probably suffered a concussion. How ironic.

Every time I blinked, pain surged throughout my head. If my skull exploded right now, I just might welcome it. That sounded as relieving as anything else.

"How long was I out?" I asked. My tongue and throat had gone entirely dry.

"Three hours," Ron said, stepping all the way into the room and stopping near my feet. He looked down at me, and I could see in his eyes he wanted to spit on me. Or maybe continue attacking me with his bat.

"Why the fuck did you break into my house?!" Ron shouted, and his words may as well have been additional blows to my head. Thank God this room was dim, or my head might have actually combusted. "Haven't you done enough damage?"

I closed my eyes, trying to get control back over my body. Even with my eyes shut, the darkness seemed to swarm around me, unable to remain still. I focused on my breathing, drawing in deep breaths through my nose and blowing out long exhales from my mouth.

"Me doing damage?" I asked, my voice weak. "You shot my house to pieces. Like an old gangster with a Tommy gun."

"Excuse me?" Ron replied. "First you break into my house, and then you accuse me of shooting at yours? Do you live in a different dimension? Or do you just get your kicks out of ruining people's lives?"

Ron's voice sounded both distant and blaring at the same time. I wasn't even sure how that was possible, but my brain was clearly in uncharted territory.

"Can I have water?" I asked. "I can't keep talking like this."

Ron scoffed, planted his hands on his waist as he stared at me with disgust, then realized he would actually need me to speak coherently. He shuffled around me toward the nightstand and grabbed the glass of water I'd seen earlier. Before he turned out my lights with that fucking bat.

"Don't try anything cute," he said when he returned, kneeling down to give me a sip from the glass. The relief was instant as the water coasted down my throat. He tilted the glass too far, and I choked. Each cough made me want to die, the pain throbbing violently.

Ron stood up and placed the glass on the dresser in front of me. The TV remained off and I could barely make out my reflection in the blacked-out glass of the screen. I underestimated Ron. Not once would I have thought he'd actually get me on the floor and tied up like a hostage in some sick game. But here I was, completely at his mercy.

"Why are you in my house?" Ron demanded, grabbing the bat he had tossed aside and leaning it against his shoulder.

"I wanted to talk," I replied.

"Talk? Who are you really? That's what I want to know. You keep showing up at the call center, asking all these questions. Sneaking around on staff computers. I don't buy a damn word you've said. Even with everything about the suicides. There's something bigger you're not telling me. And now I get a call from Patricia that you returned this morning. This is borderline harassment, and I'm inclined to get the police involved. Consider your volunteer position terminated. I don't want you anywhere near my office."

"I'm sure you don't," I replied calmly. "But I should warn you now, you won't keep getting away with this. Even if you kill me today, I have friends in the CIA still. They'll get the proper authorities involved and your house will come crashing down."

Ron's jaw hung open. He gaped at me like a baffled child. "Kill you? Jonny, what the fuck are you talking about? I'm not going to kill you. I only have you tied up because you broke into my house, and you're clearly after me for something."

Shit.

I could hear it in his tone now. He truly had no idea. This wasn't some act.

"My apologies," I said, shaking my head. Even that subtle movement sent more shockwaves. I couldn't admit to having incorrectly pegged Ron as the murderer. "I really need that list of volunteers. Trust me when I say I have no other agenda. Someone killed Kody Holt, and I believe they work in your call center."

This was it. All my chips were in the middle of the table. I studied Ron's reaction, seeing if he made any movements when I mentioned Kody and murder in the same sentence. His same bewildered look remained, however, and he looked at the ceiling in thought.

"I can't give you the list," he said. "As much as I'd like to help this cause, I just can't. I already feel guilty about sharing the information from the other night about the restricted accounts. You shouldn't know even that much. I got chewed out for that, by the way. Decided to ask my director what they knew about restricted accounts. All he said was that it was above my pay grade to worry about such things. They have their reasons for restricting accounts, and they usually come from even higher up. He wasn't pleased about my multiple attempts to navigate around the restrictions. That's on me, but I wouldn't have gone down that road if you never showed up at the office that night."

I nodded. "I never intended to get you in trouble. And I'm sorry I slipped in through your back door. I should have approached this all completely different."

"And on my day off," Ron said. "Can't I just have a few days of peace? I took three days off because I'm feeling some burnout. Been working extra hours, dealing with some problems with certain volunteers. Those positions are hard to keep filled. So much turnover. Or they think they can take whatever days off they want. And I get it, it's not a paid position, but people are relying on them to show up to answer the phones. And when they don't, it just puts more stress on my paid employees. I've always fought to get some sort of pay for volunteers—it would help with retention. But it's always a no. The government isn't going to invest in volunteers. They think giving a tax break is a fair enough exchange for their time. And maybe it is for things like picking up trash on the side of the highways. But not this. This work is too mentally taxing."

"You took the time off strictly because of burnout?" I asked.

Ron shrugged. "I know it sounds cowardly after everything I just mentioned. But when you're dealing with crises every day, burnout comes quicker than most other jobs. You question your own sanity. Hell, they don't even provide us with as much therapy for our employees as you'd think. Six therapy sessions per calendar year. We need more than one appointment every two months to get through this kind of work."

The room fell silent and we looked at each other.

"You can let me go now, Ron," I said. "I'm sorry for all this. Really. You'll never see me again."

Ron smiled. "I highly doubt that. You just said there's a killer roaming my call center. I *better* see you again, removing that person from my office."

He dropped to a knee and untied the ropes around my legs first, then moving to the one around my torso.

"Sorry for the blow to the head," he said, reaching out a hand to help me get to my feet. "Do you want a ride to the hospital?"

I shook my head. "The dizziness has finally gone away. It's just a throbbing bruise now, it feels. Mostly on the surface."

"Let me get you an ice pack. It's the least I can do."

Ron spun around, and I followed him out of his bedroom. I felt like an idiot as I went down the stairs. Sometimes there are coincidences, and I had to remind myself of that. We returned to the kitchen, where Ron dug an ice pack out of the freezer for me.

"You sure you're okay?" he asked, handing the pack over.

I grabbed it and pressed it against the tender skin on my head. "I'll be alright."

If I had just slept three hours with no issues, then it was unlikely I had a concussion. And if I did, it was mild. No vomiting. No stars in my vision. I didn't even have a headache. At least, I thought so. The pulsing pain from my scalp could have been masking other pains within. But overall, I'd manage.

"Sorry, I can't get you that list," Ron said as I headed for the back door. "A government agency like this doesn't really care what my reasons for handing over such a document to an unauthorized party are. Even for something like aiding in the capture of a murderer, they'll still fire me."

"I understand," I said, reaching for the knob and pulling the door open. "See you soon."

I left without another word, retracing my path to my car. Kody—the dog—yapped at me when I went through the gate. I shot him a wink before leaving for good.

I hopped in my car and drove off, passing by Carissa's house just to make sure it was safe. All looked right, minus the busted door, of course.

With no set destination, I drove to a Walgreens in desperate need of some pain killers. Ibuprofen would have to put up its best fight against the searing sensation on the side of my head.

Once I returned to my car and popped four pills into my mouth, my cell phone buzzed with a call from a restricted number.

"Hello?" I answered.

"Jonny," Kayla said in a grave tone. "I have it."

"Have what?"

"The name you've been looking for."

I jolted upright in my seat, damn near scraping the top of my head against the low ceiling of the Camry.

"How did—" I started, but Kayla cut me off.

"I had to call in some favors," she said. "Nothing that concerns you. But you definitely owe me dinner next time you're in D.C. Let's just say a friend of a friend of a friend works in the records division over at the Health Department. They pulled some information after we found those phone numbers from the deceased. Looks like you were on to something. There were both inbound and outbound calls to the same rep at the call center in Redwood. All four men had spoken exclusively with the same rep, some as late as three days before their deaths."

"Well, who the hell is it?" I asked, ready to jump through my windshield if she didn't say.

Kayla chuckled. "That's the interesting part, Jonny. The name is the same as the one I gave you earlier. I don't know if it's the same person, or some wild coincidence. But the rep's name is William Barnes."

Chapter 36

I couldn't fucking believe it.

We were beyond coincidences. William Barnes was Andrew Stone, and I'd fight to the death proving it was the same person. I'd already been wrong once in this case, which drastically decreased the odds of me being wrong again.

This whole time I'd been wondering what happened to Andrew Stone, and he'd been in Redwood working for the suicide hotline, speaking to the men who had destroyed his life and shattered his innocence as a teenager.

I got out of my car and ran to Ron's front door, pounding my fist until I heard him unlocking it from the other side.

The door swung open, Ron still wide-eyed. "Forget something?"

"William Barnes," I said. "Does he work in your call center?"

Ron's eyes narrowed on me. "Billy? Yes. Why?"

"He spoke with all four of the deceased men in the days leading up to their suicides."

"How could you possibly know that?" Ron asked, panic settling into his voice. He definitely didn't like me knowing more about his call center than he did.

"I told you I still have friends in the CIA," I replied. "But none of that matters right now. I need to speak with William Barnes. Immediately."

Ron rubbed his eyes. "You think Billy murdered Kody?"

"I'm not ready to make that accusation, but he's a common link between all four men. Even if he didn't kill Kody, good chance he knows something."

I absolutely believed "Billy" had murdered Kody, but I wasn't about to hit Ron with that news. If Billy was Andrew Stone, that sealed the deal. Because Andrew Stone had a motive. Those men had ruined his life, made him and his family move away and change their names. Change their identities. Never mind the scars he had to live with all these years after suffering from sexual abuse by these monsters. Shit, I couldn't even fault Andrew Stone for wanting to get his revenge, but I wasn't here to play judge or jury. And I definitely wasn't the one to decide the fairness of Andrew Stone taking these men's lives. They had never received true justice, and Stone wanted to deliver it once and for all. I suppose he and I were cut from the same cloth.

"Is Billy at the office today?" I asked.

Ron raised a finger and turned around, dashing back toward his kitchen and returning with his cell phone. "Billy is a volunteer, so I don't know his set schedule. Let me see."

I watched Ron scroll through his phone. "If not, do you know where he lives?"

"He's not in today," Ron said. "In fact, he's not in for another two weeks."

"Fuck. Where does he live?"

"Jonny, you know I can't tell you that," Ron said with a frown that said *sorry pal, nothing I can do about it.*

I reached into my waistband and whipped out my Glock, cocking it and aiming directly at Ron's face. "This is no longer a question, Ron. Yes, I believe Billy is a murderer. His real name is Andrew Stone, and he was assaulted by players on that championship team. Players who are now dying one by one. One of which we know was murdered. Now give me his fucking address, or I'll shoot you and take it myself."

I didn't think Ron's eyes could grow any wider. Sure, I felt bad for having to resort to this, but time was of the essence. I'd apologize to Ron later. For now, I needed the address even more than I had needed that list of names.

Ron gulped, his cell phone shaking in his hand as he scrolled through it. "Give me a second," he said, his voice cracking.

I didn't lower the gun, but had no plans of shooting Ron. He was just a good-hearted man looking out for his company and career. I had no reason to shoot him. Intimidate, sure. I needed vital information.

"Okay," he said. "Address is 9001 Blue Spruce Road."

"Where is that?" I asked, lowering the gun.

"No idea. Never heard of it."

I tucked my gun away. "Sorry, Ron. I needed that. And now, if you get in trouble, you can tell them I held you at gunpoint to give me that address. You even have it on camera. Cold hard proof." I gestured to the doorbell camera watching our exchange.

Ron let out a nervous laugh. I think he was trying to hold in some tears. "What are you going to do?"

I turned and started down the walkway to my car, looking over my shoulder. "I'm going to catch a killer."

I jogged to my car without another word, fumbling with my cell phone as I sat down and typed the address into Google Maps. 9001 Blue Spruce Road was clear on the north side of Redwood. Beyond the luxurious development where I had visited Ethan Stokes in Northpointe. On the map, the red pin showed the address in the middle of nowhere. It told me twenty minutes to get there, so I got on the road without wasting another second.

Most of my drive was northbound on Highway 97. Once I got on the highway, I called Carissa.

"Jonny?" she answered, her voice sounding both horrified and hopeful at the same time.

"Andrew Stone is still in Redwood," I said. I'm going to find him right now."

"Andrew Stone?" Carissa asked. "What does he have to do with this?"

"I think he has *everything* to do with this. His name was changed to William Barnes. Sounds like everyone calls him Billy Barnes. And Billy Barnes works at the suicide hotline. It just so happens he spoke with all four of the deceased men—including your brother—and he did so in the final days of their lives."

Carissa gasped. "That's impossible. He left with his family all those years ago."

"Well, he came back. And with Kody Holt murdered, I'm willing to bet this was all part of some revenge he's been plotting. He had direct access to these players from the championship team, and I'm willing to bet he's spoken to more than just the four who have passed away. I didn't exactly have time to chat with the call center's manager, so I don't have all the details. Like how long he's been working at the call center or anything like that. But that doesn't really matter to me. If I can catch him by surprise, I'll get him to confess."

"You're going there by yourself?" she asked, the concern elevating in her voice.

"I'll be fine. I have my gun. Plus, he has no idea I'm heading to his house right now, so I have the upper hand."

"Jonny, this is reckless. You can't just confront a murderer on your own."

"Not my first time, and I doubt it will be my last. I'm not worried, and neither should you. I still don't have any proof he was responsible for the murder, but he's definitely involved. If he's not the one, then he'll lead me to who is. Justice for Timmy is right around the corner."

Carissa remained silent at this comment. "Do you want me to call the cops? Where are you even going?"

"Absolutely do not call the cops. I got this. And sorry, but I'm not going to tell you where I'm going, just in case."

Carissa sighed a sound of frustration. "Be careful, Jonny. Okay?"

"I always am. Make sure no one else is shooting my house."

"Don't be a smart ass," she said, and I could hear the slightest hint of a smile in her voice.

We hung up, and I exited the highway. I turned right onto a narrow road with no signage. The map simply labeled it as "Road A."

That's how you knew you'd reached bumfuck Egypt. No street names or numbers. If I kept driving, I'm sure I'd eventually encounter Road B.

But I didn't.

After a two-mile stretch of open road, towering pine trees from the nearby Ochoco National Forest started popping up. After another mile, the trees enveloped me and I couldn't see beyond fifty feet in any direction.

The map said my turn was coming up in a quarter-mile, so I slowed down my car and waited for the turn to appear. I'd almost missed it, if not for a reflective sign attached to the fencing running along the side of the road.

A crooked street sign hung from a post, welcoming me to Blue Spruce Road.

"How the hell did anyone find a place to live out here?"

It was as off the grid as you could hope. I'd be lying if I said I wasn't jealous. This was an introvert's paradise. Complete isolation from the world and its people. All the damned people and their problems.

Even after I turned, I had to navigate a dirt road that zigzagged on bumpy terrain. After another quarter-mile, I saw the house. I was expecting a cabin-like home, but it was a house made of bricks all the way around. It didn't look the most level, so I had to assume he had built this house on his own. Or maybe hired someone from Fiverr to build it for him. Regardless, if he'd lived here and it hadn't collapsed on him, I supposed it had served its purpose.

There was no car present, which meant he wasn't home. It would be impossible to live this secluded and not have a vehicle, especially if he had to work in the city. The dirt road turned into loose gravel as I approached the house, and I parked right outside the front door.

I didn't care if Billy saw my car parked out front should he arrive soon. I had my Glock. After parking, I stepped out and took in a deep breath of the fresh air. To the right of the house was a pile of bricks matching the same style used for the exterior, and I couldn't help wonder if they matched the one currently sitting on my living room couch.

Billy kept little else outside of the house. A couple of rakes, a snow shovel, and a messy pile of firewood next to the bricks.

I strolled up to the front door and pulled out my Glock. Just in case.

No time for knocking, I tried the knob and pushed the door open. Of course, he'd left it unlocked—there wasn't a soul in sight within at least five miles.

The door opened directly into a kitchen, narrowly missing the table to my right. Everything within my immediate view was a minimal setup. The kitchen table only had one seat. The sink looked no bigger than one that belonged in a bathroom, and the adjoined counter space had room for maybe one cutting board. A refrigerator next to the counter was the largest item in the house. There wasn't even a microwave. The kitchen blended into a living room that had a lone recliner. No TV. No radio. A dinner tray stood next to the recliner, covered in papers and an ashtray full of cigarette butts.

I stepped closer to examine the papers and saw what appeared to be diagrams. A breakdown of the electrical system within a key card reader. Odd reading material, especially considering Billy had a job in the call center and didn't need to sneak in.

Then I remembered hearing about the Royal Hotel after Jackson Green had jumped from the roof. The news had mentioned the scanner had malfunctioned for the door leading to the roof access.

I moved toward the back of the house, the wooden floor creaking with every step I took. It was a short hallway that led to a bathroom at the end. The sink, toilet, and shower were cramped into a tight space, a used towel splayed across the floor.

There was only one other door in the hallway that led into Billy's bedroom, which also doubled as an office space. This was the biggest room, perhaps even larger than the combined living room and kitchen area. He had a twin-size bed pushed into one corner, and a broad oak desk in the other. A lone window provided a view to the world outside, and I looked out to see I was still alone in this desolate area of the Oregon woods.

Even more papers lay scattered across the desk. Hundreds, if not thousands, organized into crooked stacks ready to topple over. They were buried under a handful of books on cybersecurity and computer hacking. I didn't need much more than my initial glance to understand what was going on.

And to confirm my deepest fear.

Front and center lay an open, yellowing newspaper from November 1999.

REDWOOD SOARS HIGH! 1999 STATE CHAMPIONS

The headline may as well have slapped me across the face. The main image below the headline showed the team huddled around their coach, who hoisted their trophy in the air.

Below the photo was an article recapping the events of the game. Redwood had fallen down early in the first quarter, tied the game, then fell back again at halftime by a score of 21-10. After the break, they came out and scored twenty-four unanswered points to win the game, 34-21, sealing their first ever state championship.

It was a two-page spread, and on the second page was the official team portrait, likely taken before the season had even started. The caption listed all the names of the players.

Of the thirty players shown, eighteen had X's marked over their faces. Seven players had no markings, their smiles echoing through the tattered paper all these years later. One player had a circle drawn around his face. And four others had both a circle and an X-marked.

My stomach fluttered. None of this was actual proof, but I felt that anticipation of knocking on destiny's door.

I compared the names in the caption to the faces that had been crossed out. None of the names registered with me, so I moved to the ones that had been circled *and* crossed out. That's when it all became crystal clear.

Jackson Green.

Timmy Summers.

Tyrell Marshall.

Kody Holt.

The four X's over their faces stared back at me, urging me to understand this was Billy's playbook, for lack of a better word.

"Shit," I said under my breath. Only one face had a circle around it, and I matched the name of Ethan Stokes to it. "He's not just targeting those who assaulted him. He's targeting everyone he can from the team."

Of the faces that had no markings on them, the only name I recognized belonged to Mason Barker, Redwood's chief of police.

I locked eyes with those of Ethan Stokes in the picture. The tight circle framing his youthful, grinning face. I saw the resemblance to the man I had just enjoyed a glass of lemonade with a few days ago.

With so many of the faces crossed out without a circle, I had to assume they were people Billy thought impossible to reach. Perhaps they were no longer in Redwood. Lucky for them.

Beyond the newspaper, I examined the other papers on the desk. The collection included printouts of social media posts, pictures, and what appeared to be candid photographs of several men. After flipping through many faces I didn't recognize, I found the ones I knew.

I raised the newspaper and spotted a map of Redwood beneath. Circles were drawn with names next to them. The names matched those of the deceased men, along with Ethan Stokes.

A couple others jumped out to me and caused my heart to thump wildly against my chest. One circle was in the neighborhood I had just left, and the scrawled handwriting only said *Timmy's Sis.*

And the other conspicuous circle was around my house. The label Billy so kindly assigned to me was *PROBLEM!*

Okay, so Billy saw me as a threat to whatever this scheme was. I still had no physical proof he had done anything, but I couldn't stop looking.

The desk had a single drawer hanging from the right side, so I pulled it open. Three boxes of ammunition lay inside, but I saw no gun. He had a police scanner that was currently turned off. The ammo was .223 Remington. The exact type used in most semi-automatic rifles. Lying innocently on top of the boxes, however, was a car key with a faded Ford logo on both sides.

Kody Holt drove a Ford F-150. I had no way of knowing if this key belonged to Kody's truck, but my instincts were blaring frantic alarms inside.

I slammed the drawer shut and continued sifting through the papers on the desk. To the left of the newspaper, I found recent photos of Ethan Stokes. Definitely candid. He was out in town with his wife and kids. Eating at restaurants, enjoying ice cream. Even walking into the movie theater.

Beneath the photos was a handwritten list that froze my blood. The top of it said *Ethan Wife (rich bitch).*

Upon closer inspection, it wasn't a list, but a schedule:

8am - drop kids at school

8:30 am - coffee shop. Always orders a caramel frap

9:15 am - yoga

10:30 am - breakfast at cafe with yoga friends

Noon - miscellaneous...shopping, movies, some sort of activity with friends

2 pm - tennis lessons at rec

3:30 pm - pick up kids from school

4 pm - take kids to piano lessons

5 pm - take kids to swim lessons

6:30 pm - return home

On a different paper was another schedule, this one belonging to Ethan. It recapped what I now assumed was his typical day. He had golf and lunch in the mornings. What the fuck did these wealthy people actually do to earn money? The hours of four to six in the afternoon were circled, however, noting Ethan was always home at this time, no matter what he had going on during the day.

A scribbled message beneath the schedule read *make sure wife and kids enter rec for swimming lessons then pounce!*

I checked my watch. The day had completely gotten away from me, and it was already four o'clock. Billy wasn't at work, or here at home, *and* the gun I presumed he had was nowhere to be seen.

I didn't jump to conclusions often, but the pieces of this puzzle were appearing obvious. I dropped the papers back on the desk and bolted out of the room and through the house until barreling out of the front door—the *only* door.

Ethan Stokes was next on Billy's list, and I had to beat him to his house.

Chapter 37

I couldn't tip off Ethan Stokes that a murderer was headed to his house with plans of killing him.

If I had, Ethan would flee, which would only prolong the inevitable. I also couldn't hide inside his house, at least not to his knowledge. The less he knew, the better.

I had to treat this like a documentarian filming nature. The lion would maul the zebra to death, yet the film had to keep rolling. No interference.

But that wasn't entirely my plan. I wouldn't sit there and watch Billy kill Ethan, but I had to let the initial phases play out. My timing had to be impeccable. Interfere too early, and Billy could react recklessly, putting both myself and Ethan at increased risk. Wait too long, and well, you know.

I didn't take any chances when I pulled into Ethan's neighborhood, Northpointe. Billy knew my car, and if he saw it anywhere near Ethan's house, my chances of trapping him would fly out the window.

So, I parked four blocks away and had to walk nearly ten minutes to Ethan's house. Houses weren't stacked upon each other in this affluent neighborhood, and it explained why several homeowners had golf carts parked outside. The only golf carts I had seen in my hometown of Laredo belonged to the Casa Blanca Golf Course, where I worked one summer as a teenager doing landscape work.

Several pine trees towered over the neighborhood, providing a natural Oregon backdrop for the residents of Northpointe. I had arrived on Ethan's block, White Oak Way, at 4:42, worried I was too late.

But I wasn't. There were no other cars parked outside Ethan's house, so I kept my distance while hiding behind a tree trunk that kept me out of sight from any wandering eyes. The nearest house, besides Ethan's, was about fifty yards behind me.

I'd have a thirty yard dash to Ethan's front door if I needed to make a run for it. I was still fast, as I had been for all of my life, and calculated I could sprint that distance in five seconds, maybe six because I hadn't stretched my legs.

The evening was hot, sweat forming around my crown. My t-shirt clung to my back, and the Glock tucked into my waistband no longer felt cool against my flesh.

I hoped I was wrong about Billy showing up here. Maybe he was out doing anything else. Killing a man in broad daylight was gutsy. Visibility was a killer's greatest downfall, and the darkness of night only helped get away with such a crime. I reflected on the men who had already died. Timmy shot himself in the morning. Jackson jumped from the hotel roof at lunchtime. Tyrell hanged himself, but I wasn't entirely sure when he had done that. His wife had reported finding him in the morning, so it was safe to presume he had hanged himself in the middle of the night. And Kody Holt had left his house at night time before turning up dead at the high school parking lot the next day.

Could Billy—Andrew Stone—really have talked the other men into killing themselves? As an employee for the hotline, he'd have access to endless training about navigating the human mind through suicidal thoughts. Like anything good, there were always some who used their gifts for evil. How long was he at this grand scheme? To go through the trouble of landing a job with the hotline, only to hope he'd get lucky one day and speak to one of the men when they called in. From there, he'd have to develop trust with them.

During my sitdown with Avery at the call center, she had mentioned many reps would make outbound calls to follow up with people they had spoken with. Billy could have done this under the muse of kindness, and further developing that trust. It was a long, complicated game to play. Developing the trust, all while nudging them toward suicide.

Billy wasn't on the roof the day Jackson jumped, but had his words pushed the former star wide receiver?

Just like there were no other fingerprints on the gun Timmy used to take his life. Billy could have pulled the trigger via sheer manipulation.

The human mind was one of the greatest wonders of the world. It was also incredibly fragile, especially for those suffering through crisis. Or a disease like CTE.

Maybe Billy had convinced the first three men to take their own lives, but ran into issues with Kody Holt. He'd have to take matters into his own hands, and still tried to frame it as a suicide.

There were still too many questions, and while it was obvious Billy had been involved with each of the men's deaths, I had no evidence. A future trial was the least of my concerns. The police would need to come up with the evidence to present to a jury. For me, if I was about to encounter Billy, I needed the proof before facing a situation where I might have to pull the trigger on him. I had no interest in killing an innocent man based on a hunch.

But everything I had just seen at his remote house in the woods suggested otherwise. Did it even matter if Billy was the one who physically carried out the murder or not? Had he brainwashed those men into taking their lives, did that not make him a murderer, regardless?

The clock had struck five, and my hope was growing by the second that I had this all wrong. That hope promptly dissolved when a beat up car turned the corner from the opposite end of the block. A car that certainly didn't fit in a neighborhood like this. The engine rattled as it slowed to a crawl, brakes screeching when it stopped along the curb directly in front of the Stokes house.

Adrenaline filled my veins, heart jack hammering in my ribcage.

A man opened the car door, looked around the neighborhood, and proceeded up the driveway, where he disappeared along the side of Ethan's house. No knocking on the front door, but not hiding his car, either.

The face looked familiar. But I was too far to know for certain.

The car would have been visible for Ethan's doorbell camera to see. Rookie mistake if you're about to enter someone's house to kill them. Maybe it was someone else, but the splatters of mud along the base of the car had to be from driving up and down that dirt road every day.

The man disappeared completely from my sight, so I stepped out from behind the tree and dashed across the street to look inside the car. Sure enough, I saw a similar printed out map lying on the passenger seat. In the backseat, on the floor, lay an AR-15.

That was the gun that had fired all those rounds into my house. I was certain of it.

The car belonged to Andrew Stone, and he was here to kill Ethan Stokes. I ducked low and followed the same path he had taken to Ethan's backyard.

Chapter 38

As I navigated along the side of Ethan's house, it had become apparent I didn't know what I was dealing with.

Trying to form a clear picture of all the events that had happened in Redwood over the past few weeks made it impossible. On the surface, they made Andrew Stone look like a mad genius. The patience he needed to deliver all this death was unmatched by anything I'd ever witnessed.

Yet, he seemed like an absolute loose cannon. Kidnapping Carissa from her house in broad daylight. Parking his car right in front of his next victim's house. Sometimes smart people lacked the most basic common sense. This could have been that. Or criminals just love the rush. It's a high for them. What's the point of doing evil if there's no risk of getting caught?

Billy would have kept this dark secret, too. Walking in and out every day to a call center that helped people in crisis. Smiling at his coworkers. His managers. Even himself. Hell, he'd probably actually helped plenty of people avoid taking their lives. As long as they weren't people who had harmed him in the past.

Those people would get his wrath. His calm, calculated wrath.

Because of all this uncertainty, and the fact he had left an AR-15 in the car, I wasn't sure how to proceed. All I knew was that I needed to intervene as quickly as possible. Hiding and watching was no longer an option. Billy came here to kill Ethan Stokes. Whether it was doing it himself, or forcing the man to take his own life, it didn't matter. Plus, the wife and kids would be home within the next two hours, so he had a sharp deadline.

I reached the familiar backyard on my tiptoes and spotted the table me and Ethan had shared spiked lemonade during my last visit. Billy was nowhere in sight, but I didn't want to reveal myself yet.

I remained perched along the corner of the house, scanning the backyard for any movement. Nothing. Not even the dog.

My breathing under control, I peeked around the corner and saw the backdoor. I didn't have the best angle, but it looked like it had been left ajar. An inch or two.

"Shit," I muttered under my breath. I had to make a move. I pulled out my Glock and scanned the yard one more time. If Billy was hiding in a bush in the far back, I'd be dead once I stepped around the corner. But the door being just cracked open suggested I not worry about that. Billy didn't come here to hide in the bushes. And he certainly didn't come to make friendly chatter on the front porch.

I had always moved stealthily around the house as a child. For as big as I was, I navigated with the grace of a ballerina. This all started out of respect for my mother, who would sleep in late after working overnight double shifts with her cleaning crew at commercial buildings. I never wanted to wake her by creaking the floorboards or slamming the cabinet doors in the kitchen.

So I learned every creak on the floor and could dance around them without even thinking about it. But our cabinet and cupboard doors all had those annoying magnetic latches that snapped into place. Obnoxious, especially in a silent house. Instead of closing them, I'd leave them cracked open two inches so the magnets wouldn't attract. No sound. And mom kept snoozing.

That's all I thought of when I stepped out from around the corner and saw the backdoor left open exactly two inches. A door could be closed silently with enough precision, but leaving it open guaranteed no sound.

I pressed my back against the house and moved along the siding toward the door, Glock held at the ready in front of my chest. No one charged at me from the bushes once I was within arm's reach of the back door, so I stopped and craned my neck for a view through the glass door.

I saw the kitchen, but no one inside. My heart drummed, instincts sounding the alarm. There was no guarantee Billy would go inside and take his time. He could have shot Ethan already. The nature of the prior deaths made me believe otherwise, but Billy didn't always play by even his own rules.

Craning my neck further, I saw no one in the vicinity inside the house.

"Okay," I whispered. "No more fucking around."

I balled a fist and gently nudged the door open with my knuckles, not wanting to leave any fingerprints on the glass. I braced for the door to creak open, but no sound came from the sturdy hinges. God bless the new-build home.

The air grew more still—and somehow hotter—as I stepped into the house. I felt the rush of cool air conditioning, but maybe the adrenaline kept me sweating despite it. I held my breath and listened.

Silence.

I so desperately wanted to call out Ethan's name, but didn't know what that might lead to.

The kitchen split in two directions. To my left was the dining room, and to my right was a hallway that led to other parts of the house. If Billy had let himself in, he could be hiding anywhere, just waiting for his opportunity to jump out and end Ethan.

I inched toward the dining room on my left and heard a clatter from upstairs, followed by the mumble of a voice.

Then a second voice.

"He's here," I said, and relief flooded my senses, knowing Ethan was still alive.

No longer worried about Billy attacking me on the main level, I hurried through the dining room and found it connected to the living room at the front of the house. A staircase was near the front door, leading both up and down. The voices grew louder from above, but remained inaudible.

Sweat dripped down my back as I started my ascent up the stairs. The stairs spiraled, so I couldn't really see where I was going until reaching the top landing. Once there, I hid against the wall to focus my hearing on the conversation.

"I'm not going to swallow it," Ethan said in a desperate voice. "One more and it's going to kill me."

"That's the point," the other man said, his voice low with a subtle rasp. "And that's why you're going to swallow all the pills in that bottle. Every last one of them. Are we clear?"

"Why are you doing this, Andrew?" Ethan asked, his voice trembling. "I didn't even hurt you that day."

Andrew.

That was all the confirmation I needed.

Andrew laughed mockingly. "You never hurt me, Stokesy. But your father did. Let me ask, did your lawyer dad buy you this house with all his money? Or did he just give it to you for the fun of it?"

"Now this is about my dad's money?" Ethan asked.

"Of course not, you dipshit," Andrew said. "Your dad got all your friends off. I got raped by your demented teammates while everyone else watched it happen. And not a single one of them had to face justice. Case dismissed. Are you *fucking* kidding me? Not only did they all walk, they got to go about their lives like nothing ever happened. And I had to move away. Do you think my family wanted to move? We had it made here."

"Andrew, I'm sorry," Ethan pleaded. "If I had known what was going on that night, I'd have stopped it. But it all happened so fast. And we were all in shock. None of us believed what was happening. It was a surreal moment."

Andrew laughed again, a maniac sound that sent shivers down my sweating spine. "Shock. How the fuck do you think I felt?! And you could have spoken up at any time. You just admitted you saw what happened. But at no point during that sham of a trial did any of you other pieces of shit think to defend me. That's why everyone on that team is going to pay. Timmy didn't do anything to me that night, either, but look at him now."

Hearing Timmy's name made my rage boil. This sick excuse of a man had no reason to speak Carissa's brother's name.

"We can work something out," Ethan said, the desperation in his voice growing thicker by the second. "Just put the gun down."

I still couldn't see anything, but the picture was becoming clear.

"We won't be working anything out," Andrew said, confidence dripping from each word. "Your money can't help you now. There's only one price for what you all put me through. *That's* what I'm here to collect on."

"Andrew, please have some reason. Killing me isn't going to change what happened to you. It doesn't reverse it. And you'll never truly find peace."

Another laugh from Andrew. "I'm not killing you. You are. Now swallow the fucking pills before I shove them down your throat with this gun. You're dying tonight, but I'm giving you the choice of how to do it. Do you think your wife and kids would rather find you unconscious on the bathroom floor or with a bullet through your head?"

Silence.

It was time to make a move.

I stepped out from around the corner, taking a left toward the voices. The room at the end of the hallway was the bathroom they were standing in. Andrew's back was to me, his right arm raised with the gun in hand.

If I had just two seconds, I could've charged him and brought him down, and this matter would have been settled with fists.

Unfortunately, Ethan saw me through the gap between the doorway and Andrew's body, his eyes widening immediately.

I wasn't expecting Andrew to turn around so quickly. When he did, I fired a rushed shot that sailed past his head and shattered the mirror hanging on the bathroom wall. Andrew also blasted his pistol in my direction, causing me to tumble backward and swing back around the corner to the stairwell.

I lost my footing on the top step and rolled like a ball five steps down.

"YOU!" Andrew shouted as I scrambled to my feet. The thunder of footsteps stomped down the hallway toward the stairs. I fired a shot upward, knowing damn well it wasn't Ethan running after me.

That shot bought me just enough time to turn around and dash down the rest of the stairs. I knew better than to get into a shootout with someone holding the upper ground. Ethan's life was now left to chance. Andrew could either go back and kill him before coming after me, or cut right to the chase.

He chose the latter and fired two shots toward the main level. Thanks to the spiral staircase, the rounds were nowhere near me, but I caught a couple of shards of hardwood flying from the floor.

Footsteps rumbled down the stairs, which meant Ethan's life had been spared. For now. I blew a quick sigh of relief at this news, but shit was still hitting the fan.

Hopefully, Ethan was locking himself safely in a bedroom. Or better, loading up a gun to come help me.

I had no time to worry about his decisions upstairs, and backed into the kitchen while Andrew rushed down the steps. He fired randomly upon reaching the bottom landing, likely hoping to get lucky by accidentally shooting me.

From the kitchen, I backed up toward the side that opened to the hallway. Since the space had two doorways on opposite sides, I could run circles between the hallway and kitchen.

Andrew made no attempts to be silent, a critical mistake on his part. I listened as his shoes clopped along the hardwood floor, approaching the kitchen.

"You son of a bitch!" he shouted, voice echoing down the hallway. "Why are you even here? You've been fucking everything up!"

My inner smart ass wanted desperately to speak back. Taunt this poor soul before ending his life. But I couldn't. Not yet.

I heard the quick clatter of him reloading and cocking his pistol, a spent cartridge falling to the floor and getting a swift kick as it bounced into the kitchen.

"Come out, come out, wherever you are!" Andrew screamed. He sounded like he was rather enjoying himself. "What's the matter, tough guy? Can't defend yourself without your precious Carissa? I should've just fucked her when I had the chance! Silly me for thinking anyone in this world is good for their word. And silly you for actually driving back to Redwood. I hope it was worth it, because you're going to die today."

His voice grew louder as he approached the kitchen, causing me to inch closer to the other doorway connected to the hallway.

"Who are you anyway?" Andrew asked, lowering his voice to a normal speaking tone. "Seems odd for an outsider to come into town to defend all these sick bastards who ruined my life. Say something, dammit! Come out and fight me like a man."

Oh, how I wanted to. But the difference between me and guys like Andrew Stone was my understanding of picking the right spot to make a move. Loose cannons like this guy acted through their emotions. He wanted to kill me, spit in my face while watching the life slip from eyes. Rage was like a wild bull, impossible to tame without proper medication.

The more I let him speak, the more pissed off he became, which would only increase my odds. I was calm. Heart rate a tad above normal. The adrenaline had subsided. I reached a level of concentration where it was just him and me in this house. Sure, I could hear the wind chimes clanging outside from the gentle breeze. Even heard the moaning of the floorboards above my head as Ethan was surely moving around in a panic.

But that was part of my heightened senses. My mind registered these sounds, but my focus was exclusively on Andrew, his words, and the sound of each step he took.

Andrew fired a round that lodged into the wall directly to my left. He hadn't entered the kitchen yet, but seemed to know the general direction I might be hiding.

I crouched next to the counter, spotting a glass cookie jar. It was clear and cylindrical, filled with delicious chocolate chip cookies. Without hesitation, I placed my hand behind the cookie jar and thrust it forward off the counter. It sailed straight toward the back door and shattered upon impact.

Andrew fired another round, this one making the back door explode into shards of glass. I stayed low and somersaulted out from behind the counter, planting a knee on the floor and taking my first clear shot at Andrew Stone.

My slug caught him square in the stomach, but he fired at the same time, making my head ring from the cacophony of simultaneous gun blasts. My shoulder burned like it had just been branded. I saw blood oozing from the side of my vision, but Andrew remained in front of me with a twisted smile on his face.

He held his free hand against his stomach, blood spurting from between his fingers. Yet he still held on to the gun and aimed it back at me. He was off balance, so I fell to the side, pain shooting up and down my arm as I lay sideways on the kitchen floor. I still had my gun tight in my grip and quickly lined up a second shot. I aimed for his torso again and pulled the trigger.

It missed the target, but caught him in the groin.

"FUUUUUCK!" Andrew screamed at the top of lungs.

He dropped his gun and fell to his knees, one hand on his gut, the other on his crotch. Blood seeped from his teeth as he flashed a crimson smile in my direction.

"You motherfucker," he said, letting himself fall backwards.

I rose to my feet, the right side of my upper body completely numb. Blood dripped down my arm and back, but I couldn't see the bullet wound. I grew lightheaded, but not to the point of fainting.

I shuffled toward Andrew and stood over him, gun still in hand.

There he was. Live in the flesh. The man I'd been looking for this whole time. Still boyish in the face. Clean cut. Curly brown hair. He maintained an athletic build and probably could have given me a run for my money had he been larger.

He looked up at me, a blankness in his brown eyes that scanned my face. "Fuck you," he said, and spit a clump of blood that landed weakly on my shoe.

"Love you, too," I replied, shaking my head. "Was this all worth it, Andrew? Or should I call you Billy?"

Andrew smiled even wider. "Totally worth it."

I frowned. "So you wanted to die?"

Andrew laughed, a hoarse sound that turned into a cough as he choked on his own blood. "Wow, big *and* smart! I've wanted to die since I was a teenager. But could never make it happen on my own. Came really close lots of times, but it's hard, you know? It seems easy on the surface. Put the gun to your head and pull the trigger. Swallow a bunch of pills and lie down for a nap. Tie a noose and just let yourself hang out. Shit, even jumping off a building shouldn't be that complex, right? It's literally just one more step. We take how many thousands of steps each day? And just one more can end it all when you're standing on the edge. But you know what, you big dope? It ain't easy. Your brain. Your instincts. They all kick into a different gear to convince you otherwise."

"You made those men kill themselves in the same ways you tried and failed?" I asked, just wanting to keep him talking.

Andrew raised a finger. "Ding, ding, ding! You really are good. Did they teach you that during your closed-door meetings with Ron? You must not be that smart, because you looked right at me that day you were in the call center. Fucking dope!"

That was it. He looked familiar because I had seen him in passing.

"You walked right past me in the hallway," Andrew said, still grinning. "Made quick eye contact and you nodded. If I could have just shot you then, everything would still be running smoothly. I should've shot you the moment they caught you snooping around Timmy's house."

My lightheadedness grew worse with each passing second. I was losing too much blood, most of my shirt drenched with a mixture of that and perspiration. Blood, sweat, and tears. Right?

"So, you really did all of this," I said. "But how? How did you make them take their own lives?"

Andrew grew still, and his smile started to fade. The blood spilling from his stomach was now pooling beneath his body. He'd lost way more than me, and the flow appeared to be slowing.

"You can do anything with a gun pointed at someone's face," Andrew said, letting out a weak cackle. "Timmy was easy. Dude was already off his rocker. I told him if he didn't shoot himself, I'd fuck and kill his sister. He didn't need any more convincing. Jackson was more of a process, but I led him to the roof that day and was standing ten feet behind him. Just in case he chickened out. Threatened to kill his family if he didn't jump. See, love gets you killed. Love gives people a weakness. I showed up at Tyrell's house that night. We had a long talk in his garage. See, he was actually worried about me going back to the police. I was making shit up about having pictures and proof of what he'd done. And he bought it. He was even easier, seeing as his family was sleeping right inside from where we had our chat. Fastened the noose myself for him."

"And Kody Holt fought back," I said. "That's why you had to kill him."

Andrew swallowed. His throat grew slightly swollen. "I thought Kody would be a good partner for me. Kind of guy who lived on the edge. I wanted his help getting the others. When he said no, I told him he had to go. We saw how that ended for him. Maybe I should have just asked you. Look at you. Fearless. Not the slightest intimidated after all the notes. The package. Even the bullets for your house. You're still here. I'd have been halfway to Florida by now."

Andrew's eyes were turning glossy as he stared at the ceiling. The room was spinning around me and I felt off balance. I leaned against the kitchen counter, and this prompted a pathetic laugh from Andrew on the floor.

"Look at us," he said. "We're both dying. See you on the other side?"

He rolled his head back and forth, giggling at the ceiling.

My breathing grew labored. I dropped to a knee, then eventually a second one. When my thighs couldn't hold me up any more, I sat on the floor and leaned back against the cabinets.

All I could think about was Carissa. Her brother never took his life. He was murdered. They all were. As long as I could pull through, I'd get to tell her everything Andrew just admitted. Justice was served, even at the possible expense of my life.

I'd survived deadly operations in the Middle East. Just to see my life end on a kitchen floor in Redwood, Oregon.

Life truly was unpredictable.

The thoughts of Carissa gave way to my mother. I wanted her. Needed her. Her presence consumed me.

I felt at peace as I drifted away...

Chapter 39

I woke up in a hospital room, the sun bright and obnoxious as my brain pounded.

Carissa sat in the chair against the window, head tilted back, mouth agape as she slept. How long had she been here? Hell, how long had *I* been here?

A machine beeped at the rate of my heartbeat. Tubes ran up and down my arms. My right shoulder felt like it had taken a pounding from a prime Mike Tyson for fifteen rounds.

I cleared my throat, my tongue like sandpaper in my mouth. Whatever guttural sound came out was enough to startle Carissa awake.

"Jonny!" she cried, jumping out of the chair and wiping a trail of drool from her cheek. "You're up!"

She ran toward me and pressed a button on the remote I hadn't noticed lying next to my head. Her eyes were bloodshot with dark circles beneath. She caressed my arm, running her fingers up and down, right next to the mess of tubes.

I parted my lips to speak, but everything was so dry I couldn't.

A knock came from the door, and a nurse entered. She wore dark blue scrubs and a welcoming grin.

"Good morning, Mr. Mendez," she said. "Glad to see you're awake. You were incredibly dehydrated."

Fuck me. Those were words I never wanted to hear.

"We ran an IV, but you probably feel parched." She grabbed a container from the table on my left, and jammed the straw between my coarse lips. I sucked in the purest tasting water I'd ever had, my mouth and throat promptly thanking me.

I probably drank for a solid twenty seconds before pulling my face back.

"Feel better?" the nurse asked.

"Yes," I replied, looking between the nurse and Carissa, who stood on my right with her hands clasped beneath her chin. "What happened? How long have I been out?"

The nurse batted her eyes at me. "First off, hello. My name is Emily, and I'll be taking care of you today. Do you remember anything from last night, Mr. Mendez?"

I stretched my neck as the details came back. "Some of it. I was at Ethan Stokes's house. Chasing Andrew Stone. We got into a shootout and both took a bullet. I remember little after that."

"Very good," Emily said. "Your memory is fine, so I'm sure you'll remember more as time passes. No head trauma. You were incredibly lucky last night, Mr. Mendez. The bullet went into your upper trapezius muscle. No damage to any joints or bones. Another two inches and it would have severed your jugular. Since it was so close, you suffered excessive blood loss. You probably would've been fine, but you were incredibly dehydrated and your stomach appeared empty. Not a good combination."

"I didn't get much sleep, either," I said, rubbing my forehead. "Was running on fumes."

The nurse gave a warming smile. "Well, someone was looking out for you last night, or else you wouldn't be here right now. Let me refill your water and order you some breakfast. Food in your system will have you feeling much better. Your vitals have been steady, and the doctor sees no reason why you can't go home tonight."

"Thank you, Emily," I said, and she turned away to leave me and Carissa alone. I rolled my head to my right, only able to move it a couple of inches thanks to my neck's swelling. "What happened to everyone else?"

"You mean Andrew Stone?"

"Yes. And Ethan. Did he make it out okay?"

"Ethan saved your life," Carissa said, her eyes studying me. "I spoke to him last night. After the ambulances and police all left. He was in a state of shock, as you can imagine. His wife and kids showed up to quite the scene, but he told me everything that happened. He called the police while you and Andrew were playing Wild West in the kitchen. They showed up minutes after you'd been shot."

I let out a relived sigh. "Oh, thank God. A witness for once that I wasn't in the wrong."

"More than a witness, Jonny. Ethan has cameras all over his house. The entire sequence of events is all recorded and has already been shared with the police."

I couldn't help but smile. Things rarely went my way. Usually it was just me in the middle of bloody carnage. Naturally, they wanted to blame the big guy for whatever had happened.

"Why were you at Ethan's anyway?" I asked.

"Santos told me what happened. Told me to wait to show up until the authorities cleared out. It was a gamble driving up there, not knowing if Ethan would even talk. But he was good friends with my brother in high school, so he was happy to tell me everything."

Another knock came from the door, and in stepped Officer Santos.

"Well, look who finally decided to wake up," he said, holding a paper coffee cup in hand. He closed the door behind him and crossed to stand bedside.

"Good morning, officer," I said. "I take it you need an official statement from me."

Santos took a sip of his coffee and shook his head. "I do. But we can deal with that later. I just wanted to make sure you're okay first. Nurse called the station and said you're awake, so I volunteered to come take your statement." His lips parted into a grin he couldn't contain. "Chambers and Roman are walking around with their tails tucked between their legs. Chief Barker is still trying to figure out what the hell happened. He wasn't involved at all...surprise to me."

I laughed for the first time in days. The thought of Officer Roman, in particular, having to face reality that I was never the bad guy brought a satisfaction I couldn't refuse. Maybe I'd send him flowers as a joke. Asshole.

They both joined my laughter, which sent fresh waves of pain up my shoulder. "So what happened to Andrew Stone?"

"He's dead, Jonny," Santos said. "They rushed him to the hospital, tried to resuscitate, but ultimately failed. It's too bad. We would have loved to see him stand trial for what he'd done."

"You saw the video footage from Ethan's house?" I asked, raising a brow.

"Sure did," Santos replied. "It wasn't just video. Had audio, too. Not the best quality, but we heard everything Stone confessed in the kitchen. Took some digging, but we found where he lived. Went to his house and found all the evidence an officer could dream of. The notes, maps, police scanner. All of it. Even if your encounter hadn't been caught on tape, his house revealed plenty. Part of our prodding around led us to a Ron Hartman. He wanted to make sure I said 'thank you' on his behalf."

I nodded. "You can tell him 'you're welcome.'"

We all laughed again, and I craned my neck to the left to lessen the pain from the subtle movement.

"Well," Santos said. "They told me you'll be here all day. I've been up all night and could use some sleep. I'll come back this afternoon for your official statement, okay?"

"Sounds good, officer. Get some rest. I've apparently been sleeping for fourteen hours, so I doubt I'll be drifting off any time soon."

Santos nodded and knocked on the rolling table next to me before leaving the room.

I looked back at Carissa, who had inched closer. She leaned over me. "Jonny, I'm not sure how I can ever thank you. Santos told me what Andrew said about Timmy. How he wasn't involved with what they did to him that night." Tears rolled down her face. "He was always going to kill him, though, wasn't he? I guess I can have closure now, knowing his killer is dead. But it will always eat me alive knowing my brother was innocent and his life was taken just for being a pawn in Andrew's game."

She buried her head into my chest and wept uncontrollably. More pain burned in my shoulder as I lifted my arm to embrace her, but I didn't care. Her body jolted as she cried for the next minute. When she finally raised her head, those hazel eyes locked with mine. The tension was immediate, and neither of us could stop ourselves.

I grabbed her head and pulled her in. Her lips were salty from the tears, but still sweet underneath. Our tongues intertwined as we both pressed deeper. Her hands ran through my hair, pulling and tugging, nails digging into my scalp. The beeping from the heart monitor sped up, and that's when we pulled away.

Carissa laughed. "Making your heart skip a beat?"

I smiled, not loosening my grip on her arm, and pulled her back in. "It's worth it."

We kissed again, though not as intensely.

"You probably need a place to stay when they let you out of here," Carissa said. "Your house is in shambles. You're welcome to crash at my place."

She spoke these words with a mixture of hesitation and confidence, like she genuinely didn't know how I'd respond.

"Thank you," I said. "That sounds perfect. I'll stay tonight, but I'm most likely leaving town tomorrow."

"Leaving?!" Carissa shot straight up. "Why? You need to recover. You can't just leave after everything that happened."

I reached out for her hand, and she placed it in mine. "I'm sorry to say I've been in these situations before. It's best to just leave. If I stay, the town treats me like a hero. And that's not what I try to be. I don't want to be in the news, or have random people stopping me while I'm in town. Being off the grid is my sweet spot. I have a burner phone, and now it's time to get rid of it. Move on."

"Where will you go?" she asked, sorrow slipping into her voice.

"I don't know. I usually just travel around until I find somewhere I like. Redwood is honestly a rather big town compared to what I'm used to. Might need to go somewhere smaller. My nephew is starting college this fall, so I may go spend a couple days visiting him."

"What about everything here?" Carissa asked. I could tell what she really wanted to say was *what about me?* But she didn't. As much as we'd been through, even with our passionate make out sessions, our romance never got legs under it. And that was fine with me. I never planned on staying in Redwood for long.

"I have some matters to wrap up," I said. "I'll need to call Eddie and tell him what happened to the house. Hopefully he knows some guys who can help fix it up. With Andrew confessing to shooting the house, I'd imagine insurance will cover all that. Besides that, I'll just need to say goodbye to you and the Walkers. I'll miss all of you. But I just can't stick around. I hope you can understand that."

Carissa nodded. "It's hard, but I do."

We held hands and stared into each other's eyes. I liked her. And in some alternate universe, I could probably love her the way she deserved.

But this wasn't that universe. Not with danger always following me.

Buried Truth

If you enjoyed *I Hear You*, don't miss Jonny's next thrilling adventure in *Buried Truth*.

Join Jonny as he tracks down the truth behind his nephew's sinister changes after starting at a new college.

The deeper he digs, the more bodies he finds.

Jonny thought it would be a simple visit—grab dinner with his nephew, catch up, maybe hit the city. But when Andres shows up late, flustered, and distant, something feels off. Then Jonny hears whispers: missing students. A secretive group called Insight. No answers.

Driven by instinct and a growing sense of dread, Jonny starts digging. What he finds is worse than he imagined—rituals in the woods, silence among the students, a leader with too much power, and a university that looks the other way. Andres is in deep. And Jonny might be too late.

The cult demands loyalty. Dissent means death. And now, Jonny's the one being hunted.

Fast-paced, chilling, and razor-sharp—perfect for fans of *The Secret History* and *Don't Worry Darling*.

Order *Buried Truth* today at mybook.to/BuriedTruthJM3

GET EXCLUSIVE BONUS STORIES!

Connecting with readers is the best part of this job. Releasing a book into the world is a truly frightening moment every time it happens! Hearing your feedback, whether good or bad, goes a long way in shaping future projects and helping me grow as a writer. I also like to take readers behind the scenes on occasion and share what is happening in my wild world of writing. If you're interested, please consider joining my mailing list. If you do, I'll send you a free time travel thriller as a thank you!

You can get your content **for free,** by signing up at BookHip.com/KAWWBK

Author's Note

This book is the twenty-fifth full length published novel of my career. That milestone hasn't really hit me until writing this note. Twenty-five books?! Twelve-year-old Andre wouldn't believe it all came true, but here we are.

It has been quite the ride. And to think it's taken this many books to feel like I've finally hit a groove. I'm still waiting to become an "overnight success" nine years into this career. Maybe that's in the near future. Who knows? All I *do* know is something feels different with this Jonny Mendez series. Like everything I've learned about writing and storytelling is all coming together.

If you've seen the Disney movie *Soul*, you'll remember the scenes where the main character is "in the zone." Writing these Jonny books is very much like that for me. It's fresh. Inspired. And, if I may be honest with you, it feels like nothing can stop me when I'm at the keyboard working on these books.

Like any creator, maybe I'm way off the mark. We're always too close to our art to understand how it will be received. That's ultimately up to you, the reader. Speaking of, thank you.

Some of you have been with me since book number one. Or maybe you just found me because of this series. Either way, I owe you nothing but my eternal gratitude for taking a shot on me. May we have another twenty-five books together!

Now for the thank you part.

To Melissa, my editor. It has been an absolute treat working with you over the past several books. You always bring fresh ideas to make the story stronger. And know what I'm *trying* to say in the parts where I wasn't so clear.

To the Gonzalez Gang, my second family. Your engagement and encouragement never go unnoticed. Thank you for all you do!

To Arielle, Felix, and Selena. By the time you're old enough to read these books, my only hope is that you'll understand what all these long hours were for. Creating a dream life isn't easy, and I hope seeing both your mother and I working tirelessly to make it happen will rub off on you.

And to Natasha. My love. My final editor. Life has been interesting. And busy. Like, extremely busy. Yet, we power through it all thanks to you. Cheers to the day we can look back and laugh at all the struggles that got us where we want to be.

Andre Gonzalez

May 30, 2025

Enjoy this book?

You can make a difference!

Reviews are the most helpful tools in getting new readers for any books. I don't have the financial backing of a New York publishing house and can't afford to blast my book on billboards or bus stops.

(Not yet!)

That said, your honest review can go a long way in helping me reach new readers. If you've enjoyed this book, I'd be forever grateful if you could spend a couple minutes leaving it a review (it can be as short as you like) on the Amazon page. You can jump right to the page by using the link below:

https://mybook.to/IHearYou

Thank you so much!

Also by Andre Gonzalez

Jonny Mendez Series:

Never Look Back (#1)

I Hear You (#2)

Buried Truth (#3)

Arielle Lucila Series:

Time Fugitive (#5)

Time Roller (#4)

Dirty Money (#3)

Secrets in the Vault (#2)

Angel Assassin (#1)

Wealth of Time Series:

Time of Fate (#6)

Zero Hour (#5)

Keeper of Time (#4)

Bad Faith (#3)

Warm Souls (#2)

Wealth of Time (#1)

Road Runners (Short Story)

Revolution (Short Story)

Amelia Doss Series:

Salvation (#3)

Nightfall (#2)

Resurrection (#1)

Insanity Series:

The Insanity Series (Books 1-3)

Replicate (#3)

The Burden (#2)

Insanity (#1)

Erased (Prequel Short Story)

The Exalls Attacks:

Followed Away (#3)

Followed East (#2)

Followed Home (#1)

A Poisoned Mind (Short Story)

Standalone books:

Snowball: A Christmas Horror Story

Humbug (as part of the Twisted Tales collection)

About the Author

Andre Gonzalez is the international bestselling author of the Wealth of Time Series, and co-owner of M4L Publishing.

After surviving the Aurora Theater Shooting in 2012, Andre was inspired to chase his lifelong dream of pursuing a career as an author. This tragedy gave him a new appreciation for life along with a drive to make the world a better place by publishing books readers all around the world can enjoy.

He has written over twenty time-travel, thriller, and horror books after spending many years reading and studying the works of Stephen King and Dean Koontz. Keeping readers up late and their hearts pumping faster than normal is his ultimate goal. Andre was the recipient of the Rocky Mountain Fiction Writers 2021 Independent Writer of the Year award.

When he's not writing, you can find Andre buried underneath a long to-do list or chasing around his three hyper children. He and his wife are raising their family in their hometown of Denver, CO.